JULIA PARKS

The Devil and Miss Webster

Love can strike even
the most sensible of
hearts!

D0033849

ZEBRA
U.S.$4.99
CAN $6.99

EAN

ISBN 0-8217-6900-6

9 780821 769003

5 0 4 9 9

AN INTIMIDATING APPOINTMENT

"Oh, and Penny," Eleanor called. "I would like to rise a half an hour earlier tomorrow morning."

"Very good, miss," said the maid, bobbing a curtsy and heading out the door.

"A half an hour to prepare myself for a most distasteful meeting," she muttered, blowing out the candle and staring into the darkness, forcing herself to bring his face to mind.

She would arm herself, she decided, by wearing her black bombazine—an impressive gown with a high collar of black lace. There was absolutely nothing soft and pliable about the image she presented in that gown.

Sitting up, she climbed out of the bed and relit the candle, padding across the chamber to her dressing room. Lifting the candle high, she glanced down the row of gowns hanging on hooks all along the wall. There was the black gown, but there also was the lavender one, in soft wool crepe. Which gown would serve her best?

Eleanor held her breath as someone jiggled the latch on the door. Then it opened and Captain Ransom himself started inside. He spied her and stopped short.

"Oh, excuse me, Miss Webster. I'm afraid I got turned around at the corner," the devil said, quietly closing the door as he left.

Eleanor began to shake—whether with laughter or hysterics, she wasn't quite certain. At any rate, she made the decision to wear the lavender on the morrow.

After all, how could she ever manage to look formidable now that he had seen her in her nightgown?

BOOK YOUR PLACE ON OUR WEBSITE AND MAKE THE READING CONNECTION!

We've created a customized website just for our very special readers, where you can get the inside scoop on everything that's going on with Zebra, Pinnacle and Kensington books.

When you come online, you'll have the exciting opportunity to:

- View covers of upcoming books
- Read sample chapters
- Learn about our future publishing schedule (listed by publication month *and author*)
- Find out when your favorite authors will be visiting a city near you
- Search for and order backlist books from our online catalog
- Check out author bios and background information
- Send e-mail to your favorite authors
- Meet the Kensington staff online
- Join us in weekly chats with authors, readers and other guests
- Get writing guidelines
- AND MUCH MORE!

THE DEVIL AND MISS WEBSTER

Julia Parks

ZEBRA BOOKS
Kensington Publishing Corp.
http://www.zebrabooks.com

ZEBRA BOOKS are published by

Kensington Publishing Corp.
850 Third Avenue
New York, NY 10022

All Kensington titles, imprints and distributed lines are available at special quantity discounts for bulk purchases for sales promotion, premiums, fund-raising, educational or institutional use.

Special book excerpts or customized printings can also be created to fit specific needs. For details, write or phone the office of the Kensington Special Sales Manager: Kensington Publishing Corp., 850 Third Avenue, New York, NY 10022. Attn. Special Sales Department. Phone: 1-800-221-2647.

Zebra and the Z logo Reg. U.S. Pat. & TM Off.

First Printing: November 2001
10 9 8 7 6 5 4 3 2 1

Printed in the United States of America

To Doris, with love

One

September 1815

"My dear Laura, whatever is the matter?" exclaimed Miss Eleanor Webster, hurrying forward to enfold her sobbing friend in a comforting embrace.

"It is too horrible to confess!" wailed the younger woman, burying her head in the ample bosom of her companion.

"Nonsense! You cannot have done anything so horrible as you seem to think. You are not capable of committing transgressions of such a magnitude," replied Eleanor bracingly. She took her friend's shoulders and held her away from her. Again she marveled at her young friend's beauty—the dark eyes and dark hair, the porcelain complexion and fine bone structure.

She thought of the two little girls upstairs in the nursery who promised to be the image of their beautiful mother. It was lucky they didn't have their brother's red hair, fair skin, and sprinkling of freckles. A boy could carry it off; a girl would be forever trying to rid herself of those precious flaws.

"Ellie?"

The whispered name brought Eleanor back to the matter at hand, and she smiled at her friend and said firmly, "Now, tell me what is the matter, Laura, and we shall sort it out in a trice."

It was a scene that had been enacted innumerable times in the decade since she had come to live with Laura, but her friend's reaction was not what Eleanor expected. Instead of giving her the usual watery smile, Laura, Viscountess Ransom, puddled up again and threw herself back onto the comforting bosom of her friend.

Perplexed and a little apprehensive, Eleanor let her friend have a good cry, patting her slender shoulders and whispering nonsensical reassurances that everything would be fine.

Eleanor Webster was not one given to foolish starts; she was much too sensible for that, and she found it impossible to encourage such waterworks in one who used to be her charge. Squaring her shoulders, she once again held her friend at arm's length and demanded to know the truth of the matter.

Unable to look her in the eye, Laura bowed her head and began. "It all started innocently enough, right after Charles left for London that last time. You remember how upset I was," she said, looking up briefly, her dark, expressive eyes pleading for understanding. Eleanor nodded, and she continued, "He had promised me he would stay home for the harvest, but he felt compelled to return to London. I said some awful things to him; I accused him of preferring his low companions to his wife and daughters."

A little sob escaped her, and she fell silent for a moment. The story was not new. Eleanor said a little prayer of thanksgiving that Laura no longer had to endure the pain of living with the capricious husband her family had chosen for her. In their eight-year marriage, Lord Ransom had time and again demonstrated that he preferred loose women over his beautiful, willing wife, who loved him to distraction. To Eleanor's way of thinking, the late Lord Ransom had been a typical man.

Putting her feelings aside, Eleanor said, "All that is in the past, my dear. You needn't feel guilty for saying what you thought, you know. Your words did not cause Charles's death."

"Yes, but Ellie, you don't know about what I did after he left that day, and all for spite. Not that I would take it back, for if I did, I wouldn't have . . ." Lady Ransom rose and paced up and down the worn rug twice before Eleanor tugged her back down on the sofa.

Eleanor felt the hair on the back of her neck stand up, as it always did just before disaster struck. But what could Laura possibly have to say about that terrible time almost two years ago? Surely she was over the pain and embarrassment of knowing her husband died in a brothel, stripped of his dignity, his purse, and his clothes.

"You wouldn't have what?" she prodded when it seemed Laura was going to succumb to another fit of crying.

"If I hadn't done what I did, I wouldn't have Simon, my beautiful little angel," she whispered, lifting her tear-streaked face to her dearest friend and confidante, her expression pleading for understanding, for forgiveness.

Eleanor's smooth brow crinkled in puzzlement. "But Laura, you must have been with child when Charles left . . ."

She paused when Laura shook her head and dropped her gaze. Grasping her friend's wrists, Eleanor forced her to look up again. The guilt was written as plainly on Laura's face as if it had been penned in India ink.

"Merciful heavens! The baby is not Charles's son!"

Laura dissolved into tears again; powerless to stop the flow of tears, Eleanor let her weep.

After several minutes, Laura sat up and sniffed. "What can we do?"

"That depends. I assume you are concerned that when your brother-in-law finally honors us with his presence, he may become suspicious, since Simon looks nothing like anyone in either his or your family."

"No, I hadn't even thought of that!" exclaimed Laura, her eyes widening with fear. "Heavens, Ellie, you don't think he might challenge the entail, do you?"

"No, no," she replied, hoping to stave off another bout of tears. "I'm sure he will do no such thing. The man hasn't even visited home in ten years. He has no interest in this place."

"But if Simon hadn't come along, Stephen would have

inherited Ransom Hall and the title. Oh, Eleanor, what if . . ."

"As I have told you time and again, we do not play the 'what if' game in this household!"

Lady Ransom giggled like a schoolgirl, and looked up at her tall mentor with grateful admiration. At thirty-four, Eleanor Webster was still a fine-looking woman, with her golden curls and violet eyes. Although Eleanor had received one or two offers of marriage since she had come to live with Laura ten years earlier, she had turned them all down, preferring to remain at Ransom Hall, first as Laura's companion and now as governess for her daughters.

"Laura, if it isn't your brother-in-law who has thrown you into such a fit of the dismals, then what is it?" asked Eleanor, her quick mind bringing them back to the crux of the matter again.

Laura gasped, recalling her original problem. Taking a deep breath, she said, "The problem is with Simon's father; he has seen the baby."

Their eyes met.

"Victor Taylor," said Eleanor, grimacing when her friend nodded.

"He pointed out that people will jump to the same conclusion when they see them together. His eyes, his hair . . . they are just like Simon's."

"Then why doesn't he just go away?" demanded Eleanor, her lips pursed in anger. She knew what men were like, and even before Laura spoke, she guessed the source of her distress.

"He doesn't want to go away, Ellie. He wants me to . . . to . . ."

"He wants money," said Miss Webster flatly, her voice full of loathing. But Laura was shaking her head. Eleanor asked incredulously, "He doesn't want money?"

" No, not this time," she said, unable to look Eleanor in the eye.

"Not this time?" asked Eleanor, her anger rising. "Just how long has he been blackmailing you, Laura?"

"Since last June. I've given him a little money and a few pieces of jewelry; that's all. But now he wants that parcel of land I received in the will," came the hollow reply.

"Then we'll see to it he has it," said Eleanor Webster.

"But Ellie, how can we do that? It takes a solicitor, I'm sure, and you know Mr. Baxter will never agree to drawing up the papers."

"You just leave Mr. Baxter to me, Laura. I'll take care of him, and I'll deal with Mr. Taylor, too. Don't worry; I'll see to it nothing bad happens to our little Simon, or to you either, my dear. Now, dry your eyes. I'll ring for tea."

Laura sniffed loudly and blew her nose.

Her jaw clenched, Eleanor Webster rose and pulled the rope. Clasping her hands tightly, she whispered, "Just leave everything to me."

"If you ask me, Captain Ransom, that harridan Miss Webster is at the root of all the problems at Ransom Hall! She stands there with her nose in the air, telling a body how to handle his own business! A woman in business matters—what sort of foolishness is that?"

"Indeed," came the noncommittal reply.

The solicitor warmed to his subject and continued, "I told Lady Ransom she needed to wait for you to come home before she sold anything, but she wouldn't listen to me. She just turned me over to that Webster woman and washed her hands of the matter, and before I knew it, I was pushed out of the house and the land was sold! No doubt Taylor, the man who purchased the parcel, came over with a hefty sum for Miss Webster. So I say, the sooner you oust Miss Webster from your late brother's estate, the better off everyone will be!"

The lanky Captain Ransom ran a hand through his coal black hair and raised a brow; his cold-blooded scrutiny of the portly solicitor caused that man to break into a nervous sweat. Baxter would have rubbed his chubby fingers together in glee had he been privy to the captain's thoughts, but he had no way of knowing how close his worldly, sophisticated client was to turning tail and running as fast as he could back to the gritty honesty of military life, washing his hands of all familial duty and responsibility.

"How is it my sister-in-law has need of a companion?" asked the captain. "Perhaps you should just cut off the funds for her salary, and she will leave of her own free will. She won't want to stay without being paid."

"Would that it were that easy. As far as I can tell, she has ingratiated herself into the family. I don't actually pay her a salary."

"Are you telling me she works for free?" demanded the captain, his expression puzzled and displeased.

The little solicitor cleared his throat nervously. "Um, well, I couldn't really say. I mean, this Webster woman has been with her ladyship since her come-out. As I said, she is more like family, and Lady Ransom will not listen to a word against her."

"But my brother was married ten years ago! You mean to tell me this woman has been leeching off the estate for ten years? How is that? Surely Charles had something to say to the matter!"

"Well, as to that, your brother, his lordship, was frequently away from the estate. I suppose he felt her ladyship needed someone to look after her. Now that you are home, you'll be able to provide that, to act as a guide for her ladyship."

Captain Stephen Ransom reflected that he would rather face a regiment of Bonaparte's finest than face acting as guide to his sister-in-law, whom he had met only once. He believed in doing his duty, and being named the guardian of his nieces and nephew, though he didn't like the task, was a duty he could not and would not shirk. If he remembered correctly, his brother's wife—no, his widow—was an amenable creature. He should have no trouble keeping her in line; however, the Webster woman sounded like trouble. Still, he didn't believe in acting in haste.

"What else do you know of the woman?"

"Just that she is as pigheaded as . . ."

Stephen cut him off with a wave of his hand. "I mean, what else does she do besides act as companion? Is she Lady Ransom's maid or housekeeper?"

"Oh, she thinks she is too good for that. She's the daughter of a vicar, a member of the gentry, or so she would have us believe. She started out as your sister-in-law's companion, and now she acts as governess to your nieces."

"Then, in reality, she is not completely useless."

"But it is her influence over Lady Ransom that is so disturbing. If she continues to rule the estate, I daresay your wards will be penniless by the time the little viscount comes of age. I'm warning you, Captain, you must get rid of her!"

Stephen Ransom didn't like being told what to do. He tolerated it from his superiors, of course, but he had more confidence in their good sense than he did in this fat, prissy solicitor.

Rising, he said, "I have several commissions to complete while I am in London, Mr. Baxter. It may take several weeks, but then I will go to Ransom Hall and see about this Webster woman."

"But, Captain . . ."

The captain's dark eyes snapped with angry lights, and he said quietly, "I'll let you know what I decide."

Quivering with fear or indignation—Stephen neither knew nor cared which—the little lawyer rose and bowed as the tall captain passed through his door and into the outer office.

Stephen pulled on his gloves and shrugged into his greatcoat before nodding to the skinny youth to open the outer door. It was only November, and already the sky was leaden with snow clouds. For a moment, he longed for the sunny skies of Spain, but the mere thought of that country awoke memories that were best left in the past.

He pulled a watch from his pocket and checked the time before giving his tiger the signal to step away from the horses' heads. Monkey swung up behind as the racing curricle leaped forward.

"What angers *el capitán?*" called his groom with a heavy

Spanish accent. The cold wind whipped his words away, but he knew his master had heard him, for he made a rude gesture. The lad, who had earned the nickname Monkey by his ability to climb anything, cackled happily.

"Whatever it is, *el capitán,* it is not so bad. Otherwise you wouldn't give me such a salute, eh?"

Again Stephen Ransom remained silent, but he didn't repeat the gesture, and his lips curved upward in amusement.

Suddenly, Stephen growled, "To hell with the fellows, Monkey! We're going for a drive!"

"Will not Don Michael and Señor Jones be waiting on you?"

Again that rude gesture before Stephen expertly snapped the whip over the leader's left ear, and the curricle shot forward. He gave a grunt of satisfaction; it had been years since he had owned a curricle and pair, but he hadn't forgotten the finer points of driving. With people and vehicles diving to either side of the road, they left behind the busy streets of London's Temple Bar and were soon crossing Blackfriar's Bridge, heading past Magdalan's hospital and onto the Brighton Road. He let the leader have his head, and the pair's strides lengthened, eating up the earth with seemingly effortless movements.

But Captain Stephen Ransom was not a green youth bent on winning some nonsensical wager on a race, and he soon slowed his cattle, gradually bringing them down to a sedate trot and finally a walk. Monkey swung around the side of the curricle and climbed into the seat.

"Did you leave the demons behind, *Capitán?*" he asked with a cheeky grin.

"Seems like one's crawled right onto the seat beside me," replied the captain.

His master's dark eyes glittered in the late afternoon sun, but the tiger only chuckled, not at all intimidated by that sardonic stare. He was accustomed to *el capitán's* moods, and though the jagged four-inch scar that began at the capitán's right eye and disappeared into the hairline frightened some people, Monkey saw it as a badge of honor.

"If I didn't know better, I would suspect it was a woman who had put *el capitán* into such a temper. But after last night . . ."

"Quiet," growled Stephen. It was true; he had wasted no time in securing the favors of a particular little dancer upon his return to London. He felt his pulse quicken at the thoughts teasing him, and he brought the curricle to a stop.

As he began his turn, his groom gasped, looking down fearfully at the low ditches bordering the road. But he had nothing to fear; the captain accomplished his turn without any mishap, and they headed back the way they had come.

"Will *el capitán* be visiting Miss Goodbottom tonight?" asked Monkey hopefully.

"So you can visit her maid, I suppose."

The groom raised his brows and gave a lascivious laugh.

"I'm not certain what my plans are. I have to go to the club first and see what Michael and Sailor are doing. Perhaps we may pay the ladies a visit later on, but I make no promises."

The captain returned to the city at a more sedate pace, arriving at Boodle's at dusk. After instructing Monkey to take the horses back to the stable for the night, he mounted the stairs, greeting the footman at the door by name. After divesting himself of his greatcoat, he passed through to the dining room, where his oldest friends were already devouring their dinner.

"Welcome, Stephen. We expected you an hour ago," said Sir Michael, pointing his fork at the chair to his left.

Stephen sat down and picked up Michael's wineglass, draining it dry. A footman hurried forward with another glass.

"Bring us two more bottles and bring me the same thing they're having. What is it tonight? Duck?"

"Yes, sir. Will you be having the first courses, too?"

"No, just what they've got here." The servant hurried away, and Stephen said, "Ever since we went through that damnable siege where food was so short, I find it difficult to appreciate the finer points of dining."

Sailor swallowed a huge bite and nodded vigorously. "I know what you mean. I always want to say, 'Just bring me the main course quick in case we have to break camp and move again.' "

Sir Michael leaned back in his chair and observed, "I never knew how difficult it was going to be, returning to the life of a civilian." He scratched his head and pushed the unfashionable long blond hair off his face. "I don't know if I'll be able to stomach being a country vicar."

"I can't imagine you ever being one," Stephen responded with a laugh. "You drink like a fish, fight like a madman, and, as often as not, chase women with the best of us. I don't think I ever really believed you were a chaplain."

"That was early on. Now . . . Besides, as I've told you countless times, if you knew my father, you'd call me a choirboy. He gave new meaning and depth to the term 'sporting vicar.' "

"I would have liked to know the man," said Sailor Jones, favoring both of them with a vacuous grin.

"In his altitudes already," Sir Michael whispered loudly.

"What is it this time?" asked Stephen.

"M' sister's coming to town. Can't wait t' see me," said the tall, slender man, his eyes filling with tears.

"Take heart, man. She can't be as bad as that," said Stephen, giving his old friend a stout punch in the arm that practically sent him sprawling. Stephen grabbed him and righted him again.

"You don't know Hilda. My God, she's a witch. Love her like a sister of course, and she's a beauty, make no mistake, but she's got a temper on her that's worse than mine."

"I find that hard to believe," said Sir Michael, exchanging smiles with Stephen.

Lieutenant Sailor Jones had the sweetest disposition of any man on earth. He never lost his temper and was the most obliging man a friend could ask for. But he clearly dreaded meeting his younger sister again, a spinster of twenty-six who seemed determined to latch on to her long-absent brother.

Sir Michael, who was sharing rented rooms with Sailor, frowned and asked, "Where is she going to stay?"

"With a friend, but she's made it plain she expects me to squire her about." He pulled a crumpled sheet of paper from the pocket of his red regimental coat and thrust it into Sir Michael's hands. "Said something about me introducing her to all my friends home from the war. I ask you, if our great-aunt hasn't been able to foist her off on anybody in the past six or eight Seasons, how the deuce am I supposed to find her a husband?"

Michael dropped the letter on the table, pushing back in his chair as if to distance himself from such a proposition.

Stephen laughed and said, "Not I, old boy. I've heard too much about the lady."

Sailor shook his head and said glumly, "That's just it. M' friends know too much about her. And I don't have any enemies I would wish her on."

"Don't worry, we'll think of somebody. What about old Geoffrey? Think she'd like him?"

"That dandy? I don't think he would fancy the competition. I told you, my sister's a beauty, a diamond of the first water."

"True, old Geoff doesn't like anyone to outshine him."

The waiter brought another bottle, and for Stephen, a plate piled high with duck, tiny roasted potatoes, and stewed vegetables.

"Would you care for anything else, gentlemen?"

"Some sort of fruit and some cheese, if you have any." The waiter gave Michael a quizzical look but nodded and hurried away.

"I guess I've grown accustomed to the way the French do it. I like ending m' meal with a bit of cheese," said Sir Michael.

"You'll shock the good English diners if you serve that for dessert," said Sailor, putting aside his troubles and brightening up at the thought of dessert.

"Give me some apple tarts and cakes any day," said Stephen.

Sailor sighed heavily and said, "I remember our cook at home . . . ah, those wonderful little cakes she made."

Sailor sat back and closed his eyes, his voice droning on while his friends shook their heads and sipped their wine. When he was in his cups, Sailor had a tendency to become a bore, but they were accustomed to this particular foible and excused it with good grace. It was better than Michael who, if he drank to excess, would become morose and then depressed, until he could perform some suitably dangerous and foolish exploit to bring him out of the mopes. Stephen, on the other hand, would pick a fight with the nearest person and very likely call him out. Fortunately, the trio looked out for each other and had learned early on to take it in turns, leaving the two to look after the one. Tonight it was Sailor's turn, by virtue of his dire emergency—the arrival on the morrow of his harridan sister.

Harridan, thought Stephen. That was what the solicitor had called Miss Webster. He smiled as his quirky sense of humor led him to wonder what would happen if the two harridans were placed in a room together. Might be quite a thing to see.

Suddenly Stephen sat forward in his chair and thumped Sailor's chest.

"Listen to me." His two boon companions did as he bid. "What if we invite a group of the fellows to my family seat for Christmas, for a house party? Charles always said his wife loved parties, and it would save me having to go down there for the holidays by myself. You don't have anyone else, do you, Michael?"

Sir Michael opened his mouth to speak, then shook his head.

"Good, then I'll count on you. And Sailor, you can bring your sister. We won't invite that many, maybe six or eight others, but all eligible bachelors. Your sister can have her pick, and I won't be forced to endure a family gathering as the outsider!" And what's more, thought Stephen smugly, in the hubbub and excitement of entertaining her guests, his sister-in-law wouldn't even notice the absence of Miss Webster when he dispensed with her services.

"Eleanor! Eleanor! Where are you?" called Lady Laura, rushing out of her bedroom, along the corridor, and down the steps to the front hall, bursting into the drawing room without so much as a by-your-leave.

Six-year-old Mary jumped out of her chair, sending her cup flying. Eleanor caught it, the hot liquid burning her hand, but she didn't let go, only setting the cup down on the silver tray and grabbing a napkin to dab at the stains on her dark green skirt. "It's a good thing I was wearing something dark."

"But you always wear something dark," answered little Mary.

Ignoring this comment, Miss Webster said, "Really, Laura, must you take on so? Here am I trying to instruct Mary and Susan on the proper way to hold a teacup, and you come bursting in here like a veritable hoyden!"

"Only see what you have done, Mama," scolded nine-year-old Susan. "Mary, clean up this mess. Miss Webster, are you all right?"

"Yes, thank you, Susan. Don't worry. The tea wasn't that hot, and I'm sure I can get these spots out."

"I am so sorry, Miss Webster," said Mary, looking up from the floor where she was sopping up the spilled liquid.

With her dark eyes and dimpled cheeks, how could anyone not forgive the child? Eleanor smiled and signaled Laura to come forward. She, too, offered a contrite apology, which was immediately accepted.

Eleanor winked at Susan. "How can anyone remain cross with these two sweet-tempered ladies?"

Susan giggled and observed in mature tones, "No one can, of course. I suppose we must learn to live with their madcap ways."

"Now, what is this exciting news, Laura?"

Laura dropped the letter she was clutching into her

friend's lap and sat down on the blue-striped sofa by her side. She could hardly sit still, waiting for Eleanor to read the short note.

But she could not contain her excitement even that long and turned to her daughters, saying, "It is from your Uncle Stephen; he's coming home for Christmas!"

"Well, I fail to see why a visit from a virtual stranger has sent you into alt, but . . . merciful heavens!"

Laura nodded her head, her eyes twinkling and her face beaming. She turned back to her daughters and announced grandly, "Your Uncle Stephen is your guardian, you know, so we must give him a big welcome. What's more, he's bringing an entire house party of guests with him. Isn't that wonderful? We are going to have the jolliest Christmas ever!"

Mary clapped her hands in excitement. Susan, as was her wont, looked up at Miss Webster for guidance. What she saw there was not joy, but some other emotion she could not define. Rising from her chair, she stepped forward and took Eleanor's hand in hers, squeezing it gently.

Eleanor returned the letter to Laura, looked up, and smiled; it was a tight little smile. She swallowed the lump in her throat and tried again, saying brightly, "Well, isn't this wonderful news, indeed! If you'll excuse me for a few minutes, I'll just go and speak to Mrs. Brown. We have a great deal of work to do if we're to be ready for so many guests. When will they arrive?"

Laura scanned the letter again. "It doesn't say for certain. Stephen thinks he will be here next week. His friends will join him sometime later."

"And how many are there to be?" asked Eleanor, pausing at the door.

"Let's see. Yes, here it is. There will be, goodness, ten at the very least. Perhaps twelve."

"Then we will need to make up the guest cottage as well; we must see to having it cleaned. After lunch I'll sort through the linens to be certain we have enough that are in good repair."

"Thank you, Eleanor," called Laura to the thin air as Eleanor hurried out of the room.

Instead of going to the little office where Mrs. Brown could usually be found, Eleanor climbed the stairs with measured tread, entering her room and closing the door quietly. She looked down at her hand on the latch, at the key in the keyhole, and turned it. Since the death of Lord Ransom, she had never locked her door.

She crossed the room to the dressing table and splashed cool water on her face, dabbing it dry with a crisp white serviette. Turning, she moved toward the window and stared out at the gray landscape, the leafless trees allowing her to peer into the distance, to the river that lay a half mile away.

A movement caught her attention, and she looked at her distorted reflection in the glass. She wiped away the tear that was trickling down her cheek, wishing she could wipe away the memories as easily.

Two

"Will there be anything else, Miss Webster?"

Eleanor read through her neatly penned list, placing checks beside the topics they had discussed. "Let's see, Mrs. Brown. We've sorted through the bed linens, and we have agreed on the number of extra maids and footmen we need to hire, pending Mr. Punt's approval of the footmen, of course."

"I'll remember to ask him straight off after I leave your study," said Mrs. Brown, glancing down at her list. "What about the stables, miss?" she asked suddenly.

"I have it on my list, Mrs. Brown. I'll have a word with Shaw this afternoon about the stables. He's bound to need more grooms for this many guests, most of whom are gentlemen, I believe, and no doubt armed to the teeth with all manner of horses and carriages."

The round little housekeeper chortled happily and rubbed her gnarled hands together in anticipation. " 'Twill be a lovely house party, just like the old days when I was a girl," she said, licking her lips as though she were savoring a Christmas candy.

"Yes, lovely," murmured Eleanor, suddenly taken back in time to her own past, when the words *house party* had meant serving countless meals to faceless men who possessed more hands than manners.

"If you'll pardon my being frank, miss, you don't seem too pleased at the idea," said Mrs. Brown, her brow wrinkling in concern.

Eleanor shook her head slightly and smiled. "Forgive me, Mrs. Brown. Everyone is delighted over the prospect of entertaining, and here am I, thinking only of myself."

"Well, it will mean a deal of work for you, miss. I mean, the mistress is a dear, but we all know it's you who will be doing all the extra work."

"And you, Mrs. Brown."

"Ah, but I'm looking forward to it. I haven't seen Master Stephen in ten years or more. He was such a dear boy. Of course, he's grown now, but I imagine he's as handsome as ever. If only he and th' mistress . . ."

"Fortunately, that is not an option, since in the eyes of the law they are brother and sister," Eleanor said firmly. "Besides, we wouldn't wish to encourage her ladyship to form a tendre for another man who is quite content to spend his life wandering the world instead of remaining at home with his family where he ought to be."

Mrs. Brown nodded gravely and took a deep breath, sucking it through her teeth. "Of course you're right, miss. Still, it will be a happy Christmas indeed, having so many guests. I know her ladyship will charm them all with her liveliness."

"Indeed she will," said Eleanor, exchanging a fond smile with the kindly housekeeper.

Mrs. Brown rose and toddled away. Eleanor returned to her list. Assuming Captain Ransom was true to his word, he would arrive in only five days. It might be a day earlier or a day or two later. In her experience with gentlemen, they were not particularly inclined toward timeliness or truthfulness.

Why, the last thing her brother had said to her was, "See you in a few days." That was over ten years ago.

No, that wasn't true. The last thing her brother had said to her as he rode away from the shabby vicarage was that she should wed old Stokes and have a nursery full of children.

Well, she hadn't taken his advice, and things hadn't turned out so badly for her. She had been happy with Laura; in a way, it was rather like being an older sister. Laura had always seen to it that her pin money was enough to share with her "employee." In truth, since Laura's marriage, Eleanor hadn't received a single day's wages, but she wanted for nothing. When Laura bought a new gown, she would insist that Eleanor receive one, too. If Eleanor balked, saying she didn't need another gown, Laura ordered it anyway. With a half smile, Eleanor smoothed the wool crepe skirt of her gown. She would never have chosen such a deep violet color for a gown; Laura had seen the material and insisted it be made up for her companion, her friend. Charles had only laughed and applauded his wife's good taste.

As a matter of fact, the one thing about Charles Ransom she had always admired was his generosity. Though he hadn't been able to give his wife the love she craved, he had provided her with everything else—without question.

Still, Eleanor had to admit the household had become a happier place since Charles's death. Though her friend might not realize it, Laura was happier. She no longer had that haunted look in her dark eyes, and the children could sense it, too. Ransom Hall was a sunnier place to be these days.

And now Ransom Hall was hosting a house party to a group of strangers, "old friends" of Captain Ransom, another stranger to the Hall's current residents.

Eleanor rose, sweeping her skirts to one side as she circled the delicate desk where she conducted household business. She paused at the mantel, glancing up as she often did at the portrait of the children. Little Simon had grown so in the last year. In the portrait, he was only six months old, a bundle of baby smiles and wiggles. His bright blue eyes and red hair made him stand out against his sisters' yellow gowns.

What beautiful children they were. How dear . . . and sweet . . . and innocent.

Eleanor dashed the back of her hand against her wet cheek in surprise. She hadn't realized she was crying, and why on earth was she doing such a nonsensical thing? she demanded of herself, frowning and shaking her head.

She looked up again and felt her breast swell with love

and a fierce maternal determination. Her position at Ransom Hall was that of trusted confidante, cherished friend, and beloved aunt—though the blood running through her veins signified no relation to the three children staring back at her from the portrait.

This Captain Ransom had best beware if he planned to come back home after fifteen years and take over her family. If he harmed any of her children—and yes, she included dear Laura among them—he would have her to answer to.

"Damn, it's cold," growled Stephen, stamping his boot-clad feet on the ground and clapping his gloved hands together. "What do you think, Monkey? Can he go on?"

"*Sí*, I think he will be fine if we will just tie him to the back of the curricle," said Monkey, giving the gelding's leg one last pat before rising. "It is only bruised."

"Good. I don't want to have to spend the night on the road—rather pointless on such a short journey. Ransom Hall can't be more than five miles farther. Even in this snow . . ."

"If Troubadour is not carrying your weight, I think he will come to no harm. I removed the stone. When we arrive, I'll pack the hoof," said the groom, removing the horse's saddle and securing it to the back of the curricle.

"Thank you, Monkey," said the captain, grinning at his tiger before climbing onto the seat. "And thank you for not lecturing me about insisting on riding the old soldier."

"You are very welcome," said the groom with a grunt of satisfaction as he joined his master on the seat.

Stephen pulled his wool scarf over his nose and released the brake. His voice was muffled as he said, "I think you'll like the English countryside more than London. You won't feel so confined."

The young man shrugged his shoulders and said, "Are there any pretty girls?"

"I'm sure you'll find some pretty maid who will fall for your continental charms. They won't be as, ah, worldly, shall we say, as Maggie was."

Monkey gave a little laugh and nodded. "Then I shall be just as happy in the country."

"Didn't you grow up in the country, too?" asked Stephen, sending his team forward at a sedate walk, mindful of his gelding's sore foot.

His groom grunted in satisfaction at this and tucked his chin into his coat before answering. "I grew up in Albuera, but I am not certain where I was born. My mother died when I was only two or three, and my father didn't talk to us much. Finally one day, when I was twelve or so, he quit talking at all. I realized the next day he had died."

"Was he ill?" asked Stephen.

"Only from the quantity of liquor that came out of his wine bottle."

"That's why you don't drink," observed Stephen.

"Oh, I will drink, but not liquor. I do not want to wake up dead one morning."

"A wise philosophy," said Stephen, chuckling under his breath.

Captain Ransom knew that gentlemen didn't hold conversations with their servants. One didn't inquire about their past, beyond asking for references. But Stephen wasn't interested in the ways of gentlemen—at least, not in their constricting rules. He had saved Monkey's life at Badajoz—not from the French, but from the British soldiers who conquered the city and then became consumed for three days by bloodlust—raping, killing, and robbing the Spanish inhabitants. He and his friends and some of the other officers had tried to stop the senseless violence, but they were helpless.

He had found Monkey, armed with a small knife, standing over the body of a little girl, screaming obscenities at a drunken private brandishing a stolen saber. Stephen rushed forward and took the soldier by surprise, knocking him out with one blow. Then had come the task of quieting the boy without getting himself killed. In Spanish, he told Monkey he wasn't going to hurt him or his sister. He knelt down and felt for a pulse; raising his face to the youth, he shook his head. Monkey had fallen to the ground sobbing. Eventually, he had allowed Stephen to pick up the little girl and take her away, following on his heels through the ghastly scene of destruction and mayhem.

They had found a quiet spot for her. While Stephen dug in silence, Monkey had carved a crude crucifix, scratching the name *Maria* into it and placing it on his sister's grave. Monkey had then looked at his rescuer expectantly, and bowed his head for Stephen's short prayer. When Stephen explained that he had to go, Monkey followed.

Stephen soon learned that his protégé was a wonder with horses, and the young man's reputation quickly rose; other officers had offered him a fortune to work for them, but Monkey remained loyal. From that day on, he had remained close to Stephen's side.

His attention returned to the present with the sound of distant laughter and the squeals of a young child. Stephen pulled back on the reins, his keen eyes searching the meadow on his left for the source of the happy noise.

"Over there, *Capitán*," said the tiger, pointing across the meadow to the top of a small, snow-covered hill, sheltered by trees on either side.

Three figures, two small and one quite tall, were running to the top, dragging in their wake a long sled of some sort. When they reached their destination, they threw themselves onto the ground and began to slide down the hill, their cries of delight once again filling the air. The two men watched as this routine was repeated several more times before the harsh cold penetrated their cloaks and consciousnesses. Stephen picked up the reins, and they continued on their way, traveling another half mile before he turned into the wide, oak-lined drive that led to his childhood home, Ransom Hall.

He passed by the front door and drove to the stable yard, where a groom ran to the head of the team while Monkey leapt to the ground and untied Troubadour from the back. Stephen climbed down and looked around; nothing had changed. The stable consisted of a long row of stalls built of heavy stone blocks. Above the stables were the grooms' quarters. At the far end, a little apart from the stable, was a small stone cottage where the head groom lived with his wife. That would have changed, of course. Old Shaw couldn't possibly still be alive. Stephen remembered tagging after Shaw when he was only a lad, and he had thought him old at the time.

"Master Stephen, is that you?" The curricle passed in front of him before he spied the speaker—a tiny old woman with sunken blue eyes and a beaklike nose standing in front of the stone cottage.

"Mrs. Shaw!" he called, waving and crossing the snow-covered lawn in a few long strides. He picked her up and swung her around, her skirts fluttering in the breeze. Giving her a big kiss on the cheek, he set her down again.

"Naughty boy!" she exclaimed, tugging at her gown before looking up at him again and smiling. "My mister told me you'd be coming for a visit, but I didn't think you'd remember us."

"Not remember you, Mrs. Shaw? Why, you're like a second mother to me. I would never forget you," he said, his smile transforming his weathered face into that of the boy he once was. Tears sprang to her eyes, and he teased, "What's wrong? Aren't you glad to see me?"

"Lord love you, my boy. O' course I am. I'm just being a silly old woman. Has Mr. Shaw seen you yet?"

"No, I was just . . ."

"Master Stephen, I knew those horses had to belong to you!" barked a short, bandy-legged man as he crossed the yard. "We weren't expecting you till the middle o' th' week!"

Stephen turned and strode toward the man, meeting him halfway. He extended his hand for a hearty shake and then put his arm around the old groom as they rejoined Mrs. Shaw.

"See, missus, I told you he would remember us. You don't spend every waking hour at the stable for nigh on twenty years and then forget the people there."

"No, o' course not. I can see you've the right of it, Mr.

Shaw," said the tiny woman. "Come inside, the both of you. I've got gingerbread just out o' the oven."

"Are you home for good, my boy?" asked Shaw when they were settled in the neat parlor.

"I'm back in England for good at any rate," said Stephen.

"Well, glad I am t' hear that, but you ought t' be stayin' home, you know. We can use a man around here," said the groom, reproaching Stephen with a worried frown.

"Has it been so bad since Charles died?"

"No, that is t' say, rest 'is soul, your brother was not much interested in th' estate."

"So you're saying the place has gone to rack and ruin in the past ten years? I saw no sign of neglect as I drove in. As a matter of fact, I think the grounds and house look better than they did the last time I was home ten or twelve years ago."

"And so they do, but . . . Well, all th' same, it will be good to have you here to take over the reins," said Shaw.

Stephen didn't press him. Instead, he asked about their daughter and some of the other old retainers before rising and thanking the couple for their hospitality.

"You're welcome, but much as we would like it, we mustn't keep you here talking all day, Master Stephen. No doubt th' family is anxiously waiting for you to come inside. It's so good t' have you home," said Mrs. Shaw, squeezing his hand one last time before giving him a little push toward the house.

Inside, the ladies of the house were in a dither. Eleanor and the girls had just slipped inside from their sledding expedition when word came from the stables that Charles's brother had arrived. Laura promptly swooned and had to have her vinaigrette to bring her around. Eleanor, grumbling under her breath at the thoughtlessness of men who arrive several days early without warning, revived her friend, thrust the small vial into Susan's hand with instructions to keep it handy, and hurried away to the kitchens.

Eleanor found Cook nearly hysterical that the "young master" had returned before she'd had a chance to fix him his favorite dishes. Two maids sat beside Cook, comforting her as she sat blubbering into her apron; the trio was completely oblivious to the smoke pouring from the oven, where the day's bread was burning to a crisp. Eleanor threw open the oven door, grabbed her own skirts as a hot pad, and pulled the blackened mess from the smoking cavity. She yelped in pain as the heat seared the soft wool crepe of her skirt, and her hand began to tingle with pain. Immediately, Cook forgot her troubles and rushed to slather lard on Eleanor's throbbing fingers.

"I'm so sorry, miss, so sorry," she kept repeating.

"I'm fine, truly I am," said Eleanor.

Just then, the door from the kitchen garden opened, and the long-awaited Captain Stephen Ransom stepped into the kitchen.

"Cookie, my dear woman!" he boomed, opening his arms wide to invite a hug. This kindness so overset the cook that she burst into tears anew, throwing her apron over her face and running from the room. The wide-eyed maids followed the cook, leaving Eleanor to face their visitor alone.

"What the devil was that all about?" asked Stephen, his nostrils flaring as the acrid smell of smoke reached his nose. Stamping his feet to remove the snow from his boots, he held out his hand and said, "I'm Stephen Ransom. And you are . . . ?"

With her good hand on her hip, Eleanor glared at the newcomer, noting with displeasure that she had to look up to him and irrationally resenting this fact. Forgetting her injury, she pushed back the hair that had escaped its neat chignon, the gesture leaving a glistening streak of lard in her hair and along her cheek.

Her lips pursed, she said tartly, "Isn't that just like a man! You arrive three days early and expect everyone to drop everything and bow down before you! Well, Captain Ransom, you are absolutely dicked in the nob if you think I shall do so!"

So saying, Eleanor turned on her heel and fled up the backstairs to take refuge in her room, to wonder why in the world, when she was angry, she had the unfortunate tendency to fall into the most unsuitable cant. One would think she would have forgotten all that she learned while growing up at the vicarage. But no, it had a way of surfacing at the most inopportune times. How mortifying!

She strode over to the dressing table and picked up her brush. Glancing up, her jaw dropped open as she took in her scorched yellow skirt and the glob of lard in her hair. The glistening of lard on her cheek had been diminished by the streak of soot when she had swiped it with her sleeve. With a groan, Eleanor dropped the brush and turned to ring for her maid. It would take more than a quick brush of her hair and a change of clothes to make her presentable.

Whatever must he be thinking of her?

As Stephen wandered from the kitchens to the front rooms, he was thinking not at all of the outspoken female he had just encountered. Memories of childhood crowded in on each other as he crossed the threshold into the front hall. He could almost hear his mother's voice in the echoes of his mind.

"You must be Captain Ransom," said the butler, a tall, well-built man of perhaps thirty years.

"That's right. And you are . . . ?"

"I am Punt, sir, butler here at the Hall. Lady Ransom is waiting for you in the drawing room. She said if you prefer, I am to take you to your room straightaway."

"No, no. If she is willing to overlook my dirt, I would prefer to meet her first thing."

"Very good, sir. If you'll step this way." Stephen followed the priggish butler to the drawing room. The butler opened the double doors and announced in grand accents, "Captain Stephen Ransom, madam."

Laura rose, her color high, and waited for him to enter. Hiding behind her skirts were two smaller versions of her, their dark hair and eyes peeping out at him shyly.

"Stephen, do come in!" exclaimed Lady Ransom, greeting him with a warm smile.

"Good afternoon, Lady Ransom," he said, sweeping a bow and walking forward to kiss her extended hand.

When they were all seated, Laura said graciously, "Now, now, you must not be so formal. You must call me Laura. And these are your nieces, Susan and Mary. Make your curtsies, girls."

They curtsied, and then settled on the sofa beside their mother.

"I'm sorry it has taken me so long to pay my respects, Laura," said Stephen, smiling at the trio of beauties. "I hope you have been well. It's been many years since we met. I wasn't certain you would be happy to see me."

"I am delighted," breathed Laura. "It's been too long. I only wish Charles . . . but there, we mustn't dwell on the past."

"I suppose not. And how old are you, girls?"

"I'm six. I had my birthday last month right after Miss Webster's. Mama gave me a new doll and Miss Webster—"

"Hush, Mary," said Susan, regarding her uncle warily.

"What about you . . . Susan, is it?"

"Yes, I'm nine," she replied briefly.

"Now, girls, you mustn't monopolize the conversation. Susan, why don't you take Mary back to the nursery while your uncle and I become reacquainted."

"Yes, Mama," said Susan, pulling her sister out of the room.

An hour after the kitchen mishap, there was a muffled knock on Miss Webster's door, and Susan called, "May I come in?"

"Yes, dear. Do come in," Eleanor replied.

Susan opened and closed the door quietly before crossing the plush, rose-colored rug and climbing into the chair that faced her governess. Eleanor, who had washed her hair three times to rid it of the lard, sat in a dark purple dressing gown, her back to the fire as she let her long golden curls dry.

"Have you met your Uncle Stephen?"

"Yes, I met him."

"Well, what did you think of him?"

"He is very dark," came the child's solemn reply.

"You mean his features?" she asked, smiling when the child nodded. "You mustn't hold that against him, Susan. You also have dark hair and eyes, though you are much prettier than he is," teased Eleanor.

"He is well enough, I suppose, but he really is a little scary, with those dark eyes and that black hair," replied Susan.

"Well, it is not solid black," said Eleanor, recalling this irrelevant detail with exasperating precision. "I mean, there is that graying at the temples."

"Is there? I didn't notice," said Susan, picking up the tortoiseshell brush that lay in Eleanor's lap and circling her chair. With long, gentle strokes, the child brushed Eleanor's hair for several minutes before she asked quietly, "Do you think Mama will marry Uncle Stephen?"

Eleanor stilled Susan's hands and pulled her gently around to stand in front of her. She lifted the child's chin, a warm smile providing the comfort the earnest little girl so desperately needed. Susan climbed onto her lap, resting her head on Eleanor's shoulder.

"First of all, Susan, your mama—for all her capriciousness—is not a ninny. She hardly knows your uncle; she has no plans to fall in love with him. Secondly, in the eyes of the law, he is considered her brother, and she cannot even think of wedding him, so you really have nothing to worry about."

"Really?" asked Susan, sitting up and watching her governess for signs of teasing. When she saw none, she smiled and climbed down, once again taking up the brush.

"Yes, really."

"You know, I wouldn't mind it if Mama married again. I

just don't think I would like for it to be to someone like Uncle Stephen."

"Because he is scary?" asked Eleanor. "You know, he may have a heart of gold."

With perfect candor and recall, Susan said, "That is not what you were saying when you were trying to revive Mama a little while ago. You said he was inconsiderate and thoughtless . . ."

"Well, I was a little overset myself, Susan, and it was wrong of me to say those things, which were supposed to be kept to myself. I apologize. A lady should always remember to watch what she says," added Eleanor, reminding herself to be more circumspect in the future, especially around children who never missed a single detail.

Stephen had forgotten how cold it could get in a comfortable country manor house. The fire was finally beginning to take the chill off the large chamber, but it certainly couldn't be called warm by any stretch of the imagination. Still, he didn't feel he could complain, not since the virago in the kitchens had so soundly shown him the error of his ways for arriving early.

His sister-in-law had identified her as Miss Webster, the one the solicitor had called a harridan. Stephen's lips curled in amusement when he recalled her diatribe. Devil take him if she had learned that language in this house of females. A little chuckle escaped his lips as he recalled her face after her outburst. Even without the soot-smeared cheek and the dirty gown, she had gone too far, and she knew it. He had read the embarrassment in her face, quickly followed by a flash of angry defiance.

Stephen frowned. It might amuse him to cross swords with such a spitfire, but was she really the type of woman he wanted to have the teaching of his sweet nieces?

"I have arrived, Captain," announced his new valet as he entered the chilly room, sweeping one arm out dramatically while the other settled a leather case on the dressing table.

Not for the first time, Stephen wondered if his new man had been an actor before turning to valeting. But he was quite efficient, and Stephen welcomed him with a smile, saying, "Good, then perhaps you can scare up a bottle of claret or brandy for me—anything to take the chill off."

"Indeed, Captain, the temperature in this room is intolerable. I will speak to the housekeeper at once!" exclaimed the foppish servant, sweeping past his master and pulling the counterpane from the bed. He draped it around Stephen's shoulders and minced out of the room.

"Demmed dandy," muttered Stephen, throwing aside the counterpane and rising. He walked to the icy window and rubbed at it with his scarf, peering through the aperture his action had created and staring at the white landscape beyond. As a boy, he had loved the snow, the way it seemed to make everything fresh and new. Now, the very sight of it sent a chill into his bones that threatened to overtake him. He stamped his feet several times and clapped his gloved hands.

Really, this room was intolerable.

There was a brief knock and the door opened; Miss Webster stepped inside.

"I understand you find your chamber unsuitable, Captain Ransom," said Eleanor, one brow delicately arched as she stared at the newcomer. Slowly, her eyes raked him from head to toe. "It is one of the largest chambers, and it never occurred to me that someone accustomed to the privations of the battlefield would be quite so exacting in his needs."

Stephen removed his scarf and shrugged out of his greatcoat before answering. With a tight smile that held no amusement, he met her impertinent gaze with unwavering boldness, a tactic that had never failed to make his subordinates quake with fear. But on Miss Webster it had no such effect.

His tone bordering on rudeness, he said, "And I did not realize that providing guests with warmth would be such an arduous task for the household here at Ransom Hall. Such was not the case in past times, Miss Webster."

"Ah, so you know who I am."

"Indeed, Miss Webster, I know a great deal about you and

your position in this house. I do hope there will be no need to make changes to that position," he replied, his dark eyes burning through her relentlessly.

Eleanor dropped her gaze as ghosts from the past rose up before her. Her brave front fleeing, she acknowledged, not for the first time, that she would always find it difficult to confront a hostile man. Wasn't that why she had found it necessary to run away from home all those years ago? If she had stayed, she would never have been able to withstand her father's and brother's distasteful plans to wed her to the highest bidder.

Eleanor shuddered and forced herself to return to the present and the handsome man glaring at her. Playing for time to regain her composure, she turned to the fireplace and picked up the poker, stabbing at the small flames.

She looked up in surprise as the captain's hand closed over hers, and he took the metal rod from her, replacing it on the stand. His face was so close to hers, she could feel his breath on her neck; somehow, she resisted the desire to run away.

"I can stir a fire, Miss Webster; in fact, I spent the better part of the past hour trying to coax more heat out of these flames. The problem, I believe, is that the fireplace is inadequate to the task of heating such a large chamber. I would prefer one of the smaller rooms, perhaps on the south side of the house, and not a corner room with so many drafty windows."

His voice was quiet, deep, and supple, but it made Eleanor shudder and step back. She willed herself to look up, to face him boldly, but he still stood too close. She could feel the lace collar on her round gown tightening around her throat, making it difficult for her to breath evenly.

She took another step back, moving stiffly with studied composure. Finally, she met his gaze; forcing herself to enunciate clearly, she said, "I am sorry if I misunderstood your request, sir. Of course you may have another chamber. I'll see to it immediately."

"Thank you," he replied, his expressive dark eyes now

sparkling with amusement. "My trunks have just arrived with Corbin. Perhaps you can tell him where to stow them."

"Certainly," said Eleanor, her jaw tightening again. The man was laughing at her. And how dare he speak to her as if she were a mere servant!

"Oh, and Miss Webster, in the next few days I would like an accounting of the subjects you teach my nieces."

"Very good, Captain Ransom," Eleanor replied through gritted teeth, adding under her breath, "Jackanapes."

"What was that?"

"Nothing. Is there anything else I can do?" she asked sweetly.

"Yes, one other thing. My sister-in-law informs me that she is in the habit of deferring to you on most matters concerning the estate. While I appreciate your efforts since my brother's death, I'm sure you will appreciate that things cannot continue as they have been."

"I'm sure I don't know what you mean, sir," said Eleanor, trying her best not to snap, but not at all certain that she had succeeded.

"I mean, Miss Webster, that now I am here, you no longer need concern yourself with the countless details of the estate. And I will be looking into certain transactions that have taken place since my brother's death."

"What are you talking about?" asked Eleanor, hiding her consternation with indignation.

"Now is not the time to discuss it, but please understand that while I never expected to have to run the estate, I am equal to the task. To protect my little nephew's inheritance, I plan to treat this estate and its interests as if they were my very own. Do I make myself clear?" he intoned, looking down his nose at her in a manner that made her wish she could slap his cheek.

"Very clear, Captain Ransom. Now, if you will excuse me?"

"Certainly," he replied, stepping back so that she could pass before him and out the door.

Stephen grinned when she disappeared in a swirl of skirts.

Well, well, he thought with a smug nod of his head. It appeared Miss Webster had a few chinks in her suit of armor. A good strategist never allowed himself—or herself—to be rattled to the point that she revealed her emotions to the enemy.

Not that he meant to be her enemy. He didn't expect her to be around long enough to become his enemy. He had already indicated to her that her position in the household would be diminished. The next day, he would inspect her accomplishments as governess and as the estate bailiff. After a hint or two to his malleable sister-in-law, he had no doubt he could bring her around to his way of thinking. Then he would sack Miss Webster and be rid of her for good.

After that, his duties to the estate and his brother's three children would be easy.

Eleanor gave the orders for one of the cozy bedrooms on the south side of the house to be prepared for their visitor. This was the family wing; he would be just down the corridor from her room. She had hoped to force this interloper to keep his distance, but her plans seemed to be falling apart.

She grimaced as three footmen entered the room carrying large trunks and other bandboxes—not the luggage of a man who planned only a holiday stay.

"Shall I build up the fire, miss?"

"Yes, Peter. Make it a nice, roaring fire. Captain Ransom doesn't appreciate our snowy climate," she said.

"Very good, miss."

Suddenly, a tall, thin man sailed through the door. He wore a long frock coat and paused after entering, his hands on his hips as he tut-tutted and surveyed the smaller room.

"No, no, not over there! What in the world is the matter with you?" he said to one of the young footmen. Then, spinning around, he announced grandly, "Oh, this is completely unacceptable! What a pokey little room this is!"

"Excuse me, but who are you?" demanded Eleanor.

The servant pivoted in place. Looking her up and down,

he took in the richness of her gown and her haughty stare and seemed to make a decision. Sweeping a deep bow, he intoned in haughty accents, "My lady, I am Corbin, Captain Ransom's valet."

Eleanor quelled the chuckles of the footmen with a single glance. Giving Corbin a regal nod, she quickly informed the foppish valet of his mistake. "I see. Well, Corbin, I am Miss Webster, her ladyship's friend. As for the room, your master requested it; if you find it unacceptable, then you must so inform him. But if you should need anything else, please apply to Mrs. Brown; she is our housekeeper here at Ransom Hall."

"You are most gracious, Miss Webster," he replied with his nose slightly elevated. Then, under her scrutiny, he swept another bow. It was obvious he hadn't made up his mind exactly how deferential he should be to her ladyship's friend.

With another nod, Eleanor left the room. She heard footsteps coming toward her and swiftly slipped inside her own room. With the door cracked, she watched as the captain made his way down the hall to his new room. She listened hopefully for some explosion similar to the valet's about the unsuitability of the room but none was forthcoming, and she closed the door, sagging against it with a sigh.

Then, with her customary firm step, she crossed the room and sat down at the small escritoire. If the captain wished to take over, then he needed to know about the repairs to the tenants' cottages that required immediate attention. Eleanor picked up a pen and dipped it in the ink, but it dried before she had written a word.

The good captain had only just arrived and already he was making his presence felt in the butterflies fluttering around her stomach. It would not be simply for the duration of the house party, but forever. Suddenly the position of honor and influence she had grown accustomed to here at the Hall was in jeopardy. For the first time, Eleanor keenly felt the uncertainty of her situation. While Laura and the children treated her as a beloved aunt, Captain Ransom certainly didn't, nor was it likely she could win him over. She had understood his veiled threat; at the very least, he meant to reduce her influence in the household. At worst . . . but she would not allow herself to think about that.

Besides, she reminded herself, it was not just her position that was being threatened. While he probably had no intention of making difficulties for Laura, if he insisted on investigating the "sale" of that parcel of land to Taylor, it would mean trouble.

What if he had discovered they had signed over that bit of property to buy Taylor's silence? she thought, panic rising in her breast.

But no, she reassured herself, it couldn't be that. And anyway, that property had been willed to Laura, something extra to go with her widow's jointure; she could dispose of it as she pleased. Still, if Captain Ransom chose to question the reason for the "sale," Laura would find it impossible to explain.

And if he did discover the reason, he might challenge little Simon's paternity himself. After all, with Simon declared illegitimate, the estate would pass to Captain Stephen Ransom.

Taking a deep, steadying breath, Eleanor vowed that such an event would never happen, not while she had breath in her body to prevent it.

The sooner they saw the back of Captain Ransom, the better!

Three

"I cannot tell you how happy we are that you are joining us for Christmas, Stephen. And bringing guests as well. It will be wonderful to have Ransom Hall full of life again," said Lady Ransom at dinner that evening, bestowing a happy smile on her brother-in-law.

Eleanor smiled, too. How could she not when Laura was so happy? To see that little frown of worry erased from Laura's brow was enough to make her forget her own problems. It was almost like old times when Charles had been at home—one of the many times he had vowed he was going to settle down and his adoring family had believed them. Tonight, Laura was smiling again, dressed in a silk gown in a brilliant shade of blue; she was still a beauty, even at the age of eight and twenty and with three children upstairs.

Eleanor glanced from her friend to the captain and was startled by his handsome features. She had been so vexed by his arrival that afternoon, she hadn't properly studied him. When he smiled, his looks were quite extraordinary, with his dark hair touched by silver and those beautiful dark eyes fringed by heavy lashes. His teeth were even and bright white against his tanned skin. He was wearing a black coat of excellent cut. New, she guessed, most likely by Weston. And his cravat would be the envy of any group of fashionables. She wondered if he tied it himself or had his dandy of a valet to do it. The latter, probably. There was nothing of the dandy about Captain Ransom's manner or appearance, she thought, her mouth tightening in a smirk.

Eleanor gulped when she realized the captain had turned his dark gaze on her and was watching her intently. Even Laura had turned to her and was waiting, presumably for a response to some question.

Eleanor refused to acknowledge that she had been inattentive, so she nodded and murmured, "Indeed."

This seemed to satisfy Laura, but the captain's eyes began to dance, and he lifted his wineglass to her in a silent salute. Eleanor developed a sudden interest in the asparagus on her plate.

"Well, you mustn't work too hard, Stephen," Laura continued. "You need to enjoy yourself after so many years of hardship and deprivation."

"You're a very considerate sister, but I am grown so accustomed to hard work, I daresay I would find it difficult to lay about and do nothing all day. As I told Miss Webster, I intend to wade right in. No, it is not only my duty that brings me home, it is also the satisfaction I will get from seeing Ransom Hall brought back to its former state."

"It hasn't exactly gone to rack and ruin," murmured Eleanor.

"Now, I'm certain Stephen meant no such thing, Ellie. But I am also sure you will be happy to be relieved of the task of looking after the tenants and such." Laura leaned toward her brother-in-law and whispered in a loud aside, "I have heard dear Eleanor say time and again how we really should hire someone new to tend to estate business."

"Really? Then you are not much taken with my brother's bailiff, Miss Webster?"

"I did not say that, Captain, and I believe Mr. Lamb served your brother well, but he has difficulty dealing with a woman. I'm certain you are much more qualified to judge such a matter, so you must decide for yourself," said Eleanor with a tight little smile.

"Yes, I believe I must, Miss Webster. It is understandable that he might resent taking orders from you," he added before turning back to his sister-in-law, who was eyeing the pair with a little frown creasing her smooth brow. "Now, no more business at the dinner table, I promise. Tell me, Laura, when was the last time you went to London for the Season?"

Like a girl of eighteen flirting with a favored beau, Laura trilled a little laugh; some lessons were never forgotten, thought Eleanor with a grin.

"It has been several years, Stephen. It is so difficult, with the children, you know."

"Of course, but you must go up for the theater from time to time. I mean, it is only an hour or so away."

"I'm afraid not. We always seem to be too busy for such a journey," came the wistful reply.

"Well, now that I am here to look after things, you should make plans to go up to town in the spring. The children will be fine here at home with me."

Laura looked uncomfortable, and Eleanor jumped to her rescue. "I daresay Laura would prefer to wait until Simon is older."

"Ah, yes, Simon. When will I be allowed to meet the little viscount? How old is he again?"

"It's hard to believe, but he is fifteen months old."

"Then he was born well after . . ." he began, before realizing how tactless his observation would seem. "That is, having met my nieces, I can only look forward to meeting the youngest member of the house."

"I'm sorry, Stephen, that he was asleep when you arrived this afternoon, and he'll be asleep again before the tea tray is brought in, which is when the girls usually join me and Eleanor in the drawing room. Of course, if you don't wish to have the children come down in the evenings, we will discontinue that habit," said Laura, automatically leaving the decision to him, just as she had always deferred to her husband.

Eleanor's gaze narrowed as she watched him. No matter what he might do to her, if he didn't take pleasure in the children, then he would remain forever in her black books.

But the captain smiled and shook his head, saying, "You mustn't change anything on my account, Laura. I am not here to disrupt your household."

Except for inviting a horde of people for the holidays

without so much as a by-your-leave, thought Eleanor, raising her brow as she watched Laura simper and smile at her brother-in-law.

She wondered how closely Stephen Ransom resembled his late brother. Certainly the similarity in their appearance was startling, though Stephen's hair and eyes were darker, lending him a satanic quality unless he was smiling. What was more to the point, did the captain possess his brother's restless spirit? To spend so many years in the army, a man must be restless, she decided. Still, she shouldn't judge him too harshly yet; she would wait and see.

Laura rose and declared that they would leave the captain to his port. Stephen pushed away from the table, too.

"If you ladies don't mind, I'll just bring it along to the drawing room. Can't bear to drink alone."

"Of course we don't mind," replied Laura, taking his arm.

Eleanor hesitated only a moment before accepting his other arm. He was acting the part of a true gentleman, at any rate.

When they entered the blue and yellow room, the girls were waiting for them with their nursemaid, Jane. The servant kept one hand on each girl to prevent them from running across the room as they usually did. This was hardly necessary, especially with Susan, who was still too much in awe of her uncle to behave in such a carefree manner.

Stephen seated his sister-in-law and Eleanor on the sofa before going toward the girls and saying, "Good evening, ladies. I'm so happy you could join us." He looked up and smiled at the maid, who blushed a furious red when he added, "How do you do? I am Stephen Ransom. And you are . . . ?"

"Heavens, sir, I mean, Captain, I'm Jane, nursemaid to the young ladies."

"I'm very happy to meet you. Your charges have very pretty manners. I assume we may thank you for that."

"Heavens, sir, you're welcome, to be sure, but I think Miss Webster is the real one you should be thanking."

Still smiling at the maid, he held out his hands to Mary and Susan and led them across the room to their mother. When they were seated between Eleanor and Laura,

Stephen sat down in a chair, asking politely, "Do you ride, Susan?"

"No. Yes. That is, I can, but I prefer not to," she replied nervously, looking up at Miss Webster, her eyes pleading for rescue.

"Really? I am surprised; I thought all girls loved horses."

"I do!" cried the exuberant little Mary, unable to remain silent another moment, much to her sister's relief. "I have my very own pony; I named him Mr. Applegate."

"So you are the horsewoman, eh?" he said, turning his gaze on the younger child, who fairly bounced with nodding her head, her black curls springing up and down like countless yo-yos.

"Then what do you like to do, Susan?" he asked.

His gaze caused her to blush. She was much more comfortable allowing her younger sister to be the center of attention.

But he was still waiting for an answer, and she cleared her throat and managed bravely, "I like to read and play music."

"Is that so? I also like to read, but I have had little time for it until recently. And your music; do you play the pianoforte?"

"Yes, sir."

"Would you play for us tonight?" he prompted.

Susan glanced up at Miss Webster before replying. It was obvious that the thought of performing for him was causing her anxiety, but she nodded bravely and rose.

"Why don't we play that duet we have been practicing?" asked Eleanor, rising and following her grateful pupil to the instrument.

"Thank you, Miss Webster," whispered Susan, sitting down while Eleanor pulled up another chair.

They began playing, their efforts laborious at first until they both settled into a creditable version of "Greensleeves." When they finished, their efforts were met with an outburst of applause.

"Well done, Susan," said the captain, rising until they were once again seated. "And well done of Miss Webster, too," he added.

"I am learning to play, too," said Mary, climbing unabashedly onto her uncle's knee.

"Well, you practice very hard and perhaps you can play something for the house party," he said, tweaking a silky black curl.

"Speaking of the house party, Stephen, tell me about your friends who are coming for Christmas," prompted Laura.

"Mostly old soldiers, all particular friends of mine. There will be five single gentlemen, two of whom are bringing their sisters. Then there is Virgil Prentiss, a retired major, and his wife, and finally Lord and Lady Reading, who may bring along their son, a lively lad of six or seven."

"How delightful!" exclaimed Laura. "Won't that be wonderful, girls, to have a visitor in the nursery."

"Yes, Mama," said Susan dutifully.

Eleanor gave Susan's hand a little squeeze and smiled down at her sympathetically. Susan was the sort of child who disliked change. Any alteration in her schedule was cause for disquiet. But she was also a very thoughtful child, and Eleanor knew she would make their young visitor feel welcome.

"What sort of entertainments did you have in mind?" Eleanor asked, looking up at the captain.

"I really hadn't thought about it. They all know each other, so I'm sure there will be no end of conversation. As long as there are some cards handy, a few bottles of port, and the fellows will be happy."

"There is usually a foxhunt between Christmas and the New Year," said Laura.

"Splendid! All the gentlemen like riding and hunting, as does Mrs. Prentiss. And is there still a billiard table here?"

"Oh, yes, Charles loved to play," said Laura. With an eager gasp, she added, "What about a ball? Don't you think we should give a Christmas ball, something to reintroduce you to the neighbors?"

"I'm sure all the ladies would love a ball," said the captain, chuckling as he watched his sister-in-law send her elder child across the room to find paper and pencil, which she gave to Miss Webster.

"Is there enough time to organize a ball? I don't wish to be a nuisance," he added.

"Organizing a ball will never prove inconvenient to Laura," said Eleanor dryly, who knew the majority of the tasks would fall on her own shoulders.

Even knowing this, Eleanor couldn't help but join in with her friend's enthusiastic plans. Soon they were indulging in a lively discussion, throwing out a melee of ideas for the proper theme, the most tempting menus, and the best decorations. The captain sat back and watched with a bemused smile as the two ladies, with Mary sitting between them now, sailed through a long list of details with the precision of well-trained troops.

When it was quiet again, Laura took the list Miss Webster had been writing and announced, "Very well, we will have the ball two days before Christmas. As such, we will decorate the ballroom with the usual Christmas greenery and bright bows. We will hire some musicians from Chipping Barnet. You girls will have your own fete. We'll invite the vicar's children and Mr. Powell's nephew."

"May we watch the ball from the balcony?" asked Susan.

"Of course you may," said Eleanor, tempering her permission with, "until eight o'clock."

"Ten o'clock!" said Mary, frowning fiercely.

"Nine o'clock, puss," said Eleanor, patting Mary's cheek. The little girl giggled and nodded.

"What do you think, Stephen?" asked Laura.

"I think it sounds absolutely marvelous. I can't wait."

"Good, that settles that. On Christmas Eve we always attend the midnight services and then come back for a Christmas feast."

"A charming tradition," said Stephen.

"I'm glad you think so, Stephen, because I would like for you to play Father Christmas!" said Laura with a girlish giggle that sent both her daughters into whoops.

"And what, precisely, does that mean?" he asked.

"In my family, Father Christmas, who always wears a long

velvet robe and whiskers, acts as the host of Christmas Eve," said Laura.

"And you think I would be a good Father Christmas?" he asked in a deep, pompous voice that set his nieces laughing again. Their uncle wagged a slender finger and admonished them soberly, "Be careful, ladies. You should never mock Father Christmas!"

When they were quiet again, little Mary whispered, "Miss Webster, what does mock mean?"

"It means it is time for bed, I think," said Eleanor, signaling to the maid, who hurried forward and gathered up her charges despite their vocal objections.

Eleanor rose also, and Laura followed her lead, albeit with a reluctant grimace.

"I suppose it is getting late, and you must be wanting your sleep after your journey," said Laura.

"Oh, I think I'll go try out that billiard table before I seek my bed," said Stephen.

"Then we'll bid you good night," Eleanor said firmly when Laura seemed to be hesitating.

"Yes, good night, Stephen."

"Good night. May I have a quick word with you, Miss Webster?"

"Certainly," she replied calmly, watching Laura walk out the door, leaving her alone with this stranger. By sheer strength of will, she managed not to flinch when he took her elbow and escorted her back to the sofa, sitting down by her side and studying her for a moment before speaking.

"Miss Webster, you seem to be a remarkable woman," he began. When she made no reply, he continued, "I wanted to warn you that I intend to visit the schoolroom tomorrow at ten o'clock."

"Very good, sir," she replied, keeping her gaze down and her back ramrod straight.

"There is another matter I wish to discuss with you, but I fear this is not the appropriate time."

Eleanor raised her chin, meeting his eyes boldly. "I am not so weary that I cannot hold up my end of a discussion, Captain."

Baxter had warned him that Miss Webster did not consider herself a mere servant. Nonetheless, Stephen was taken aback by her brashness, though he recovered quickly and commented, "Very well, Miss Webster. I have some concern about the way you have been allowed to manage this estate since my brother's death. I also have concerns about decisions you have made regarding the estate."

Eleanor could not keep the spark of indignation from her fine eyes as she replied, "When was the last time you deigned to visit Ransom Hall, Captain?" When he would have replied, she held up a hand for silence. "You needn't answer since I have been here for ten years and have only just made your acquaintance today. Given that fact, do you not think that it would be better if you inspected the estate before forming an opinion?"

Without waiting for his response, Eleanor rose, looking down at him, outwardly calm but seething inside.

Rising also, Stephen Ransom had the grace to nod and say, "You may be right."

"Then I will bid you good night, Captain. Until tomorrow morning," she added, giving him a regal nod before sweeping past him and out the door.

Stephen expelled a quiet whistle of admiration—not only for the battle Miss Webster had just won, but also for the flash of trim ankle he had glimpsed as she retreated.

She really was a remarkable woman. He almost hoped to discover the solicitor had been wrong, that she had not been playing fast and loose with his nephew's inheritance. But he doubted it very strongly.

He could remember as a child of perhaps six, his father trying to juggle their finances so that he didn't have to sell off part of the estate. It was one of the only lessons he recalled learning at his father's knee.

"No matter what, boys, you must keep the estate intact."

Charles had asked, "What's intact, Father?"

"Together. Ransom Hall is like family; never split it up because you can never replace it."

Stephen shook his head, his dark eyes clouding with emotion. As it turned out, his father hadn't been able to keep the family together. His mother had left for the first time when he was only eight; things had never been the same.

With a snort of derision, Stephen shoved these maudlin thoughts back into the dark recesses of his memory. He couldn't allow the past to cloud his objectives for the future. His little nephew's interests came first, and if that meant ridding the household of Miss Webster's presence, then so be it.

Eleanor found sleep elusive that night. While her maid Penny chattered endlessly about the captain's rugged good looks, she listened with only half an ear.

What was there about the man that set up her back every time he opened his mouth? Was she that insecure in her position here? After all, Laura was still Lady Ransom and the mistress of the house. In all her years as governess and companion, hadn't she forged a close enough tie with Laura that she needn't fear for her position? Surely Laura would not be so influenced by this stranger's opinions that she would cast aside all their years together.

Of course, her real worry was not her own position, but the baby's position as rightful heir to the title and to Ransom Hall. That was why she had to be wary.

Suddenly, she recalled the captain's interest in meeting his nephew. In her experience, men seldom cared to be around babies. Perhaps he already suspected that Simon was not his brother's offspring. Had Charles written to his brother regularly? She didn't think so, but she determined to question Laura on the subject as soon as might be. She knew Laura had flaunted her flirtation with Victor Taylor in front of her husband, in a futile attempt to make Charles jealous. Although the flirtation hadn't gotten out of hand until after Charles had left home that last time, might he have suspected Laura of having an affair with Taylor and written to his brother about the possibility?

And now the good captain had finally come home to discover if he was the rightful heir, instead of his so-called nephew.

"Will that be all, miss?" asked the maid.

"What? Oh, yes, thank you, Penny. Oh, and Penny, I would like to rise a half an hour early tomorrow morning."

"Very good, miss," said the maid, bobbing a curtsy and heading out the door.

"A half an hour to prepare myself for a most distasteful meeting," she muttered, blowing out the candle and staring into the darkness, forcing herself to bring his face to mind.

She would arm herself, she decided, by wearing her black bombazine—an impressive gown with a high collar of black lace. There was absolutely nothing soft and pliable about the image she presented in that gown.

Rolling over, Eleanor hugged the pillow to her breast and closed her eyes, only to have them pop open seconds later. Sitting up, she climbed out of the bed and lit the candle. Padding silently across the spacious chamber, she opened the door to her dressing room. Lifting the candle high, she glanced down the row of gowns hanging on hooks all along the wall.

There was the black gown, its stiff fabric and linings causing it to stand out from the wall, farther than the others. Then she spied the lavender gown in soft wool crepe. She loved the gown and knew it complemented her violet eyes.

Which gown would serve her best in this instance? Should she try to look soft and vulnerable for the devil who was threatening her very living here at Ransom Hall? Or should she try to face him down, looking as intimidating as a judge in the Inquisition?

Eleanor chuckled, then held her breath as someone jiggled the latch on the door. It hadn't occurred to her to lock that door; there had never been any need. And here she stood in her thin and faded muslin nightrail with her candle held high.

The door opened, and Captain Stephen Ransom started inside, spied her, and stopped.

"Oh, excuse me, Miss Webster. I'm afraid I got turned around at the corner. I should have gone right instead of left. Pardon me," the devil added, quietly closing the door.

Eleanor began to shake—whether with laughter or hysterics, she wasn't quite certain. At any rate, she made the decision to wear the lavender on the morrow.

After all, how could she ever again manage to appear formidable to the captain now that he had seen her in her nightgown?

"Very good, Mary. Why, you've gone all the way to fifty. I am very impressed," said Eleanor, smiling at her younger pupil the next morning, trying not to look at the clock, which told her it was only fifteen minutes until her nemesis arrived. "Now, Mary, can you write your letters?"

"Yes, miss," said the child, returning to her small table and continuing her work.

"I can't remember, miss. When did we lose the colonies in North America?" asked Susan, studying the globe.

"In seventeen-eighty-one," said a deep voice.

Three sets of eyes turned automatically to the doorway, where Stephen leaned against the opening. Mary recovered with a squeal of delight and left her work behind to go and jump into his arms. He gave her a hug and set her back down. Looking at his mangled cravat, Eleanor thought smugly that that would teach him to come and visit the schoolroom. But he made no effort to straighten his attire, following Mary to her table, where he seemed intent on his conversation with the gregarious six-year-old.

"I can write all my letters," announced Mary.

"And a very good job you are doing of it," said her uncle, adding, "I would love to see that when you have finished." Mary set to work with a will.

Still smiling, the captain approached Susan. Eleanor decided to remain seated; she would not act like a servant and rise when the "master" entered the room. She regretted her decision almost immediately when she realized she could either fix her eyes on his waist or crane her neck to look up at his face. Neither choice was advantageous. He solved her dilemma by sitting down on the end of the table and leaning over the globe.

Pointing to the former colonies, Stephen asked, "And who was king at that time?"

"Our present king?" Susan replied tentatively.

"Quite right. It's really a shame that we lost them. It's a beautiful country."

"You have been there?" Eleanor found herself asking.

His dark gaze turned on her, almost taking her breath away.

"Yes, though it was not the best of circumstances. Part of my regiment was sent over briefly to help during the last American conflict. We arrived just as it was ending in eighteen-fourteen and then were summoned back almost immediately. A good thing, too, since Bonaparte escaped the following March," he said, his words for Susan, but his eyes resting on Miss Webster.

She was a handsome woman, he thought, especially in that violet gown that matched her eyes so perfectly. Why on earth had she never married?

"How exciting," breathed Susan, unable to contain her curiosity or her admiration.

Stephen tore his eyes away from Miss Webster's charms and replied, "I confess that I was not particularly thrilled to be getting back on the ship; I hated being at sea."

"Don't tell me you get seasick," said Eleanor, meeting his gaze over the top of Susan's head, her violet eyes twinkling with amusement.

"No, just a little queasy. Mostly I hated being confined on the ship."

"But a ship is in the middle of a huge ocean," said Susan, her brow furrowed. Then she remembered her audience, and she ducked her head shyly again.

"Ah, I can see you have the heart of a sailor, Susan—to them there's nothing like the open sea. But I'm afraid to me, if I can only stride twenty paces before having to turn round, I feel very confined."

Susan lifted her head and gave a solemn nod to signify that she understood this sentiment.

Her uncle pointed to a spot on the North American coast and said, "This is where we landed. It's a beautiful spot, all green and lush. I would have liked to see more of it, but I hope to return one day as a simple traveler, not a soldier."

Susan's eyes shone with eagerness, and she began, "Might I . . . ?" Losing her courage, she looked back at the globe.

"Perhaps, when you are older, you might like to go with me, Susan," said her uncle, and the little girl smiled shyly and nodded. "Well, we shall keep that just between us. I daresay your mother would not like to hear about you journeying around the globe just yet."

"You won't forget?" she asked shyly.

"Certainly not. And we have Miss Webster here as our witness." He grinned at Eleanor, and she felt a strange tremor race down her spine, ending somehow in her stomach.

"I'm finished!" announced Mary, rushing from her place and thrusting her slate under her uncle's nose.

He took it from her and studied it for a moment before announcing, "What pretty handwriting you have, Mary. I don't know very much about children, but I think to be able to write your letters so neatly at this age, you are quite a remarkable young lady." The little girl beamed with pride.

"Mary is a very good student," said Eleanor, "but sometimes she tires of sitting still."

"Surely you take them out for exercise, too," said Stephen sharply, suddenly recalling the reason for his visit to the schoolroom.

"Of course, but a child must have discipline, too," replied Eleanor.

"Yes, I recall the type of discipline required by my tutors only too well." There was an edge to his voice that made Susan slip out of her seat and take her sister by the hand, leading her back to her little table.

"I do not beat the children," said Eleanor quietly, her jaw set with ready anger.

"I did not accuse you of such a thing," he replied, taking

a deep breath and looking away at his nieces for a moment before continuing. "I apologize, Miss Webster. I fear I let my own experiences cloud my conversation. I meant no offense. One has only to look at the girls to know that they admire you, that they have no fear of you."

"Fear of me? I should hope not! Although sometimes I fear them," she added, before recalling her audience and blushing furiously.

With a teasing smile that made her heart do a somersault, he asked, "Now what on earth could you possibly fear about those two little angels?"

Eleanor could not tell him the truth—that she was afraid she loved the girls too much, like a mother. No, it would be giving him too much power over her. Hadn't she learned at an early age from her own father never to reveal how dearly one held something? Any time she had loved a kitten or a book, she had been forced to give it away to some "more needy child." It was the only time her father had ever exhibited a tendency toward charity—to give away something his only daughter prized.

Instead, Eleanor managed a rueful smile and said, "I fear I will never be able to keep up with them. You have no idea how active they can be!"

Sensing the lightening of tension in the air, Susan allowed the exuberant Mary to return to their side, joining them herself at a more restrained pace.

Bouncing from one foot to the other, Mary asked, "Uncle Stephen, do you like to go sledding?"

"I suppose. I haven't gone sledding in a long time, however. I may have forgotten how."

"We can teach you!" crowed Mary.

"Perhaps he doesn't want to go," said Susan, her eyes pleading with him in a way that words never could.

"But of course I want to go! Only, I'm not sure there is enough snow today."

"We have a secret spot," said Susan. "Miss Webster found it for us. It's a wonderful hill, and the snow lasts for days because it is in the shadows."

"But what about your lessons?" he asked.

"We will finish our morning lessons before we go," said Susan. "You said we might go back today, Miss Webster."

Eleanor smiled at the girls' upturned faces and agreed, "Yes, we can go back after you have finished with your mathematics and Mary has finished her reading."

"Huzzah!" they shouted.

"And Uncle Stephen may come with us?" asked Susan.

"If he wishes," she replied.

Both girls turned hopefully to their uncle.

"How can I refuse?" he asked, earning another "Huzzah!"

Then Susan took Mary's hand, and they set to work on their lessons.

"Exactly where is this magical hill?" he asked.

"Beyond the home wood going toward the Miller farm. It's not too tall, but they have a good time."

"Did you take them there yesterday, too?"

"Why, yes, but they had finished . . ."

"No, no, I didn't mean to accuse you of being lax in your duties, Miss Webster. It was just that we saw three figures from the road, sledding and laughing in the distance."

Her cheeks turned quite pink, and she said, "It was very probably us. Sledding is never a quiet sport."

"Indeed, not," he murmured, before rising and taking his leave of the girls.

Puzzled, Eleanor followed him out the door and asked, "I thought you wanted to know what subjects the girls are learning, Captain."

He turned, shaking his head; his dark eyes appeared black in the shadowy hall, but Eleanor didn't feel the least wary or intimidated. He radiated a warmth she found impossible to fear—or to resist.

"I don't think that's necessary, Miss Webster. I am convinced you are all that you should be as a governess to my nieces. Until this afternoon," he added with a nod before leaving her in stunned silence.

Four

Stephen made his way downstairs to his brother's study. He looked around at the white walls and ceiling. By the fire were two inviting chairs covered in red leather; across the small room was the desk, its top void of papers, but with a vase of silk flowers on the corner. No, not his brother's study. He recalled his brother's habits—he was a careless man who needed an army of servants to pick up after him. Oh, he had known how to get things done. His achievements at university had been hard . . . make that impossible to follow. Stephen had hated every minute of university life, and after only six months he had wrangled a commission in the army out of their tight-fisted grandfather, thanks to Charles's eloquent pleas.

He shook off those reminiscences and walked over to the desk, sitting down on the delicate chair. Another innovation of Miss Webster's, no doubt.

He wasn't certain what to make of this lady. It should have been obvious even to the most dim-witted of fellows, like his brother's solicitor, that Miss Webster *was* a lady. Whether or not she was a manipulative, conniving sort of lady was yet to be determined. With this thought in mind, he opened the top drawer and pulled out the ledger for the house.

Scanning the past month's expenses, Stephen thought he had never seen anything quite so meticulous as the entries for each household expenditure, from the purchase of several new mops to the wages of every servant. There was even a column titled PIN MONEY where Miss Webster had recorded in that same neat hand the purchase of such minute items as new ribbons and lace for refurbishing one of Susan's old gowns for her little sister.

Stephen closed the book and opened the drawer to take out the estate ledger. Frowning suddenly, he closed the drawer and opened the first ledger again. He skimmed through the past several months, his frown growing with each page. He remembered Baxter spouting some nonsense about Miss Webster working for nothing, but after another close scrutiny, he had to admit that nowhere was there a listing for Miss Webster's wages. Closing it once more, Stephen rose and searched out his sister-in-law.

He found her in the back sitting room that overlooked the gardens, reclining on a fainting couch, a copy of *La Belle Assemblee* in her lap. Nearby, her son and his nurse sat on the floor, playing with blocks.

"Good morning, Stephen," she said, moving her feet to one side and patting the blue velvet cushion for him to sit down.

He ignored her invitation and approached the child, placing his hand on the old servant's shoulder when she started to rise.

"So this is Simon, Viscount Ransom," he said, squatting down to be nearer the child's eye level. "How do you do? I am your Uncle Stephen."

Simon scrambled onto his nurse's lap and eyed the stranger warily.

"Now, that's no way to act with yer uncle, my boy," said the nurse. "I'm sorry, sir. He's not much used to bein' around gentlemen."

"I don't mind, Nurse. It will take time, but we'll become better acquainted."

Turning to smile at his sister-in-law, he was startled by the intensity of her regard, and by the utter whiteness of her complexion.

"Are you feeling quite all right, Laura?" he inquired solicitously, rising and hurrying to her side.

"I'm fine," she whispered, then added a weak laugh to further confound him. Looking past him, Laura held out her arms, and the little boy toddled into her embrace.

After burying her face against his hair for a moment, she looked up with a bright smile. "Sometimes it is so difficult to think of Simon growing to manhood without Charles. You must forgive a mother's sentimentality."

"Of course. It hadn't occurred to me. . . . He is a handsome little fellow, but he doesn't look at all like his sisters, does he?" commented Stephen, tousling the red hair of his nephew, who had fixed him with a blue-eyed stare.

"Now, Simon, you mustn't be rude to your uncle. Won't you give him a smile?" said Laura, tickling his tummy. The baby looked solemnly from his mother to the stranger and back again. Then, climbing down, he toddled back to his nurse and the brightly colored blocks on the floor.

"Babies are not very obedient," she said, once again patting the end of the fainting couch.

Stephen sat down, the frown returning to his face once again as he recalled the ledgers.

"Is something wrong?" Laura asked anxiously.

"Not wrong, precisely. Could we have a word in private perhaps?" he asked, nodding toward the servant and his nephew.

"Certainly," replied the viscountess. "Nurse, take Simon up to the nursery, please."

"Very good, m' lady," said the old woman, clambering to her feet and picking up the child. She held him close to his mother who gave him a perfunctory kiss.

When they were alone, she said breathlessly, "Now, whatever has you looking so unhappy?"

"Not unhappy, Laura, only I have been going over the ledgers for the household and have noticed a very curious thing."

Laura breathed a sigh of relief and relaxed against the velvet cushions once more, waving away this concern with a flutter of her lace handkerchief.

"Stephen, you really should speak to Eleanor about such

matters, not me. She has been keeping those books for years."

"Even before Charles died?" he demanded.

"Of course. Charles didn't wish to be burdened by household matters, and I'm afraid I never had the head for such nonsense. So after we married and dear Eleanor volunteered to look after it, I'm afraid I haven't given it another thought."

"I see."

"So you should apply to Eleanor if you have any questions, Stephen."

"I would, but the question I have is rather delicate. Miss Webster has kept wonderfully clear records, very detailed, but there is nothing there about her wages. How is she paid? And what is more to the purpose, how much is she paid?"

"Why, I don't know."

"You don't know? Then who would know?"

Laura was sitting up by now, her smooth brow creased with worry—not that she had been cheated, but that her brother-in-law might be unhappy with her and therefore with Ransom Hall. She certainly didn't wish to make him angry. Why, he might decide to leave and take his guests with him.

"Is it really so important?"

Stephen sat back in his chair and shook his head at his sister-in-law. He had never realized what a ninnyhammer his brother had married. Oh, she was delightful to look at and as charming as could be, but she lived in an ivory tower.

His lips curved into a slight smile, which Laura returned with wide-eyed interest.

"Perhaps you can enlighten me on this one point, Laura. Where do Miss Webster's wages come from?"

"Well, I suppose you could say I pay her. We never really discussed money. I told you I have no head for it, and since Charles didn't wish to be bothered with it, it was arranged that an account would be set up for my pin money, and Eleanor's wages would come out of that. Of course, she manages that account for me as well."

"How much is it?"

"My pin money? I haven't the slightest idea, Stephen. I

told you, Eleanor manages all that. I suppose it has increased over the years, but I am only guessing. I mean, if I have need of something, I simply buy it. Eleanor always manages to settle the accounts."

He shook his head in earnest now.

"You know, Stephen, if you were planning to remain here at Ransom Hall for good, I daresay Eleanor would be only too happy to have you handle the household accounts, too. I mean, she spends a dreadful amount of time each month working in that study."

"Do you never glance at the ledgers?"

"She tried to teach me when we first came here to live, but I never understood a bit of it, I'm afraid."

"She could be swindling you out of a fortune, Laura, and you would never know it!"

"As if she would!" came the beauty's loyal reply. "Perhaps you shouldn't speak to Eleanor, Stephen. I wouldn't want you to upset her with such absurd accusations!"

Stephen chuckled. "I promise you, Laura, I shan't upset her. I would be a fool to do so when she obviously holds your entire fortune in her hands. But I *will* speak to her— later, when I have become better acquainted with your Miss Webster."

"Good," said Laura, satisfied with this. She glanced out the French doors that led to the stone terrace and the garden beyond and exclaimed, "Isn't that the most beautiful sight you have ever seen? Since the snow covered the ground two days ago, I have spent almost every morning here, looking outside at the bright snow with the evergreen trees lining the far side of the garden."

"Yes, it is beautiful, but also very cold. I am going sledding with the girls this afternoon," he said.

"How delightful. It would be wonderful if there was a little hill close enough that I could watch from inside."

"Why don't you come with us, Laura?" he asked.

"What? I haven't gone sledding since I was a child."

"So what? You're younger than Miss Webster, and she

goes sledding," he observed, wondering why he had mentioned it. Ladies did not go sledding!

But Laura turned her head to one side and said thoughtfully, "I hadn't thought of it like that. You know, Stephen, I believe I *will* go with you and the girls, but you must promise to teach me again."

"I promise," he said, "as soon as I relearn myself."

"I must go and find something suitable to wear, something warm," she said, holding out her hand for him to help her rise.

When she was gone, Stephen shook his head, still unsure why he had urged her to come along. Laura was the perfect hostess, the epitome of social grace, and it was obvious that she doted on her children, even if she never went sledding with them.

Who would have thought he would be urging his sister-in-law to follow Miss Webster's example?

He smiled, remembering the squeals of laughter as the very proper Miss Webster and her two charges careened down the hill.

Perhaps they all had lessons to learn from Miss Webster.

When Eleanor discovered Laura was going on the sledding expedition, she decided to remain behind, claiming to have too much work to prepare for their guests. Laura didn't quibble, but Stephen suspected that Miss Webster simply preferred to avoid his company as much as possible.

While they were out of the house, Eleanor again met with the housekeeper, Mrs. Brown, and relayed to her the complete list of guests they could expect. After working out who would sleep where, they discussed menus. Finally, she made a list of those items unavailable in the village so they could send someone to London for them.

When Mrs. Brown had left her in the study, Eleanor made several entries into the ledger before closing the book and putting it away. It was then she recalled that the ledger had been on top of the desk when she first entered the room that afternoon. Her thoughts flew immediately to Stephen Ransom. She had expected to show him the books, but that he had gone behind her back, rifling through her desk without permission . . .

Eleanor caught herself before she continued on in this vein. She reminded herself that as Simon's guardian, he had every right to inspect the household accounts as well as the estate ledgers.

Perhaps it was just as well he had arrived and wanted to take an active part in the running of the estate. She was in danger of forgetting that she was only a trusted employee, not a family member or a permanent fixture.

What would happen when the children were grown? Or perhaps Laura would wed again, marrying a man who didn't want his wife to have a "companion." Such was not an impossibility, especially since the captain was bringing in new people and encouraging Laura to go to London for part of the Season.

A tremor of uneasiness swept over her, but she shook it off, remonstrating with herself for such selfish thoughts. She wanted Laura to be happy, and obviously this required having a man about her. She was positively glowing since Stephen's arrival—the captain's arrival, Eleanor corrected herself.

Really, thought Eleanor, she was in danger of falling into a case of the dismals. What she needed was some sort of physical activity. With this in mind, she sent to the stables and ordered her horse saddled. She needed another ball of blue thread to finish the reticule she was making for Laura's Christmas present, and she had promised to stop in at the vicarage and get the list of parish poor so that baskets could be made up for each family.

Dressed in a bottle-green habit and half-boots, she settled a sensible bonnet on her head and threw on a caped greatcoat before heading for the stables. Her mare, a large bay with a black mane and tail, greeted her with a soft wicker. Eleanor slipped her half of a carrot and stroked her glossy neck before allowing the groom to throw her into the saddle. With a little wave, she turned the mare toward the woods, choosing the back route into the village.

It was a lovely afternoon, crisp and bright, snow lingering only in the deepest shadows. She was glad she had been able to get away by herself. The girls were wonderful, but every once in a while she enjoyed having only herself for company. Even as a girl, she had ridden about the countryside alone, mounted on some dilapidated old hack that her sporting father had forgotten existed. His stable had been full of blood animals, but she had feared showing an interest in any of them. They would have been sold immediately.

She let the mare amble through the woods, making her way slowly toward the village of Church End, her mind wandering just as her horse was doing. Breaking free of the woodland path, she entered the road, nodding to another rider who passed by and stopping to say hello to Mr. Miller, who was returning from the village.

It took her little time to transact her business, and soon she was heading back home, feeling content and refreshed. When she rode into the stable yard, the head groom came out and helped her down himself.

"You'd better hurry on up to the house, miss. Miss Mary hurt herself when they were out sledding," said the old man.

"Is she badly hurt?" Eleanor asked, her heart beginning to pound.

"I don't think it's too bad, but they've been asking for you this past hour."

"Thank you, Shaw. You'll see to Daisy?"

"O' course, miss," he replied, stroking the mare's nose while Eleanor rushed toward the house.

She threw off her coat and bonnet when she reached the hall and hurried up the stairs, not taking the time to check her appearance or change her clothes.

Entering the girls' bedroom, she blanched at the sight of the physician bending over the little girl. Laura was sitting in a chair close to the bed, knotting and unknotting her lace handkerchief while tears flowed down her cheeks unchecked.

When she spied Eleanor, she rushed forward, exclaiming dramatically, "Thank God you are here! Mary has been asking for you this age!"

"Is she all right, Mr. Powell?" she asked, hurrying toward the bed and taking up her position opposite the doctor with Laura by her side, clinging to her for support.

"I think she will be fine by tomorrow," pronounced the physician, winking at his patient. "Won't you, Mary?"

"I'll try," she said in muffled tones.

Eleanor looked up at the physician for an explanation.

"It's nothing to worry about. As I understand it from Lady Ransom, Mary was going a bit too fast and took quite a tumble. She cut her lip and chin, as you can see, and bit into her tongue, which accounts for her fuzzy speech." The man smoothed the blanket and smiled at Eleanor.

"But she will recover?" Laura asked anxiously.

"Of course she will. And I was very careful sewing up that chin. She's so young, there shouldn't even be much of a scar," he said, tearing his eyes away from Eleanor and glancing at Lady Ransom.

"I wish you had been with us, miss. We had tho much fun," lisped the little girl sleepily. "Uncle Thtephen rubbed candle wax on the runnerth tho we could go fathter."

"Candle wax! Has the man taken leave of his senses? Those sleds were quite fast enough, especially for a six-year-old child!" exclaimed Eleanor.

Patting Eleanor's hand and giving her a warning smile, the physician added, "She's had a dose of laudanum to calm her down." He closed his bag and put on his black coat, saying, "I'll check on her in two days. I really think she will be fine after a night of rest. I'll see myself out."

"Thank you for coming so quickly, Mr. Powell," said Eleanor.

"Actually, he was passing on the road when it happened," said Laura, "and came to our rescue immediately. Wasn't that lucky? We couldn't all fit in the carriage, of course, so Stephen is bringing Susan home on foot."

"How very timely of you, Mr. Powell," said Eleanor with a grin. "Let me see you out."

They left the room with Laura watching her now-sleeping daughter.

Conversing easily as they walked down the stairs, Eleanor once again thanked the physician and added, "It really was quite lucky you were passing."

He stopped and gazed at her for a moment before admitting, "I wasn't just passing, Miss Webster. I was coming here to see you."

"Really, Mr. Powell, I have explained to you . . ."

"I know, but that doesn't mean I can't see you anymore, does it? Surely we can still be friends."

"Certainly you are welcome here at Ransom Hall at any time," replied Eleanor.

With a tender smile, he stretched out his hand and brushed a lock of hair from her forehead. Eleanor reached up and smoothed her hair, apologizing for her windblown appearance. The physician took her hand in his and raised it slowly to his lips, giving it a chaste salute.

"Well, well, Mr. Powell, I am surprised to find you away from your patient's bedside," said Stephen, climbing the stairs and stopping a few steps short of them, his gaze taking in the blush that was stealing across Miss Webster's countenance.

"I have already attended my patient, Captain, and she is asleep with her mother by her side."

"May I see her?" demanded Susan.

"If you are quiet, certainly," replied the physician, watching the child disappear up the stairs before turning back to the captain. "Mary is going to be fine, as I was just telling Miss Webster."

"Is that what you were doing?" said Stephen, one sardonic black brow rising in disbelief.

"I was just showing the doctor out," stammered Eleanor.

"Then by all means, show Mr. Powell out," he said, stepping to one side with a sweep of his hands.

Lips pursed tightly, Eleanor took the physician's arm and

hustled him down the stairs and out the front door. When it had closed, she turned and glared at the captain, who still watched from his high vantage point, a small smile playing on his lips.

Hands on hips, she exclaimed with a snort, "Candle wax!"

With a perfectly derisive swish of her skirts, Eleanor disappeared through the nearest door.

Stephen's smile widened. He had never known himself to enjoy taunting a woman as much as he did Miss Webster. He continued up the stairs, pausing when he had reached the girls' room, his thoughts on the woman belowstairs and the little tête-à-tête he had happened upon between the governess and the physician.

Perhaps that was the best solution to the problem. If he encouraged a liaison between the couple, he would have no need of sacking Miss Webster. She would leave of her own free will to wed the good doctor.

The thought made him sneer, and he experienced an overwhelming desire to punch the wall. Puzzled by this sentiment, he recalled the obvious warmth in the physician's eyes when he looked at Miss Webster, and the intimate gesture he had witnessed when Powell touched her hair and took her hand, kissing, not the back of it, but the palm.

He had half expected the proper Miss Webster to slap the physician's face. But she had simply stood there, her hair mussed and her color high.

Bam! Stephen winced and whipped his throbbing hand behind his back just as Susan threw open the door, blinking up at him in surprise.

"I'm sorry. I tripped and nearly fell," he lied before passing her and crossing the room to look down at the bed where Mary lay sleeping.

Following all the drama of the day, dinner was a silent affair. Eleanor had considered dining in the schoolroom with Susan, but the day had taken its toll on the child, too, and she was already washed and dressed for bed when Eleanor dropped in.

So Eleanor had retreated to her room and changed for dinner, joining Laura and Captain Ransom in the dining room after all. Even Laura made little effort at conversation, throwing out a few queries from time to time but mostly content to remain silent.

The captain, Eleanor noted with grim satisfaction, had evidently injured his hand while sledding, for he had it wrapped in a bandage. He made no effort to enliven the conversation, giving only monosyllabic replies to the few queries that came his way.

When Laura rose, Stephen stayed where he was, saying, "If you ladies don't mind, I think I'll just have a glass of port and then retire for the night."

"Are you sure you wouldn't like for me to make up some liniment for your hand, Stephen?" asked Laura.

"No, it will be fine," he said, moving his fingers gingerly.

"If you should change your mind . . ."

"Thank you. Good night, ladies."

In the hall, Laura said, "I am so glad we will have the opportunity to speak in private, Ellie. Why don't we go up to the nursery. I want to look in on the girls and Simon."

"Certainly," she replied, moving toward the stairs. "Nothing is wrong, is it?"

Laura put her finger to her lips and shook her head. When they reached the nursery, all was quiet.

Entering the schoolroom, which separated the girls' bedchamber from Simon's little room, Laura pulled two chairs away from the table and sat down, drawing her shawl closer around her shoulders. Eleanor waited patiently for her friend to speak.

"Stephen met Simon today."

"Yes? How did it go?" asked Eleanor.

"Oh, Ellie, I'm not certain. He didn't seem to be suspicious—although he did comment on how different Simon is from the girls."

"But that is not so unusual; surely that happens in many families."

"Yes, but that is not the whole of it. He is also going over the books. He was quite adamant about learning your salary, for some reason."

"Well, there can be no harm in that. What did you tell him?" said Eleanor, smiling at Laura. On this one count, she knew she had nothing to hide. There were no skeletons in her closet!

"Why, I told him he had best ask you, since I know almost nothing about such matters."

Eleanor nodded confidently and said, "We have nothing to worry about, Laura. The truth is, I don't really give myself a salary. Your pin money is very generous, and we live very quietly here. I settle all of our bills, yours and mine, out of it each month. The remainder, if you'll remember, goes into a separate account at the bank."

"Good," said Laura, but the frown creasing her brow was still visible. Shaking her head, she said, "How I wish all we had to worry about were the guests and the ball and such!

"That is all you should be worrying about," said Eleanor, patting Laura's hand.

Laura lifted her face and tears shone in her eyes. "I am so afraid Victor Taylor will come back with more demands."

"I inquired at the vicarage today about Mr. Taylor. He has gone to London for an extended stay, or so Mrs. Shell believes. She is delighted to see the back of him. I understand he makes a very poor neighbor," she added, hoping to tease Laura out of the doldrums. Laura smiled, but the frown was still there. "Anyway, I think you may rest easy, dear, and enjoy this house party."

"I hope you may be right, Eleanor, but I have the most sinking feeling in my stomach that something is going to go very wrong in the next few weeks."

"Stuff and nonsense! You are merely overtired after the excitement this afternoon. Now, you go on to bed. I'll check on Mary to make certain she is comfortable."

"Thank you, Ellie. You always make me feel better," said

Laura, rising and giving her companion a fierce hug before heading out the door.

Eleanor remained frozen, trying to convince herself that what she had just told Laura was the truth. In reality, however, she had been having that same sinking feeling for the past thirty-six hours—ever since Captain Stephen Ransom had arrived at the Hall. Shaking it off, she checked on the sleeping children before turning toward her room.

Passing the small room Jane occupied next to the girls' bedchamber, Eleanor heard someone weeping. She knocked on the door; red-eyed and sniffling, Jane opened it a moment later, throwing herself into Eleanor's arms without ceremony.

After a few minutes, the maid pushed herself away and wiped her face, apologizing profusely.

"Whatever is the matter, Jane? Are you unwell?"

"It's just foolishness, miss." She sniffed. "Just a woman's foolishness."

"Ah, so you and Mr. Punt haven't made up yet."

"No. He says he's too busy to have time . . . for . . . me," the maid managed before sobs overtook her again.

"You must be understanding, Jane. He does have many worries right now, with all the guests who are coming for Christmas. Most of the time, there is little enough for Mr. Punt to do, but now he must train the extra footmen we have hired, make sure there is enough wine and ale—all manner of things require his attention right now. You must be patient."

"I'll try, miss, but it's that difficult, it is."

"I know," said Miss Webster, patting the maid on the back. Grimacing, she asked cautiously, "You and Mr. Punt haven't . . . that is, you aren't perhaps . . . in trouble?"

"Good gracious, no! Why, I never! I mean, really, miss, I never . . . you know!"

"Of course, Jane. I do hope you aren't offended, but I needed to ask." Squaring her shoulders, Eleanor smiled and said confidently, "Then there is no reason you cannot be patient, is there? You'll see, your patience will bear fruit."

"I hope you may be right, miss. But I've kept you from

your bed for too long, though I'm thankful you stopped to chat."

"You're welcome, Jane. Good night."

Eleanor made her way down the stairs to the family wing. Passing the room the captain now occupied, she was surprised to see that the door was wide open. There was a cold draft coming from the room and she could smell smoke; rushing inside, she discovered a sight so ridiculous, she burst out laughing.

"Well, don't just stand there," snapped the captain. "Come in and help open the windows!"

Still chuckling, Eleanor entered and closed the door, hurrying across the small chamber to the row of windows that Stephen and his valet were trying to open.

Pounding on the windowsill, which had been painted shut, she called merrily, "What happened?"

"This deuced valet of mine was trying to warm my slippers and placed them too near the fire. Then he fell asleep . . ."

"I am so sorry, sir! Absolutely mortified to have allowed such a thing to happen."

"Do be quiet and open the blasted windows!" barked the captain.

Within minutes the smoke was almost gone, and they relaxed against the wall until Eleanor's teeth began to chatter.

"For heaven's sake, Corbin, get a blanket for Miss Webster. Not that one, man; it smells of smoke!" he added when the valet reached for the counterpane on the bed.

"Of course, immediately," said the valet, hurrying from the room.

Stephen shook his head and said, "I really do think he was an actor. He's certainly not much use as a valet, except that he knows how to care for boots and clothes."

"Well, you can't have everything," said Eleanor, unable to keep the amusement out of her voice, although she prided herself on not laughing again. "You can have the room next to mine," she added, sobering completely at the thought.

"Thank you. I don't think this one will be comfortable

until it's been thoroughly cleaned. I gladly volunteer Corbin's services for that job. He's the one who nearly burned the house down."

"I'll take you up on that. The maids have quite enough to do getting ready for all those people you have invited." Eleanor gasped at the incivility of her comment.

Corbin arrived with a blanket and threw it around her shivering shoulders.

"Let me show you to the other room," she said, leading the way.

Standing to one side, she allowed him to enter his new quarters before she began a halting apology.

Stephen raised his dark brows and let her dangle in misery before he finally asked, "Does my sister-in-law feel the same as you obviously do, Miss Webster? Is she displeased about the arrival of my guests?"

"No, Laura is delighted."

"Then that is all that really matters, isn't it?" he added, his gaze cold and distant.

"Yes, Laura's wishes are the only ones that matter," said Eleanor.

"Then we have nothing further to discuss. Good night, Miss Webster."

The door closed softly in her face.

Angry and mortified, Eleanor sought her bed, finding sleep elusive for the second night in a row.

Five

Stephen reined in Troubadour, a deep-chested gelding of sixteen and half hands that was feeling fresh after being confined for two days with a bruised hoof. The bailiff's mare caught them up, already winded after an hour's undemanding ride.

Looking down at the big man with the stained waistcoat and shabby greatcoat, Stephen felt only contempt. There was one thing a good soldier always took care of, and that was his horse. The bailiff was both tall and heavy, and the mare he was riding was dwarfed in comparison.

Endeavoring to keep the scorn out of his voice, Stephen observed, "You might want to think about buying another horse, Lamb. That plug of yours is hardly up to your weight."

"Certainly, Captain, if you think I need a new horse, I will purchase one," said the bailiff. "I can go up to London tomorrow and . . ."

"That isn't necessary. Have Shaw find one for you. He'll know just the thing."

"It would really be better if I choose my own. Shaw and I don't exactly see eye to eye," replied the bailiff with an obsequious smile.

"So I gathered from him, but he'll oblige me if I ask him," said Stephen, sending his horse forward again. He pulled up a few minutes later and pointed to a low-lying field. "What's all this water doing here?"

"I told Faraday to dig a drainage ditch at the bottom of that rise over there, but the man won't listen. Every time there is a little rain, or even snow such as we've been having, the field floods. It's not too bad now, but it's useless for planting in the spring—sort of like Faraday is all the time."

"That would be Tom Faraday?"

"No, that was his father. This is his son Christian—a fancy name for a fellow who almost never attends services on Sunday and is as lazy as the day is long. Of course, he's not the only one. You'll find most tenant farmers are willing to live on your land and take your charity. Faraday just adds being a nasty customer to idleness."

Stephen glanced at the man by his side with distaste. Robert Lamb was an educated man; his family was of the gentry but had fallen on hard times, scraping together enough of the ready to send their son to university, where he had met Charles Ransom. When Charles left school, he offered Lamb the position of estate steward at Ransom Hall, where he had been every since. Stephen wondered why his brother had done such a thing; Lamb was never a very likeable sort of fellow.

"As far as I can tell, all the Faradays are that way," the bailiff continued. "I offered the daughter a position as housekeeper in my house. She turned me down flat; ran off and married some gypsy, I think. They're all just worthless."

"I seem to remember Tom Faraday was an excellent tenant," said Stephen, frowning as he searched his childhood memories. It was no easy task getting past all the bad episodes to recall what life at Ransom Hall had been like when his father was still alive and vital.

With a snap of his fingers, he said, "I have it now. I remember my father telling me that Tom Faraday was such a shrewd farmer that with a little luck, he would probably be able to buy his own farm before long. I wonder what happened."

"That was more than twenty years ago. I guess his luck ran out," said the bailiff with a grunt of satisfaction.

"Still, I think I'll ride over and speak to Faraday."

"I wouldn't. You'll never meet a young man with such a temper. I would avoid him if I were you."

Stephen stopped his horse and turned his dark, sardonic stare on the bailiff, saying curtly, "But you're not me."

Lamb looked away first, then pointed to the orchard of bare-limbed fruit trees in front of them.

"I told your brother to plant these when I first arrived. They produce enough fruit each year to supply Ransom Hall and the entire village, if we wanted."

"What do you do with the excess?" asked Stephen.

"We give some of it away to neighbors."

"And the rest?"

"Birds have to eat, too," the bailiff said.

"Wouldn't it be better to give it away to the poor or something?" asked Stephen.

"If you start giving away food, nobody will work for it. They'll just be standing there with their hands out," added the bailiff, nervously twitching the reins to one side as he kicked his tired horse and turned down the path that ran the length of the orchard. "Let's go this way. I want to show you the gatekeeper's cottage."

"That's where you live, isn't it?" asked Stephen.

"Yes, though it's not easy. It's so small and old."

"Small? It has six or eight rooms, surely enough space for an unmarried man such as yourself."

"Yes, but it's in need of refurbishing, and the garden is a shambles," said Lamb, ducking his head.

"That's a shame. Old Morely, who was my father's bailiff, kept the place like a palace, especially the gardens."

"Well, he probably had help," grumbled the bailiff. "I don't have any help except one girl from the village who comes in to do a bit of cooking and cleaning. I suppose if I had a wife, people wouldn't mind helping, but they don't want to work for a bachelor."

Privately, Stephen thought that if Lamb managed to find himself a wife, she would probably be as slovenly as her husband. But he was being harsh on the man; perhaps the gatekeeper's cottage really was in need of repairs. It was well over a hundred years old.

It was called the gatekeeper's cottage because it had been

built beside the old iron gates that at one time led to Ransom Hall. The former entrance led almost directly into the village, but his grandmother, who loved visiting town, had persuaded her husband to move the entrance to the other side of the estate so that it was closer to London. The driveway leading to the house had eventually grown over with trees and brush, leaving only a small path. The charming stone cottage had fallen into disrepair until someone had the notion of letting the estate steward live there.

Just then, the structure came into view, and Stephen had to restrain himself from cursing. To say that the place was in need of repair was putting it mildly. The grounds more closely resembled a jungle than a garden. Weeds had overrun the flower beds and pathways, and the house, covered with vines and shadowed by huge trees, was practically invisible. There was no excuse for allowing the place to go to ruin, thought Stephen, keeping his temper tightly reined.

Sliding to the ground, he followed the bailiff into the house. It was dark and dingy, with little light managing to find its way through the windows.

"You see? The place is a shambles," said Lamb. "Sally! Sally! Where are you, girl?"

"Who is Sally?"

"The girl from the village. She was supposed to come in today and clean." He sniffed the air, his nostrils flaring angrily. "Lazy slut."

"Now, there's no need . . ."

A girl of perhaps fifteen entered the room, her eyes on the floor and her hands twisting nervously in her apron.

"Where were you?" demanded the bailiff.

The girl recoiled as if he had struck her. Her voice barely audible, she said, "I'm sorry, Mr. Lamb. I was hanging out the wash."

"Well, go and fetch us some glasses."

"That's not necessary," said Stephen, backing toward the door. "We'll let you get back to work, Sally."

She bobbed a curtsy and disappeared again.

"You see what I mean? Lazy and worthless."

Stephen thought he understood very well what was happening since his brother's death—perhaps even before Charles died. Judging from the state of the gatekeeper's cottage, little or no money had been spent to keep the place in order. No wonder the bailiff was in such a foul mood.

"What are you going to do about this place, Captain Ransom?" demanded the bailiff.

"First, we'll have the gardeners from the Hall down to put the garden and grounds in order."

"They won't come," said Lamb, shaking his head dolefully. Leaning closer to Stephen, he said confidentially, "It's that Webster woman. She won't allow anyone to work anywhere except at the Hall. I thought that solicitor was going to tell you about her and her high-handed ways."

"But you're the bailiff; you should have the last say on how the estate is run. And why is she keeping the ledgers for the estate? I can understand her keeping the household accounts for Lady Ransom, but surely you are in charge of the estate."

"You'd think so, wouldn't you? I mean, whoever heard of a woman running a big estate like Ransom Hall? That's not the way to get things done, I can tell you!"

Stephen gave a noncommittal shrug of his shoulders and stepped outside again.

"I've seen enough for today, Lamb. I plan to speak to the tenants in the next week, and I'll certainly have your house taken care of."

"Thank you for that," said the bailiff, rubbing his hands together at the prospect.

"You're welcome. I'll also speak to Shaw about finding you a suitable mount."

"I knew I only needed to bide my time until you came home, Stephen." He gave a nervous laugh and corrected himself, saying, "I mean, Captain. I told myself that when you got here, you would set that Webster woman straight, and I was right!"

Swinging onto Troubadour's broad back, Stephen said,

"We'll see that the cottage is put in order, Lamb. You can count on that."

Stephen sent the big gelding cantering along the old road, taking the long way around the estate to the current entrance. He had the strangest desire to take a full bath and wash away the experiences of the morning. Robert Lamb might have come from gentry stock, but he was the most repellent man Stephen had ever had to deal with, and that included the lowest-born soldier in His Majesty's army.

Perhaps that was the reason he so wanted to blame Lamb for all the problems on the estate—the crumbling fences, the tainted pond, and the flooded field. It was easier to think Lamb was the reason than it was to lay the blame at Miss Webster's door. He had to admit that, despite the solicitor's dire warnings, he found it difficult to think ill of her.

Stephen rode into the stable yard and jumped to the ground, leading Troubadour to his stall.

"Good afternoon, Capitán," said Monkey, appearing out of nowhere and speedily removing the big horse's saddle. He replaced the bridle with a halter, tethering the gelding to his stall. With vigorous strokes, the groom began to brush the damp saddle marks.

"I missed you this morning," said Stephen.

The groom's brush moved swiftly across the withers of the big horse.

"I asked Shaw where you were, but he said he hadn't seen you since yesterday. He also said one of the horses was missing."

"I had something to do."

"I see," said Stephen, picking up another brush and turning his attention to the gelding's head. "Did that something take you back to London?"

Monkey's hands stopped in midstroke, and he walked slowly around the gelding's head. Stephen continued to brush the bridle marks away, turning his head slightly so the groom could not see his grin.

Finally, Monkey dropped the brush and declared angrily, "This England of yours, there is no slavery, is there?"

Stephen straightened his face and drawled, "No, no slavery, but we do hang people for stealing horses." He couldn't hold it back any longer and began to laugh.

Monkey retrieved the brush he had dropped. Waving it at his master, he warned, "Next time, I will tell Maggie that you no longer care for her mistress, Miss Goodbottom!"

"Not that!" laughed Stephen. Poking his head around the horse's neck, he added, "Next time, ask permission to use one of the horses . . . and ask me if I want to go, too!"

Chuckling, Monkey continued brushing Troubadour, his off-key whistle breaking the silence of the afternoon.

Stephen left the stable, turning over in his mind the implications of all he had seen that morning and all that Lamb had told him. If Lamb was telling the truth, then Miss Webster was being foolishly tightfisted about expenditures for the estate. According to the ledgers, money had been paid for many of the improvements and repairs Lamb had mentioned. Obviously the money had not been used for these purposes. Then where were those funds?

When Stephen was at the edge of the stable yard, the head groom called to him, and he turned around, a dark scowl on his face. Shaw hesitated and approached with more deference.

"I'm sorry to disturb you, Captain, but may I have a word with you?"

Stephen closed his eyes and sighed. Opening them, he made an effort to replace his scowl with one of polite interest. "Go ahead, Shaw."

"It is your niece, sir."

"Which one? What's happened?" demanded Stephen, turning back toward the house.

"Nothing, sir. Nothing at all," said the surprised groom.

"Then what is it?"

"The last time the girls went for a ride, I remarked to Miss Susan that she would soon need to trade in her pony for a horse." The old groom expelled a short whistle and shook his head. "The look of terror in that child's eyes!"

"She told me she doesn't like to ride," said Stephen.

"It's more than that. She's terrified of horses. Partly, I think it comes of her following her papa around the yard here when she was just a little mite and getting stepped on."

"I didn't know about that."

"Oh, it wasn't much. The horse stepped on the tip of her shoe and it pinched her little toes something fierce, but she didn't come to any lasting harm. At the time, it scared Lord Ransom more than it did Miss Susan."

"Surely she doesn't even remember that."

"I don't know about that; Miss Susan is a downy little thing. After that, she was often out here when Lord Ransom was home, and she was happy enough on her pony. What she really liked was to ride up on your brother's horse Aster."

The old groom scratched his head and added, "She's not a coward, Master Stephen. I just hate to see the child so frightened of the horses."

"I appreciate the family history, Shaw, but I don't see why it's so important that Susan like to ride."

"That's what I wanted to tell you. Miss Webster came out here right after I said what I said about her needing to change her pony for a horse. She told me to purchase a gentle mare for Miss Susan, and I have done that. That was a month ago, and Miss Susan won't even come to the stables and look at her; she gets hysterical and starts crying."

"I see," said Stephen, frowning. "That doesn't sound like the Susan I have come to know."

"Miss Webster seems to think you could persuade the child," said Shaw, shuffling his boot in the dirt.

"Oh, she does. Well . . ." Stephen fell silent. He had to admit that Miss Webster, even if she was an embezzler, was a wonderful teacher. The children plainly adored her. If she was willing to place that much trust in him, then he would accept the challenge.

"Very well, I will do my best. Have Monkey ride the mare for an hour or so, first thing in the morning. That should take the edge off her, and I'll bring Susan down around eleven o'clock."

"That should do the trick, Master Stephen," said Shaw, grinning happily as he returned to the stables.

Stephen continued toward the house, his stomach starting to growl as he neared the path that turned toward the kitchens. The smell of something wonderful in the oven made him forgo his chat with Miss Webster in favor of Cook's pastries.

"Wash your hands, Mary," Cook was saying when he walked through the door.

Mary spied him first and rushed toward him, her flour-covered hands outstretched, crying, "Come and sit with us, Uncle."

Laughing, Stephen caught her hands and led her back to the old wooden table that stood in the center of the room where the three children and their maid sat, their faces smudged with white powder.

"Still letting the children help you with your baking, I see, Cookie," he teased, inspecting the empty chair at the table for flour before sitting down on it.

"My children always help on pastry-making day," said the Cook, a large woman with rosy cheeks.

"I remember you always had a soft spot for grubby little boys," he said fondly.

"I still do. Now, you go wash your hands, and you can have one of my apple tarts fresh from the oven. Those were always your favorite."

"Right you are," said Stephen, rising obediently and pouring fresh water into a basin. "I see you are already training Master Simon here on the finer things in life," he called over his shoulder.

"Yes, and he needs his hands washed, too, if you think you can manage," said the ruler of the kitchen.

Stephen obediently dunked a clean cloth into the water and turned to his nephew, who was on his knees in a sturdy chair, warily watching his uncle's approach.

"Let me do that," said Jane, the maid.

"No, no, I can manage," said Stephen, looking at the little boy and chuckling. "You have so much flour in your hair,

Simon, my boy, you look like a miniature judge." The girls giggled, but Simon began to howl indignantly at having his face and hands scrubbed.

"Now, that's much better," said his uncle, looking down at his coat. It would probably give Corbin a case of the vapors. "And just in time! Here come the tarts."

"Let me see your hands first," said Cook, inspecting each pair with a critical eye. Stephen, holding out his own as well, made a funny face, and the children giggled merrily. Cook wagged a plump finger at him and said, "None of your sauciness, Master Stephen!"

"I'll be good, just let me have one of those apple tarts!" He sank his teeth into one, rolling his eyes and moaning with pleasure. The girls giggled again, and he asked, "Which is your favorite, Mary?"

"I like the cherry ones best."

"And you, Susan?"

"I like the apple, too," she replied, reaching for one.

"I am sorry to hear that," said her uncle, pulling the plate toward him possessively. "I'm afraid you'll have to choose another flavor. The apple tarts are all for me, aren't they, Cookie?" he added, throwing his arms around the Cook's wide waist as she set another plate of the bite-sized tarts on the table.

She gave his hand a playful slap, saying, "Go on with you, Master Stephen. You'll share like everyone else."

Stephen leaned forward, staring at each of the table's occupants in turn. One brow raised, he said, "I may share, but I'm not going to like it!" So saying, he grabbed another tart and popped it into his mouth, sitting back and sighing with contentment. The girls began to laugh at his outlandish behavior.

Before anyone knew what he was about, Simon climbed onto the table and shook his finger at his uncle, saying firmly, "No, no. You be nice."

Jane grabbed the baby as Stephen roared with laughter, wiping tears from his eyes. After a moment of uncertainty, the baby's deep, throaty giggles joined in, and he shook off the maid's grasp and scrambled into Stephen's lap, patting Stephen's face with his chubby little hands.

Stephen looked up to find misty violet eyes watching the scene from the doorway. Eleanor glided across the room and joined them at the table.

Stephen put his forehead against Simon's and said confidentially, "I see we have another devotee of Cook's pastries."

"Everyone loves Cook's pastries," said Susan. "That's why you have to come to the kitchen when she makes them so you can be sure to get your share."

Eleanor pulled up a chair and sat down. Smiling at the captain, she said primly, "You really should wash before you sit down at the table. You have flour all over you."

"Ah, but our hands are clean," came his smiling reply. "That is the only thing Cookie requires."

He looked into her twinkling eyes until she dropped her gaze. The desire to see her smile again made him forget all about the warnings from Baxter and the neglected repairs around the estate. If only she would smile again, she might feather her nest all she pleased. Without deliberation, he reached out and lifted her chin so she would look at him again.

Their eyes met, and he dropped his hand.

She began to tremble and looked away.

"You have flour on your chin now, Miss Webster," said Mary.

Slowly, Eleanor turned her head and smiled at the child. "Then I should go and wash my face," she said gravely, rising and leaving the room despite the children's vocal protests.

Stephen pulled his unruly thoughts back to the children and made a silly face. "I certainly hope she doesn't expect us to save her any."

"But we have to save some for Miss Webster," wailed Mary. "We have to share!"

"He's only teasing, silly," said Susan.

The wide-eyed little viscount looked from one sister to the other and then back at his uncle. Hugging Stephen's neck, he said, "You be nice."

* * *

More than anything else in the world at that moment, Eleanor wanted to escape and hide but Laura came running up to her in a state of excitement, and she set aside her own feelings and asked, "What is it, dear?"

"We just received a note from some of Stephen's friends. They are arriving early—either tomorrow or the next day!"

"Tomorrow!" exclaimed Eleanor, wresting the paper from her friend and reading it quickly. "At least they had the fore-thought to send ahead and warn us," she grumbled. "Excuse me, Laura; I must find Mrs. Brown."

As it turned out, Mrs. Brown had already heard the news and was well on the way to finishing the last-minute prepa-rations for their guests.

"You are a treasure, Mrs. Brown," said Eleanor, heaving a sigh and pushing back the blond curls that had escaped their pins.

"Thank you, my dear. It really wasn't so much. The guest house is ready for the single gentlemen, and there are enough bedchambers ready for our other guests. When they do ar-rive, all I need do is have the fires lighted and make sure the beds are properly aired."

"Has anyone warned Cook?"

"Yes, yes, she was finishing her baking, and she told me she had made extra just in case. If they arrive tomorrow, for dinner, we'll start with some trout and have a bit of roast beef and ham with the second course. There's also a venison pie that she was going to prepare for tomorrow morning, but she'll put that off for dinner instead."

"That sounds wonderful."

"Everything will be fine, Miss Webster. You should go upstairs and rest before the guests arrive. You'll be needing all your strength in the days to come. I told the mistress the same thing, though she is so excited—bless her heart—I daresay she will find it impossible to sit still. But you mustn't worry about anything else. We're ready for them, whenever they decide to show themselves. Do run along and wash that flour off your chin," added the housekeeper with a wink.

"Thank you, Mrs. Brown. I shall go and wash my face right now before I forget," said Eleanor, wiping away the flour as she hurried to her room. The action pulled her back to that moment in the kitchen when she had thought she would drown in those dark eyes. What an absurd notion! she told herself firmly, pausing in the hall and glancing at a mirror on the wall to be certain the flour was gone.

"There must have been some flour in the chair when you sat down," said Susan, coming up behind her and brushing at the back of her gown. "That didn't get it all; you'll have to change."

"Thank you, dear, I plan to do just that. I'm afraid there will be no time for music lessons this afternoon. Some of your uncle's friends are arriving early, and I have things to do."

"That's all right, Miss Webster," said the girl, looking at the carpet and shifting uneasily from one foot to the other.

"Did you need something, Susan? Why don't you come to my room?" she asked, placing a gentle hand on the child's slender shoulder. Susan fell into step beside her, and they were soon settled in Eleanor's room on the comfortable damask-covered chairs beside a cozy fire.

Eleanor waited patiently for Susan to come to the point. She was such a pensive child, people sometimes mistook her quiet ways for flatness. In truth, Susan had a brilliant mind and an engaging personality once she grew comfortable with people.

This afternoon, it was obvious to Eleanor that something was bothering Susan, but she was taking her time deciding how to phrase it.

Finally, she asked bluntly, "Miss Webster, don't you like Uncle Stephen?"

"Don't I . . . but of course I like your uncle. He's a very nice man, don't you think?"

"Oh, yes, I quite like him. You were right, Miss Webster, I just needed to give him time. He is so kind and funny.

When we were coming back from sledding yesterday, just the two of us, I didn't think about the cold because he was telling such wonderful tales about the army."

"Surely not about the battles!"

"No, no, he didn't talk about that, except to tell me it wasn't for my ears. But he told me about his men and the other people he met. They did the oddest things," said Susan, giggling at some remembrance. "And he introduced me to his groom, who is from Spain."

"Really? I didn't realize he had any servants other than his valet."

"Yes, but you'll never guess his name," she said with a gurgle of laughter. Without waiting, she said, "It's Monkey. Isn't that funny?"

"It's certainly unusual," Eleanor replied. "But I'm glad you like your uncle, Susan. And believe me, I do, too; it's just that it is different for me . . . it's . . . Oh, I can't explain it."

"That's all right, as long as you like him. I was afraid, in the kitchen, that you were angry with him."

"No, not at all. I just remembered things I needed to be doing since our guests are arriving as early as tomorrow!" Eleanor told herself such a small lie couldn't hurt. Susan would never know that she hadn't found out about their guests arriving the next day until after she had fled the kitchen.

"Even the little boy?" Susan, who never forgot anything, asked glumly.

"Yes, I believe he will be here, too. You will make him feel welcome, won't you?"

"Of course," she said. "And I'll make sure Mary does, too."

"Thank you. That is one less worry on my shoulders. Now, run along and let me change my gown."

When Susan was gone, Eleanor removed her round gown and put on a soft wool wrapper. Pulling her chair closer to the fire, she stared into the flames and forced herself to remember.

The touch of his hand on her face had awakened long-ago memories she thought had been forgotten—memories of a time when she still believed her father loved her, a time when she had still believed in love.

She had known Henry Mason all her life. It had seemed the most natural thing when he said he loved her and asked her to be his wife. Her father had deemed the boy unworthy of her hand—in other words, too poor. Looking back, she felt certain Henry would not have made her happy, but she had thought she was in love with him. What did a girl of seventeen know? Or a boy of nineteen, for that matter? How sweet and innocent their kisses had been!

That was when it all began; that was when her father had realized that his beautiful daughter might actually have a value beyond being his housekeeper, if he could sell her to the highest bidder. If he had given her to the first one, a prosperous farmer, it might not have been so bad. She had been appalled at the idea of wedding a man of forty who already had five or six children; had she only known of the indignities that lay ahead for her, she would have leapt at the chance. But her brother had gone to London for the first time and had incurred heavy gambling debts, and her father had turned the farmer down, telling her that she would have to wed someone with enough cash to pay off Michael's debts.

Eleanor shivered despite the warmth of the fire. Next had come Adrian Chapman, a dandy with painted palms and long ringlets, who appeared on the doorstep of the little vicarage, demanding to see "the Webster chit." Eleanor closed her eyes; she could almost hear his high-pitched tones as he took her chin in his hand and turned her head from side to side, a sneer on his painted face.

"Egad, Webster, you'll never sell this 'un. She's too demmed tall. What's more, she's built like a farmer's daughter . . . or the farmer himself!" he added, cackling like a hen laying an egg. Eleanor had run to her room and locked the door. Her loving father, the village vicar, had left her there on bread and water for two weeks, trying to change her buxom figure into something more fashionable and willowy.

With a snort of anger, Eleanor rose and rang for Penny, going to her dressing room to select a gown suitable for accompanying the butler to the cellars to select wines for the next few days. She wasn't very knowledgeable about such matters and relied heavily on the rigid butler.

It took all her fortitude to return to the kitchen, but she needn't have worried. The captain was gone and only Jane remained, the maid's attention riveted on their stuffy butler.

Eleanor watched for a minute, undetected by the couple at the table. For the life of her, she couldn't understand what the maid saw in Punt, but Jane was head over heels in love with the man, who seemed quite content to accept her adoration without giving anything in return.

"Miss Webster, are you ready to inspect the cellars?" he pronounced formally when he looked up and found his mistress watching.

"Yes, I'm ready," she replied.

"You may go about your business, Jane," he said, looking down his nose at the maid, who looked ready to burst into tears. She managed to make her exit before she succumbed.

"I don't understand why you must be so harsh with Jane," said Eleanor as they descended the uneven stone steps.

"I beg your pardon, miss? I didn't realize it was harsh to tell her to fulfill her duties. And if you are referring to more personal matters, you should know that I have offered her absolutely no encouragement."

Eleanor cocked her head to one side and studied him for a moment before saying, "Forget what I said. It is none of my affair."

"Thank you, miss. Now, you'll see over here we have the bordeau and the brandy. Farther down the row . . ."

"You don't think it's inappropriate to have the girls dine with us this evening, do you, Eleanor?" asked Laura, biting at her bottom lip as they sat together in the drawing room before dinner that evening.

"Not if your brother-in-law doesn't mind," said Eleanor.

"Mind? It was his idea. I was so surprised, but what he said made sense."

"And that was . . . ?"

"Possibly this will be the last night we will be *en famille,* just the five of us, and Stephen thought it would be a good idea if the girls were allowed to join us the entire evening. I confess I am quite looking forward to it. They adore Stephen, and having him here has made everything so much easier."

"Easier?" asked Eleanor. That was not how she would put it.

"Well, certainly more pleasant. It is so wonderful to have a man to turn to again," said Laura, heaving a delicate sigh.

"Yes, so wonderful," said Eleanor dryly.

"I'm so happy you agree, Miss Webster," said Stephen, slipping silently into the drawing room and joining them.

She opened her mouth for a tart rejoinder, then thought better of it. Elevating her nose half an inch, she signaled her opinion of his comment.

"Now here comes Susan. Remember what I told you, Laura," he whispered urgently. "We must stick to the plan."

"What are you talking about?" demanded Eleanor, who was rather piqued at not knowing what was going on. Since when was Laura keeping secrets from her? And with the captain!

To her further outrage, Laura shushed her, and Stephen whispered, "Just follow my lead."

Since she had no idea what he was talking about, Eleanor was mystified when the two greeted the girls and began speaking of polite nothings. It hardly sounded like a plan, she thought sourly. Punt announced dinner, and Stephen offered one arm to each niece, though Mary had to walk on tiptoe to keep her hand in place.

The dining-room table had been turned and pushed against the far wall. In its place was a small round table that allowed the five of them to converse easily.

"Did you enjoy your inspection of the estate today?" Laura asked Stephen.

"Yes, it was a pleasure to see all the familiar places, though there are definitely things that need improvement. And I would like to speak to the tenants. Of course, it's been so many years, I don't know them anymore, and they certainly won't know me. I do wish I had someone to ride along with me and perform the introductions—someone the tenants would recognize as belonging to the Hall."

"Yes, that would be most helpful, but I don't know who in the world could do so. I'm afraid I am much too busy at present preparing for our guests, as is Miss Webster. Can you think of anyone?" she added, turning to Eleanor, who was frowning in confusion.

Eleanor began to suspect Laura and the captain had scripted this part of the conversation, though she could think of no reason for them to behave in such a bizarre manner. Mary and Susan exchanged puzzled glances but said nothing.

"No, I'm afraid I can't," Eleanor replied, playing for time.

"I know!" exclaimed Stephen, doing his best to appear thunderstruck.

Eleanor tried not to laugh out loud at his poor acting, and she applied her serviette to her lips to cover her smile.

Turning to Susan, he asked earnestly, "Susan, do you think you might accompany me to the tenant farms?"

"Oh, I don't know . . . I really think I have too many lessons tomorrow. Don't I, Miss Webster?"

Suddenly, Eleanor understood the plot that Laura and the captain had hatched. Though she secretly thought they were much too obvious, she willingly picked up the baton.

Looking at Susan's worried frown, her heart went out to the child, but she shook her head and said, "No, I think we have had enough lessons until after Christmas. Even the students at Oxford go home for the holidays."

"I'll go with you, Susan," said Mary.

"I'm afraid your pony wouldn't be able to keep up. You wouldn't want to make Mr. Applegate sick," said Stephen hurriedly.

"No, Uncle, I suppose not," said Mary with an apologetic glance for her sister.

"Besides which, I can certainly take care of Susan by myself. I took care of a hundred men when we were in Spain."

Susan was not a fool, but she was nine years old, and she was obviously torn between her fear and the desire to please this new uncle.

Stephen continued telling his tale, saying to the table at large, "I remember one lad of perhaps seventeen who had never been away from home. He was so unhappy at first. I assigned one of the older men to look after him, and he did just fine. When I checked on him a few days later, the boy had all the confidence in the world, and he was having the time of his life."

Susan looked at each of them in turn and then lifted her chin defiantly. "I'll go with you, Uncle Stephen, but I warn you, I do not plan to enjoy myself."

"That's my girl," he said, and then wisely turned the subject. "Now, how are the plans for the Christmas ball coming along?"

The remainder of the meal passed without any more plots surfacing, much to Eleanor's relief. Eating little, she studied the captain surreptitiously as one course followed another. With his dark eyes and black hair, anyone would pick him out as the late Lord Ransom's brother. Stephen was taller and more powerfully built, but they were both fine figures, especially in evening clothes, she thought. Stephen had one other advantage in her eyes: so far, he had not yet disappointed her or the tender hearts in his care.

Laura led the way to the drawing room, where Susan and then Mary played the pianoforte while their uncle sat close by. He turned the pages for Susan, encouraging her when she lost her place. Giggling, she resumed her performance.

Eleanor shook her head and took another stitch in the handkerchief she was embroidering for Mrs. Brown. He had been there only a short time and he already had all of them hanging on his every word, even Susan. Stephen Ransom was a charmer, there was no doubt about that. But she was still waiting for Captain Ransom to turn into his late brother, she thought, glancing up and finding him smiling back at her. When he smiled, he was impossible to resist.

So had his brother been. And Charles could play the perfect husband and father for perhaps two weeks at a time. Then he would disappear for several days. In the early stages of his marriage to Laura, his departures would be preceded by a day of arguments and crying. Toward the end, he would simply make some excuse about business in London and ride away. Laura saved her tears until he was out of sight.

Susan, who had been seven when her father died, would spend days moping for him. When he was home, she was his shadow. To his credit, he never seemed to mind; his patience was limitless with both his daughters—as long as he was home.

She often wondered if having Simon would have changed Lord Ransom in any way. Of course, he didn't have Simon, thought Eleanor with a grimace. Victor Taylor had given them Simon.

"A penny for your thoughts, Miss Webster," said the handsome captain, joining her on the sofa. When she didn't answer, he added affably, "Ah, you are hard at work, even as we sit here enjoying the music."

"This is hardly work, sir. I enjoy embroidery."

He lifted one corner of the handkerchief and studied the tiny stitches for a moment before asking, "Lavender?"

"Yes, that's right. It is one of a set of four, each with a different flower. They are for Mrs. Brown."

"How thoughtful of you," he said, giving her that sardonic grin that made her want to box his ears. Suddenly, he turned the topic again, asking, "I wonder whatever is the matter with Jane this evening."

Eleanor looked at the maid, who sat glumly against the wall, staring into space.

"It is none of our business, Captain Ransom," she replied primly.

"But you know what is troubling her, don't you? Miss Webster knows all and sees all!" he teased.

"Pray do not be absurd," came the tart reply.

"Will you slap my knuckles with a rod?" he demanded, the laughter in his tone causing her to glare at him.

Eleanor realized her mistake immediately. She should never have met that dark, powerful gaze when he was sitting so close. Her heart turned over in her breast, and she stabbed herself with the needle, the blood stealing rapidly across the white fabric.

She tore her eyes away from his, muttered a hasty excuse to Laura and the girls, and escaped.

Six

The next morning, a determined Eleanor decided to meet her fears headlong, so she marched down to the breakfast room, ready for battle. Her sharp greeting was met with a muttered response from behind the morning newspaper. When the captain put forth no further effort at civility, Eleanor pursed her lips and made up her mind to ignore him, too.

It was difficult to ascertain if this tactic was having the desired effect since he never looked up. Her thoughts on his discourtesy, she helped herself to hot tea from the sideboard, adding a spoonful of sugar and a few drops of cream before taking her first sip. She managed not to spew it across the table, but she pushed it away with a grimace.

"It's coffee," said the figure behind the paper.

She thought she could detect amusement in his tone, but she ignored that, too, ringing for a fresh cup and tea.

"Sorry," said Stephen, lowering the paper.

She was right; his eyes were dancing.

"I learned to drink it in the army. I like tea, but I prefer coffee. Since you ladies don't usually come down for breakfast, I suppose Punt only brought in my coffee. Couldn't you tell the difference from the smell?"

"I shall remember that," said Eleanor, relenting beneath his smiling gaze. Such was the way of a rake, a devil. She would simply have to beware of him, making certain she kept her head and didn't lose her . . . She couldn't complete the thought. It was too absurd.

Stephen set aside his newspaper and said, "I visited the gatekeeper's cottage when I rode out with Lamb yesterday."

"Indeed?" she said, taking a bite of her toast.

"I was shocked at the state of the cottage and the grounds."

Eleanor raised her brows in surprise, saying, "If Lamb is content to live in squalor, there is nothing we can do about it."

"But the cottage belongs to the estate, not to Lamb," he said, as if explaining things to a child. "Anyway, I spoke to Shaw and Archer and told them to go over there and fix the place up."

"Really?" she asked with an infuriating little smirk. "And what did they say?"

"Nothing. What would they say? They will do as they are told," said Stephen, frowning at her.

"Of course," she replied, taking another sip of her tea to hide her amusement. She really ought to explain to him why the cottage was in such bad shape, but he was being insufferable. It would serve him right if she stepped back and allowed him to take over completely. Just let him issue his orders; he would soon discover the results—or lack of them.

Eleanor sighed. The men would ignore the order and the captain would be furious—with her, with them, with everyone. She couldn't let that happen. She supposed she would be forced to smooth things over. But she wouldn't tell Captain Ransom about it.

Instead, she asked, "What time are you and Susan going out for your ride?"

"Eleven o'clock. Monkey is out riding the mare now to take the starch out of her. I don't want any mishaps. By the way, you played along admirably last night."

"Why, thank you. Susan saw straight through your plan, you know."

"I didn't really think we were fooling her. Shaw told me that you were the one who suggested she might be willing to ride in order to please me."

"Yes, and now you must be patient with her."

"Of course. I am not—let's see—completely 'dicked in the nob,' " he said, that sparkle returning to his eyes.

"I was overset that day when you arrived unexpectedly. I should not have spoken so. I apologize, but a true gentleman would never bring up the incident."

"There you have it. The crux of the matter. Anyone will tell you, Miss Webster, I don't give a fig for the rules of gentlemanly behavior. Most of the time I just please myself, and the devil take the hindmost."

"Odd," she said, pausing to take a sip of tea before she continued, her violet eyes widening innocently, "I thought I was speaking to the devil."

"Now, Susan, this mare is as gentle as a lamb; there's no need to be frightened," said Stephen.

Susan had mounted the mare without balking, but now she sat rigid, her eyes closed.

"Open your eyes, Susan."

She obeyed, fluttering them open for a second before exclaiming breathlessly, "It's too high!"

Stephen frowned and waved Eleanor and Shaw away. "Very well, if you are not going to open your eyes, then I will simply lead you around the yard, the way one does with babies who are put on a pony for a little ride."

After two or three excruciating minutes of this activity, Susan opened her eyes and called, "Stop, Uncle Stephen. I don't need you to lead me."

"Are you ready to ride by yourself?"

She looked around for Miss Webster, gazing at her in order to gather her confidence, before nodding.

"Miss Webster, you mean to go with us, don't you?" asked Stephen, clearly daunted by the prospect of riding out alone with his jittery niece.

"I would be delighted," said Eleanor, who was already in her riding habit and had her horse saddled and waiting.

They rode three abreast across the lawns, progressing at a sedate walk with Susan between them. When they reached the path through the woods, Eleanor led the way with Susan behind and Stephen bringing up the rear. The weather had turned warmer, but in the shadows of the bare trees it was still chilly.

The first tenant farmer was relatively new to the estate, replacing an old couple who had died three years earlier. He and his wife had four children, all under the age of six. Stephen observed that they all greeted Miss Webster warmly and offered them mugs of steaming cider.

Stephen led Paulson outside and questioned him closely on his plans for spring planting. Then he commented on the condition of the cottage and his small barn, which looked to be in excellent repair. Paulson revealed that his father and brothers had come over from the next parish and set everything to rights before he and his wife moved in.

Stephen frowned and demanded, "But surely that was the duty of your landlord, my brother."

Paulson set his jaw and clamped his mouth closed after saying simply, "I'll not speak ill of the dead."

Eleanor and Susan walked out of the cottage, where they had been admiring the new curtains Mrs. Paulson had made. They said their good-byes and mounted again. This time, Susan had a little more confidence, although she protested when Eleanor started her mare off at a trot.

"Next, we'll visit the Faradays," said Eleanor, dropping back to a walk. "You probably remember the family."

"Yes, I knew the present tenant's father, a hard-working man. I understand his son has quite a temper," said Stephen, before muttering under his breath, "I only hope he doesn't want to punch me in the nose."

"Temper? Well, he is a bit impatient, but he is always polite to me."

Faraday was everything Eleanor had said and more, greeting Miss Webster and Susan like good friends and offering his hand to Stephen. He introduced the captain to his young wife, who was expecting their first child at any moment, and again they were offered refreshments.

"I noticed that field the other day. If the bit of melted

snow we had caused it to flood, I hate to think what spring rains will do," said Stephen.

"True, but we'll have a new drainage ditch dug before spring," said Faraday, winking at Miss Webster. "It won't be as hard as you think. There used to be a ditch there, but it has caved in and become overgrown with time. Now, when the rains come, the ditch just can't handle it."

"But you're going to take care of the problem before planting this spring."

"Oh, yes, we've got it well in hand," he said, giving Miss Webster another wink.

Stephen rose, saying curtly, "Come along, ladies. We have a great deal to do."

They rode away from the neat cottage, past the marshy field, and toward the orchard, where the path widened and allowed them to ride three abreast again.

Finally, Stephen could stand it no longer, and he barked, "What was the meaning of all that winking back there?"

"Winking?" asked Eleanor with wide-eyed innocence. "Oh, you mean Mr. Faraday. I thought he had something in his eye."

Without thinking, Eleanor urged her mare to a trot, and Susan's mare followed suite. Caught off guard, Susan screamed, and her frightened horse reared up on its hind legs and jumped forward. Stephen dove for the bridle, kicking free of his stirrups and jumping to the ground, where Susan lay stunned.

Eleanor leapt down also, sinking to her knees and cradling the child's head in her lap.

"It's all my fault," she moaned, looking up at Stephen, wide-eyed with fright.

"Stop that! You're just going to frighten her more if she wakes up and sees you hysterical," snapped Stephen, feeling Susan's limbs for any breaks. "Besides, she's going to be fine. She's already coming around."

Susan's dark eyes flew open, and she started up only to have her uncle restrain her. Breathing hard, she whispered in awe, "I'm not dead?"

"Dead? Of course not! Does anything hurt?"

Gingerly, the child moved around in Eleanor's embrace and then shook her head.

"You're fine. I think you may have scared your poor mare to death, but you haven't come to any harm at all. Don't you know better than to scream like that when you're around horses?"

"Oh, Stephen, don't scold her," said Eleanor.

Their eyes met in surprise as they each realized what she had called him.

With an impudent grin, the devil replied, "If you say so, Eleanor."

She was trapped. She couldn't very well scramble to her feet and get away from him with Susan lying in her lap. Instead, with a haughty toss of her head, the proper Miss Webster said, "I think we have had enough excitement for one day. Susan, would you like to ride with me on Daisy?"

Susan took her uncle's hands and allowed him to pull her to her feet. Still holding his hand, she asked, "May I ride with you, Uncle Stephen?"

"Of course you may," he replied, holding out his hand to Eleanor, who ignored it and rose unassisted.

She walked away from him stiffly; he resisted the urge to brush the dirt and grass from the back of her skirt. He waited for her to ask for his assistance, which she grudgingly did. After helping her mount, he handed her the reins to Susan's mare. Then he swung up on Troubadour's back and leaned down to pull Susan up in front of him. The bedraggled little troop turned toward home.

"You're very quiet, Susan," said Stephen when they had been riding several minutes.

"I don't have anything to say," she replied, leaning against him with total confidence.

"What did you mean, when you first woke up? You said, 'I'm not dead.' "

She twisted around and pierced him with her trusting eyes. "Papa died while riding a horse; Miss Webster told me so—only she told me not to talk to Mama about it because it made her too sad," she whispered, tears pooling in her eyes.

"I see. You know, Susan, it probably wasn't the size of your father's horse, but the speed or the terrain that caused the accident."

"But I rode with Papa, and he was the best rider that ever lived. He never rode too fast, and if it was raining and slippery, he didn't ride at all. Besides, I know how tall his horse was. That's why he died."

"And that's why you have been afraid to ride your mare?" She nodded, and he gave her a squeeze.

"You know now that you can take a tumble and not be badly injured, don't you?" She nodded against his chest. "Good; then you will ride with me again?"

"I suppose so," she whispered, "but we must be very careful. I don't want to hurt Mama anymore."

Stephen didn't answer her. He just hugged her tight.

When they arrived back at the house, Stephen went straight to the study, searching out paper, pen, and ink. There was something going on between Faraday and Miss Webster. Considering that Faraday and his wife seemed to be quite happy, he couldn't suspect a romantic link. Recalling Lamb's description of Faraday's hot temper, he could only assume that Miss Webster and Faraday had some sort of business arrangement. Stephen remembered there was an entry in the ledger that indicated that money had been paid to dig that drainage ditch, yet it hadn't been done. He flipped through the ledger again. There it was, dated over three months earlier. This, along with Eleanor's odd reaction when he told her that he was having Lamb's cottage restored, raised his suspicions to the point where he could no longer ignore them.

He shook his head in disgust. Well, there was only one thing to do at this point. Penning a quick missive to Baxter, his late brother's abhorrent solicitor, he requested that the man search the banks for an account in Miss Webster's name.

Signing off, he slipped the letter into an envelope and placed it in his pocket. He would have Monkey take it to London that very afternoon.

If Miss Webster was lining her own pockets at the expense of her mistress and the household, she would have to put the money someplace. In her room, a maid might find it. No, someone of Miss Webster's infinite efficiency would no doubt have found a way to secrete any ill-gotten gains in a bank. If she had, he would soon know about it.

There was a knock on the door, and Stephen straightened, calling what he hoped was a casual, "Come in."

Miss Webster entered and favored him with a smile, saying, "Congratulations. I think it went very well."

"Really?" asked Stephen, wondering if the letter in his breast pocket had somehow caught on fire; it seemed to be burning into his flesh. Ignoring this, he said, "She believes her father died just because he rode such a big horse."

"She what?" asked Eleanor. "That is the first I have heard of it!"

"That's what she told me. She said he was too good of a rider to have an accident because he never rode too fast or even in the rain. It hasn't occurred to the child that Charles was only being cautious when she was riding with him."

"I feel so terrible," said Eleanor, a worried frown creasing her brow. "Perhaps we were wrong to concoct that story of Lord Ransom's death."

"And tell her what?"

"I don't really know, but it seems the only pleasant memories she had of her father were tied up with horses and riding. I hate to think we have robbed her of those memories."

Despite his suspicions of her wrongdoings, he put a comforting arm around her, saying, "You were right not to tell the child the truth about Charles's death, you know. Sometimes a lie is quite justified. I'm of the opinion that she should never discover the truth."

Eleanor looked up at him with wonder in her eyes.

A crooked little smile playing on his lips, he asked, "What is it? What's wrong?"

Gulping down a lungful of air—since she had forgotten
to breathe—Eleanor moved out of his embrace and put on
an awkward smile, saying nervously, "Nothing. I just had a
chill. If you'll excuse me, I should go and change in case
the guests begin arriving."

Without waiting for a reply, she scurried from the room
and up the backstairs, hoping to avoid meeting any of the
servants. Eleanor hurried to her own room, wanting a bath
before their guests arrived. She had been pleased with the
morning—until that moment in the study when he had put
his arm around her.

When she entered her dressing room and found the maid
there with the steaming tub of water, she exclaimed, "You
are a wonder, Penny."

"It was just a lucky guess, miss. You see I have all the
extra cans of water heating by the fire just in case it got cold
before you arrived," said the maid, helping Eleanor remove
her bonnet and coat. "How did it go with Miss Susan?"

"Well, I think. I believe as long as her uncle is with her,
she won't mind the occasional ride, and that's all we were
really hoping for. Has there been any word from the guests?"

"Yes, miss. Lady Ransom received a note around noon.
Her maid told me they will be arriving today for sure."

"Then I mustn't linger too long," she said, stepping out
of her habit.

Penny turned and put her elbow in the water. Using her
apron, she picked up two more cans of water from the hearth,
adding them to the bath.

"That should do it, miss. Oh, wait, I forgot your rosewater.
You'll want to smell nice for the gentlemen," said the maid
with a grin.

Eleanor let the remark pass and slipped into the copper
tub. She stretched out one leg to bathe it with the scented
French soap Susan had given her for her birthday. Her mus-
cles were stiff from the tension of the morning. She was
delighted with the result, however, and would always thank
Stephen for his part in helping Susan get over her fear.

The soap shot out of her hands as she lost her balance

and slipped down in the warm water. Sputtering, she grabbed the sides of the tub with soapy hands and slipped back again. When she finally managed to right herself, her hair was soaked and her temper frazzled.

"What on earth happened, miss?" asked the maid, rushing in from the bedchamber.

"I . . . I slipped," she said.

Well, that was true enough. She certainly wasn't going to tell Penny, who had a reputation as the household gossip, that thinking of the captain by his Christian name had sent her into a tizzy! But the maid appeared satisfied with this explanation.

Standing back with her hands on her hips and clucking like a mother hen, Penny said, "You might as well wash your hair now, miss."

"Yes, I suppose so, but it will never be dry in time to greet guests this afternoon."

"I'll build up the fire in the bedchamber, miss. That should do the trick."

A few minutes later, Laura popped into the room to announce excitedly that the guests were coming up the drive.

Her face fell when she realized Eleanor was dressed in her wrapper with her hair freshly washed.

"Whatever were you thinking?" she asked.

"I'll be down as quickly as I can," Eleanor said calmly. "Captain Ransom"—she had almost said Stephen again— "will be there to help you entertain. Now run on."

Laura brightened and said, "Yes, you're right, but you will hurry, won't you?" She kissed her fingertips to her friend and floated out of the room.

As it was, Eleanor's hair was still damp an hour later when she finally gave up and told the maid to twist the dark gold curls into a knot at the nape of her neck. She wasn't really fond of that particular style; it was too severe, but Penny brought out the curling rods and framed her face with soft, wavy tendrils.

Standing up, Eleanor took a last look at her reflection and nodded, smiling and thanking the maid. She was ready to face anybody, dressed in a dark green silk gown with a high waist and a low décolletage. She might not be willowy, but she was slender, except for her generous bust. There was nothing she could do about that!

The guests were already in the drawing room when Eleanor made her way downstairs. Hoping to slip in unobtrusively, her heart sank when Laura called her to her side; with a fond smile, her friend introduced her to the new arrivals.

"Ellie, this is Lieutenant Jones and his sister, Miss Hilda Jones." Her arm still around Eleanor's waist, Laura turned to the other newcomer. Eleanor stared up at the tall, lanky man and felt goosebumps rise on her arms. Laura was still smiling and said, "This is Sir Michael . . . I'm sorry, Sir Michael, I didn't hear your last name."

The gentleman in question stepped closer, extending his hand to Eleanor in a friendly manner, though his gaze was still on the beautiful Laura. "It's Webster, my lady. Sir Michael Webster."

Eleanor gasped, "No!" and twisted out of Laura's hold. She stumbled from the room, throwing open the front door to the astonishment of Punt and several footmen and running headlong away from the house.

Once down the front steps, Eleanor picked up her skirts and dashed across the wide expanse of lawn and into the woods, her cheeks flaming from the exertion as well as the flood of emotion that had robbed her of her good sense. She plunged deeper into the woods, branches tearing at her carefully coifed hair and her elegant gown.

How in the world had such a thing come to pass? How, after all the years of carefully guarded serenity, had her painful past found her? Was it just cruel fate that had brought her brother to her very doorstep?

Winded and weary, Eleanor stopped and spun around, looking at the trees and wondering if she was truly lost until she spied a familiar landmark and heaved a sigh of relief. Stumbling toward the boulder that overlooked the deep pool hollowed out by the stream dividing Ransom Hall from the

Millers' farm, Eleanor sat down and quickly realized how very cold she was. A rasping laugh broke the silence of the woods, and tears began to flow, a trickle at first, turning to a flood.

The burst of emotion warmed her for a few minutes, but the pervasive cold cut through her thin gown, and she began to shiver in earnest.

"Fine thing to do," she grumbled, "killing yourself over a ghost from the past."

And why? It wasn't as if Michael could hurt her. It had been years since he had sided with their father against her. Eleanor sniffed and pulled an embroidered handkerchief out of her sleeve, dabbing the last tear from her cheek. Really, things had turned out very well for her—except that she was in the middle of the woods and freezing to death.

Frowning, she rose and turned back toward the house, bending her head against the sharp wind that whistled through the trees. Just when she thought she couldn't go on, she looked up to find Stephen blocking her path. Pride kept her from throwing herself into the warmth of his embrace as she lifted her chin and one supercilious brow.

"Well, that was an odd episode for the very proper Miss Webster," said Stephen, his expression inscrutable.

Eleanor pursed her lips in silence and glowered at him. Hunching her shoulders, she resumed walking toward the house. Her teeth were chattering so, she would have found speech impossible. Stephen, however, didn't want to listen; he wanted to talk. Removing his greatcoat, he threw it around her shoulders and fell into step by her side.

"I realize things may seem a little awkward for you and Michael, but I have to ask you to set your feelings aside."

"You knew!" she managed as she shot him a look of wounded outrage.

Stephen shook his head and continued, "No, as a matter of fact, I didn't know. He never mentioned having a sister. And I know it is a great deal to ask, but I hope you'll be able to continue politely, for the sake of the house party and, more importantly, for the sake of Christmas."

"Not fair," she added simply.

"No, I agree, but will you do it? Surely, whatever passed between you and your brother—it's in the past."

Eleanor stopped for a moment, head bowed. Stephen leaned down, cocking his head to one side to study her tear-streaked face. She drew a deep staccato breath.

Stephen resisted the urge to gather her into his arms to comfort her. Instead, he forced himself to smile and say, "For Laura's sake?"

Another breath that was like a silent sob, and she nodded.

It was all Eleanor could manage; the cold was overwhelming. Her slippers were soaked through from the damp ground; even the hem of her gown and petticoat were soggy. She looked across the wide lawn at the house and doggedly put one bruised foot in front of the other, leaving him behind.

"Come here, Miss Madcap, and let me help you."

Eleanor stopped, thinking he meant to put an arm around her to help her along. Instead, he lifted her into his arms as if she weighed no more than a feather and strode effortlessly across the lawn.

Looking down at her, Stephen laughed and said, "Yes, I know you want to plant me a facer for treating you like a child. A true gentleman would undoubtedly allow you to crawl the rest of the way home just to save your pride. But, as I believe we established in the kitchens that first day we met, I am *not* a true gentleman. Now, close your eyes and pretend it is only a dream. We'll be there in a minute or two."

"And think about England," she whispered against his chest.

He gave her a puzzled smile, but fortunately he didn't ask what she was talking about. He probably thought her mad, which was perhaps not far off the mark. Eleanor buried her head against his broad chest, savoring the scent of his cologne, reveling in the warmth of his body against hers.

Stephen carried her through the kitchen, where he firmly ignored her whispered plea to put her down. He passed Cook and several other servants with a silent nod, and Eleanor decided the lesser of two evils was to close her eyes again and allow him to carry her up the backstairs to her bedroom. Once inside her room, she fairly jumped out of his arms, the effectiveness of this act of righteous indignation suffering from the fact that she stumbled and had to cling to him for support.

Deciding to be gracious, Eleanor said stiffly, "Thank you, Captain Ransom."

"Sit down," he commanded, leading her to one of the chairs by the fire.

Again she thanked him, but the humiliation wasn't over, she realized, when he sat down in the matching chair across from her and pulled her legs into his lap, removing her shoes and rubbing her numb feet vigorously all over, even up to her ankles.

"Captain! Stop that at once!"

The door opened and Penny entered, her eyes widening at the sight of her mistress being handled so. "My word!" said the servant, rushing forward. "You're half frozen, and here you are with damp hair and all!"

"Penny, go and get help immediately," said Eleanor, trying to push her skirt down to cover her feet.

Stephen interrupted, barking with military precision, "Go and get some warm water and towels, and send Corbin to me at once."

"Yes, sir!" she said, backing out the door.

"How dare you tell my maid . . ."

"Look, I've seen the effect of frostbite; you would not like it, Eleanor."

"That is for me to . . . and I never gave you leave to call me Eleanor!" she snapped, withdrawing her feet.

"No more did I, but I distinctly recall you using my name this morning when Susan fell off that horse," he returned, grabbing her feet and continuing to rub them vigorously.

"A gentleman would not . . ."

"And I also told you I don't care to follow some foolish gentleman's code when it's being deuced silly," he growled.

"There is no need to forget your manners, Captain Ransom," she said haughtily, once again trying to draw herself away.

But he would have none of it and pulled her feet into his lap again. "If you would try to be less exasperating . . ."

"What is it, Captain?" asked Corbin, his long coattails flapping furiously as he hurried into the room.

"Where the devil have you been? I want you to make up one of your special punches for Miss Webster."

"For . . . Miss Webster?" he asked, his eyes flying about the room, settling anywhere but on his master's lap and Miss Webster's feet.

"Yes, man, can't you see she's in need of a restorative?"

"Very good, sir," said the valet, prancing toward the door. There, he paused for a second before asking cautiously, "Do you want me to include all of the ingredients?"

"Yes, all of them!" barked Stephen, twitching Eleanor's skirt out of the way and continuing his task. "Stop your wiggling! I swear, you are worse than Simon."

"I am not!" came her petulant reply. "It is just that . . ."

Stephen's hands slowed, and he waited patiently for her to put her thoughts into words. Suddenly, her breath caught on a sob and tears welled up in her eyes, spilling over the dark lashes like a waterfall. He put her feet down and pulled her forward to take her into his arms.

The door flew open, and Lady Ransom sailed into the room.

"My poor darling! Your brother told me all about it."

Stephen was pushed aside as Laura threw her arms around Eleanor, their tears mingling in a perfect torrent of feminine emotions.

Shaking his head, Stephen retreated to the sanctity of his own room, where Corbin was mixing his famous punch.

"I'll take a cup of that," growled Stephen, tossing it down as soon as it was poured. "Once again." He took this offering and strolled to the window, staring at the gathering dusk outside.

"Shall I take the remainder to Miss Webster?" asked the valet.

"Yes, this will do for me. When you come back, I'll dress for dinner," said Stephen, walking back to the fire and sitting down. Even in his greatcoat, he had been chilled to the core while searching for Miss Webster; it hadn't taken him long to warm up, however, while rubbing her feet and ankles.

A lascivious grin replaced his melancholia, and he drained the second cup.

"An excellent punch, Corbin. You have outdone yourself," he added. "Here, help me remove these boots before you go."

The valet left off stirring his punch and hurried forward, exclaiming in horror when he saw the state of his master's boots. "Oh, they were such lovely boots," he mourned.

"I have no doubt that you'll be able to salvage them."

"I only hope you may be right, sir." The valet finished his task and returned to the hearth, where he had placed the bowl to gently heat the potent punch.

"I believe several more of your friends arrived while you were, uh, out, sir."

"Did they? Good. Well, you had better take that along. Tell her maid to be sure her mistress drinks at least two cupsful of it. She had quite a chill," said Stephen, grinning at the thought of a tipsy Miss Webster. "On second thought, you'd better make it three."

"Very good, sir. I have ordered hot water for a bath for you, sir. I will attend you when I return."

"Thank you, Corbin. You're a prince among valets," said Stephen, frowning when he was alone again. He put one hand to his head, which was beginning to spin. He hadn't had a bite since breakfast and it was not wise to drink the valet's punch on an empty stomach.

He looked around the room and spied a covered silver tray. Good old Corbin, he thought, standing cautiously before making his way to the table.

"Where is Miss Webster tonight?" asked Stephen when he managed to separate his sister-in-law from the other guests in the drawing room before dinner that evening.

"She was so sound asleep, I told Penny not to wake her."

"But she came to no harm through her foolishness."

Laura pursed her lips and narrowed her eyes at his smiling face. "I still find it difficult to believe you didn't realize your friend and Eleanor were brother and sister."

"I promise you, Laura, it never occurred to me. Michael never even mentioned he had a sister. Did Miss Webster ever mention him to you?"

"No, I don't believe she did. They must have had a terrible row," said Laura mournfully.

"Come, come, put on your smile again. People are beginning to stare," said Stephen, turning and greeting the Prentisses.

Dinner was a convivial affair, and Laura was the perfect hostess, just as he had suspected she would be. She had said that she and Charles entertained only sporadically, but she was born to the role, making sure each guest was well fed and amused. This was not such a difficult task, thought Stephen, waving away the venison pie. The tray Corbin had provided had done its work too well. Though it had cured him of his light-headedness, it had also robbed him of his appetite. A shame; Cook had outdone herself again.

"Captain Ransom, you are going to waste away to nothing," exclaimed the motherly Mrs. Prentiss, taking a generous portion.

Stephen chuckled and said tartly, "You must try to remember that we are no longer your boys. If we continue to eat the way we did while on campaign, we will not be able to fit through the doors."

"Ha, as if you would ever lead such a life. Since your arrival here, I wager you have ridden and walked as far as any days on campaign."

"Oh, I have been a veritable slugabed," he teased. "Most days I don't rise before noon, and I rarely move beyond my own chamber."

"With a lovely thing like that in the house?" she asked, pointing impolitely at her hostess at the far end of the table.

"My sister-in-law?" asked Stephen.

"Yes, your sister-in-law. She's quite a beauty, and you're a good-looking lad. Oh, I know it wouldn't be proper, but when is love or lust ever proper?" said the salty dame.

"You're right, but I assure you, I regard Lady Ransom as my sister in every way. I hadn't really considered . . . Now that you mention it, I suppose she is a beauty. And she's very sweet-tempered," he added thoughtfully.

"Aha!"

Stephen shook his head and leaned toward Mrs. Prentiss confidentially. "Not for me. But what about one of the other chaps here? Which one do you fancy would be suitable for her?"

It was like teasing a dog with a bone. Mrs. Prentiss's eyes lit up as she looked from one young man to the next.

"Not Sir Michael. He's too old for her."

"He's my age!"

"Still, thirty-six or so is too old for the lady in question. What about Beauchamp? He's a family man already, since he inherited his sister's children; he could use a wife, a mother for those babies."

"Too many children. Lady Ransom has three of her own, you know."

"True, that would make for a full nursery, and Beauchamp would probably want his own heir."

"Besides," said Stephen, "he told me he and his sister are only staying a night or two before going on to their other sister's house. Hardly enough time for romance."

Mrs. Prentiss nodded, and her eyes drifted down the table, narrowing as she settled on another possible candidate. "Now young Ardmore . . ."

"He's a gudgeon, and too young, to boot," said Stephen succinctly. "A friend of mine, to be sure, but the lady in question needs a bit of guidance."

Mrs. Prentiss grunted and said, "She's a bit of a ninny, eh?" Stephen shrugged, and she continued her appraisal. "Well, there's Norton, but he just doesn't seem the marrying type. Besides, he needs a rich wife. What about Jones?" she asked, turning her head and meeting Stephen's speculative gaze with a smile.

With a gleeful cackle, Mrs. Prentiss added, "That's the one. You just leave it to me."

Stephen grinned but didn't attempt to temper the lady's enthusiasm. Mrs. Prentiss had followed her husband, Major Prentiss, all over the Peninsula until a wound sent him home for good. They had no children of their own, so she had adopted the young men who served with her husband, affectionately calling them her boys. She was happiest when she was dabbling in matching one of them with some female.

Now she tapped his arm and whispered, "You had better tend to your other dinner partner. She's looking decidedly pouty."

Stephen looked at his friend's sister, who had been placed on his left hand. Hilda Jones was a beauty in her own right, but her expression, as far as he could tell, was always petulant.

Leaning toward Mrs. Prentiss once more, he said, "Very well, but please do not attempt to play the matchmaker for me. I am only playing host; I have no interest in that direction."

"I wouldn't dream of being so presumptuous!" she replied with a sly grin.

Stephen turned to Hilda Jones and engaged her in conversation for the rest of the meal. Mrs. Prentiss gave him no choice, since she seemed to be completely taken with her dinner partner on her other side.

"Did you go to London last Season, Miss Jones?" he inquired.

"No, I had had enough of London. I did go to Brighton while the Prince was in residence there. Have you seen the pavilion, Captain? It quite took my breath away."

"No, I'm afraid I haven't visited there yet."

"Oh, but you must. And the entertainments! His Highness is quite the best host around, present company excepted," she added with an endearing little smile.

We'd Like to Invite You to Subscribe to Zebra's Regency Romance Book Club and Give You a Gift of 4 Free Books as Your Introduction! (Worth $19.96!)

If you're a Regency lover, imagine the joy of getting **4 FREE Zebra Regency Romances** and then the chance to have these lovely stories delivered to your home each month at the lowest price available! Well, that's our offer to you and here's how you benefit by becoming a Regency Romance subscriber:

- **4 FREE** Introductory Regency Romances are delivered to your doorstep
- **4 BRAND NEW** Regencies are then delivered each month (usually before they're available in bookstores)
- Subscribers save almost $4.00 every month
- You also receive a **FREE** monthly newsletter, which features author profiles, discounts, subscriber benefits, book previews and more
- No risks or obligations...in other words, you can cancel whenever you wish with no questions asked

Join the thousands of readers who enjoy the savings and convenience offered to Regency Romance subscribers. After your initial introductory shipment, you receive 4 brand-new Zebra Regency Romances each month to examine for 10 days. Then, if you decide to keep the books, you'll pay the preferred subscriber's price.

It's a no-lose proposition, so return the FREE BOOK CERTIFICATE today!

Say Yes to 4 Free Books!
Complete and return the order card to receive this $19.96 value, ABSOLUTELY FREE!

If the certificate is missing below, write to:
Regency Romance Book Club
P.O. Box 5214, Clifton, New Jersey 07015-5214
or call TOLL-FREE 1-888-345-BOOK
Visit our website at www.kensingtonbooks.com.

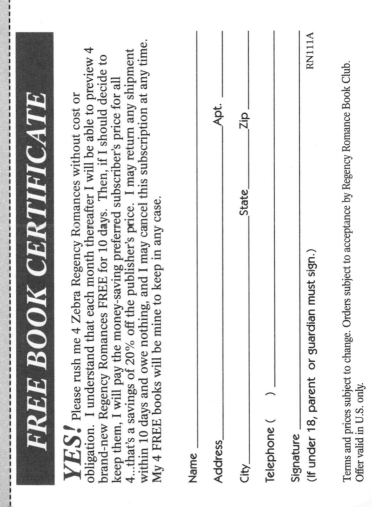

FREE BOOK CERTIFICATE

YES! Please rush me 4 Zebra Regency Romances without cost or obligation. I understand that each month thereafter I will be able to preview 4 brand-new Regency Romances FREE for 10 days. Then, if I should decide to keep them, I will pay the money-saving preferred subscriber's price for all 4...that's a savings of 20% off the publisher's price. I may return any shipment within 10 days and owe nothing, and I may cancel this subscription at any time. My 4 FREE books will be mine to keep in any case.

Name _____

Address _____ Apt. _____

City _____ State _____ Zip _____

Telephone ( ) _____

Signature _____
(If under 18, parent or guardian must sign.)

RN111A

Terms and prices subject to change. Orders subject to acceptance by Regency Romance Book Club.
Offer valid in U.S. only.

llₗₗ.ₗₗlllₗₗ.ₗₗlllₗₗₗₗlₗₗₗₗllₗₗₗₗlₗₗₗₗₗₗllₗₗₗₗₗₗllₗₗₗₗₗₗllₗₗₗₗₗₗllₗₗₗₗₗₗlₗₗ.l

REGENCY ROMANCE BOOK CLUB
Zebra Home Subscription Service, Inc.
P.O. Box 5214
Clifton NJ 07015-5214

PLACE
STAMP
HERE

Looking at her beautiful face, Stephen could feel the parson's mousetrap being set . . . and he was the mouse.

It was well past one o'clock before the merry group disbanded for the night. All the ladies had had their turn at the pianoforte, and Lieutenant Jones and Sir Michael had been pressed to sing a duet. As host, Stephen had tried to move from group to group, but no matter where he went, Hilda Jones always managed to drift along with him. Every once in a while, Mrs. Prentiss would catch his eye and smile at him knowingly.

Finally, the travel-weary guests began to drift toward their beds. Stephen bade everyone a polite good night, all the while biding his time impatiently so he could speak to his friend Michael in private.

"A word with you, if you please," he said, laying his hand on Michael's sleeve.

The smile Sir Michael Webster had been wearing all evening faded, replaced by infinite weariness.

Shaking his head, the man asked softly, "Can it wait, Stephen?"

Stephen hesitated, then nodded. It was really none of his business what had made Michael, their company chaplain, forget he ever had a sister, or what had made Eleanor flee from her brother as if she had encountered the devil himself.

"Certainly. Good night, my friend," he said, placing his hand on Michael's shoulder and giving it a gentle squeeze.

As if words were beyond him, Michael nodded and left the room.

Stephen climbed the stairs to his room. Hesitating at the door, he looked thoughtfully down the corridor to Eleanor's room. It was really none of his business to check on her, either, but he made his way along the dark hallway and knocked quietly on her door. When there was no answer, he opened it and peeked inside.

In the chair beside her bed, the maid Penny dozed noisily. Stephen crossed the room silently and stood looking down at Miss Webster. She was turned on her side, and her face in repose looked like a child's, serene and innocent, with her golden hair plaited in a single braid. One curl had escaped its bonds and fell across her brow. Stephen smoothed it away with a gentle touch. His smile faded, replaced by a frown.

What in the world was he thinking? He might not care about society's code of conduct, but others did, and to be caught in a lady's bedchamber in the dead of night while she slept would either label him a lunatic or—once again—the mouse in the parson's trap.

He crossed the room, silently closing the door before leaning against it and taking a steadying breath. When he was back in the safety of his own chamber, he reflected on one startling fact with brutal honesty: being the mouse for Eleanor's trap didn't instill the same terror in his breast as being Miss Jones's mouse had.

And just when had he begun to think of her as Eleanor?

Despite retiring at such a late hour, Stephen rose early and went out for another ride around the estate, this time by himself. If he had trouble focusing his thoughts on what his eyes were seeing, he wasn't willing to delve into that yet. Miss Webster, as he firmly called her once again, was only a thorn in his side. That was why she was taking up so many of his thoughts.

When he rode into the stable yard, his groom was dismounting from his own hack. Another groom took away this horse, and Monkey led Troubadour to his stall, picking up a brush and beginning to brush his glossy coat.

Stephen followed, keeping his steps even with some effort. He watched for a moment before commenting quietly, "You made very good time, Monkey. Do you have any news for me?"

"*Sí*, the weasel-man sent his man out immediately after I arrived. He put me in a small bedroom above his office for the night. I didn't stay there the whole time, though," said the young man with a lewd wink.

Stephen grinned and asked, "And how is Maggie?"

Monkey licked his lips and said, "Maggie is very good, *Capitán*. And her mistress, Miss Goodbottom, sends you her regards and hopes you will soon come back to London."

Stephen felt a strange impatience at this remark and returned to the reason for Monkey's journey.

"Just tell me what you found out."

"I don't know. It is all here in this letter from the weasel-man."

"Baxter," Stephen corrected the tiger.

"Perhaps I should call him a badger instead. That is close to his name, and he is short and fat like a badger."

Stephen took the envelope and tore it open; reading rapidly, the hope he felt turned to disappointment and then to anger. Folding the letter and stuffing it into his pocket, he pulled out a gold coin and flipped it to the groom.

"Your silence."

"You think it necessary to pay for my loyalty?" snapped the groom, his swarthy complexion darkening with anger.

Stephen paused, studying the young man before smiling and giving a small bow.

"I apologize, Señor Montoya, for my behavior. If you would care to return the coin . . . ?"

The groom flipped the coin into the air, caught it, and dropped it into his own pocket. "No need, *Capitán;* I will take good care of it."

Stephen's smile faded, and he turned away.

"It is bad news, *Capitán?*"

Leaning against the rough wooden post, Stephen said softly, "I didn't realize exactly how bad the news would be to me. I guess it never does to trust a woman too much."

With a heavy tread, he walked toward the house, letting the anger overtake him again. It was much easier to deal with than the disappointment that had washed over him when he read Baxter's revelation that Miss Webster did indeed have a large account at one of the banks in the city. Stopping at the study and going inside, he closed the door.

"Damn you, Eleanor."

"I beg your pardon?"

Stephen's head snapped up, and he found himself staring into the violet gaze that had occupied his thoughts the better part of the morning.

Seven

Eleanor rose from the desk where she had been working on the ledgers. Her delicate brows arched in surprise, she waited for a reply. When none was forthcoming, she said, "Captain Ransom?"

"What? Oh, it's nothing. I mean . . ." He paused, frowned, and pretended to sneeze. "I think I've caught a deuced cold thanks to your little episode yesterday."

"You did not have to follow me," she said quietly. "And I still haven't granted you permission to use my Christian name."

"Turnabout is fair play," he said.

"A gentleman would not bring that up," came the petulant reply. Her head was aching abominably from that valet's punch, and when she had woken up in the middle of the night, her thoughts had gone immediately to Stephen. And now here he was, making her head spin all over again.

Stephen wanted to rail at her, to shake her until her teeth rattled and demand an explanation for that bank account. She certainly couldn't have earned that much money as a companion or governess, not in a lifetime, much less in the ten years she had been with Laura.

Instead, through clenched teeth, he said, "I told you before, I don't care anything about your gentleman's code of honor."

"So you did," she said quietly, her shoulders sagging.

She really wasn't up to this repartee. She had sought refuge in the study to avoid the possibility of meeting her

brother in the breakfast room. She knew she had to face him
some time, but she wasn't ready for that yet. She looked up
to find Stephen's dark gaze on her, watching her with an
almost frightening intensity. She wasn't up to that either, she
thought.

"If you wish to use the study, I can leave."

"No, that's not necessary. I was wondering if you had
spoken to Michael yet."

"No, I haven't, but you needn't trouble yourself over that
matter. I don't intend to make another scene."

"Good, good. Well, I have business to attend to," he lied.
"Good day," he said formally, giving a little nod and slipping
out the door.

Eleanor leaned against the desk, her thoughts drifting to
that moment yesterday when she had looked up and found
him waiting for her. The expression on his face had fooled
her into thinking he cared. His attention to her, carrying her
to the house and even rubbing her frozen feet, had fooled
her, too.

"I don't care!" she whispered fiercely to the empty room,
her eyes filling with tears. "I'm thirty-four years old, too old
for such nonsense!"

There was a soft knock on the door, and she turned away,
wiping the tears from her eyes as Punt entered the room.

"Excuse me, miss, but her ladyship wanted a word with
you in the steward's room."

"The steward's room? Of course, I'll go immediately,"
said Eleanor, passing the butler and hurrying toward the back
of the house, a puzzled crease in her brow.

The steward's room was little more than a storeroom, almost never used, where they had placed a discarded sofa and
several chairs from the drawing room. The servants sometimes used it as a sitting room, and she had the occasional
meeting there with the head gardener or groom, since it also
had a door that led into the garden. Laura never used it.

Eleanor pushed open the door and froze.

"Please come in, Miss Webster."

Eleanor entered and closed the door, leaning against it for

support. "Good morning, Mr. Taylor. What are you doing here?"

"Now, now, that's no way to talk between neighbors. I just came to inquire about the little viscount. I trust he is well," he said, patting the spot beside him on the worn sofa. He was smiling, but the expression didn't reach his eyes. The coat he was wearing looked new, and his linens were white and freshly pressed. His red hair curled around his brow, reminding her forcefully of little Simon.

Ignoring Taylor, Eleanor spoke to Laura, who was sitting stiffly on a chair against the far wall. "Are you all right, Laura?"

"Oh, yes, Lady Ransom is fine. I wouldn't do anything to harm her," said Taylor.

Eleanor moved forward, standing between Laura and Taylor. "I asked what you're doing here."

"Oh, I just called to say hello; it's the neighborly thing to do at this time of year. Speaking of this time of year, do you have any idea how expensive being a landholder is? Alms to the servants and so forth. It costs a small fortune, I can tell you. And then, spending several weeks in London . . ."

"You want more money," Eleanor said flatly.

He rose, taking two steps and closing the gap between them until he was so close she almost gagged on the smell of his stale breath.

"Money or jewels."

"I told him I didn't have anything else," wailed Laura.

"Let me see now. You're hosting a ball, and you're having a house party for a dozen or so people . . . you've got the money," he sneered.

Laura gasped, but Eleanor jutted out her chin and said defiantly, "What if we refuse?"

The force of his hand sent Eleanor reeling. Laura caught her before she fell, and she shook her head to clear it. Pushing away from her friend, Eleanor glared at the red-haired fiend.

"Five hundred quid should do it," he said affably. "Of course, if you prefer, I can always apply to Captain Ransom."

"No, we'll get the money, but we'll have to sell some jewelry, and it may take a week before I can get to London, what with our guests here."

"I'll give you the week. You have the money by the night of the Christmas ball and I'll keep my mouth shut." He moved toward the door, pausing before he left. "Oh, one other thing. I haven't received my invitation to the ball yet. An oversight, I'm sure. I'll receive it in the next day or so, won't I? Good day, ladies."

"Oh, Eleanor, what are we to do?" cried Laura, jumping to her feet and wringing her hands.

"We'll do just as I said," replied Eleanor, moving to the small fireplace and looking at her red cheek in the mirror over the mantel.

"That will be a bruise by nightfall," said Laura, coming up to stand behind her friend, her dark eyes brimming with tears.

"It can be covered, and if anyone asks, I ran into a door. Did anyone see him come in—like your brother-in-law, I mean?"

"No, I don't think so. The children were in the salon with me. Mr. Jones and his sister were there also, but I don't think they actually saw him. Punt came in and told me he was here, but I didn't allow him to come into the drawing room."

"Good. It wouldn't do for any of the guests, but especially the captain, to see Taylor and Simon together. They might jump to conclusions."

"Oh, Ellie, what will happen when he comes to the ball?" breathed Laura, turning pale.

"I don't think we need worry about that. There will be too many people here for Taylor to stand out. And Simon won't be at the ball, either."

Laura shook her head vehemently, her dark curls bouncing like little Mary's. "I would do anything to make this nightmare go away."

Eleanor put a bracing arm around her friend's shoulder and said firmly, "We are doing everything there is to do. Now, let's go to your room and look through your jewelry chest. We must decide which pieces to sell that won't be recognized."

"I'm running out of the jewelry Charles gave me since we married," said Laura dolefully. "Soon the only pieces left will be family heirlooms, and I can't sell those."

"We only need half of the sum from that. I think I can squeeze two hundred and fifty from your pin money and the household accounts. As for the jewelry, we may have to take some of the stones out of the heirloom pieces and have them copied so we can sell the genuine articles," said Eleanor, putting her arm around Laura as they left the room. "People do it all the time. Don't worry. We'll manage."

"But this won't be the end of it, Ellie."

"It will take care of it for now. After Christmas, we'll see if there isn't something else to be done, something more permanent."

She and Laura decided to remove the amethyst out of an ornate old necklace as well as a ruby ring. The necklace was in one of the ancestral portraits in the gallery that ran along the south side of the house, but it was no longer fashionable, and Laura had never worn it.

Laura placed the pieces in the bottom of her dresser drawer in a black velvet pouch. Eleanor assured her that she would find an excuse the following week to go up to London and would take the pieces to the same discreet jeweler who would pay for the two stones and make copies to place in the original settings.

It had been such a horrible morning, Eleanor decided to salvage what was left of it and go for a ride. It was good to get away from the house and all of the complications of the house party. Once a refuge of peace and comfort, the drawing room was never free of company, and the morning room was no better. It was a good thing she had given the girls leave from their pianoforte lessons since practice would have been impossible with the parade of people constantly passing through.

It was to be expected, Eleanor told herself, with so many people living under one roof. The gentlemen found many ways to pass their days, from shooting to riding, but the ladies were usually underfoot. She admitted that they were a much more genteel lot when compared to the house parties her father had given for his rowdy friends. They had done nothing to make her feel uncomfortable, except by their constant presence.

Still, Eleanor thought, taking a deep breath of cold air, it was good to get away from everyone—including Laura and the children. Most of all, she didn't have to worry about another run-in with the captain, or anyone else who might upset her day.

"Well, well, if it isn't Miss Webster. You don't usually drift this close to my cottage."

Eleanor's head jerked up at the sound of Robert Lamb's oily voice. She cursed herself for not watching where she was going. Trying to hide her displeasure at their encounter, she said evenly, "Good afternoon, Mr. Lamb."

So much for freedom from worry. So much for peaceful quiet.

"I guess Captain Ransom told you that he's having the cottage fixed up for me. And giving me a new horse. Sounds to me like you're on your way out, missy," said the bailiff, spitting on the path in front of her.

He reached for Daisy's bridle as she tried to pass him. "What's the matter, missy? Don't tell me you're afraid to be out in the woods all alone with a . . . Let's see, what was it you called me? 'The poorest excuse for a bailiff you'd ever seen?' "

"Stand away from my horse, Lamb," she said quietly, trying to keep the loathing she felt for the man out of her voice. It would only enrage him.

He released the mare. "Oh, I'll stand away. I just wanted you to know how things are going to be from now on. I'm the one in charge around here now."

Eleanor grasped her riding crop and turned so that her booted foot was close to Lamb's face if he should try anything. Looking down at him, she said coldly, "I'm glad I came across you, Mr. Lamb. It will save me a call on you. Captain Ransom has ordered the men at the Hall to repair your place, but we both know they won't make a move without my say-so. While they are at the cottage, if you interfere in any way, I will pull them and tell Captain Ransom exactly what happened the last time. You remember that, don't you? When Lord Ransom gave you the money to pay the workers and it somehow disappeared? I wonder if your personal affairs would stand up under close scrutiny."

He gave a cringing bow and stood aside.

"Do we understand each other?" she asked. He nodded, and Eleanor turned Daisy around and headed back to the Hall.

For once she wished she had taken a groom with her. Lamb was a coward and would not have accosted her if there had been a witness.

If only Simon's inheritance didn't lie in the balance. She would raise such a ruckus with Captain Ransom about all manner of things!

But she couldn't. There were too many lives at stake— Simon's, Laura's, and her own.

Eleanor vowed to keep to her room the remainder of the afternoon. The blow Taylor had dealt her had darkened, but it wasn't as bad as she had feared. At least her eye wasn't turning black. With Penny's help, she thought she would be able to mask it.

During her ride, Lord and Lady Reading had arrived with their son. Eleanor decided a visit to the nursery was in order, and climbed the stairs wearily. Susan, Mary, and Simon were making the acquaintance of Lord Reading's son, Peter, who was not six years old, he quickly informed them, but eight.

"I am very happy to make your acquaintance, Peter," said Eleanor, smiling at the bright-eyed boy. "I am Miss Webster."

"Are you a maid?" he asked, obviously puzzled about her place in the scheme of things.

"No, silly," said Mary. "Miss Webster is our governess."

"Governess, what's that?"

"Our teacher," said Susan.

"I don't have a governess. I have a tutor," he announced grandly. "He's not here, though. My father allowed him to have a holiday."

"How kind of your father," said Eleanor. "Well, Jane here will be happy to look after you, too, Peter."

"I can look after myself," he said, standing with his legs slightly spread and his chest out.

"Oh? You take care of your own clothes and meals?" Susan asked tartly.

"No, I don't do that!" he replied, frowning up at her.

Eleanor deemed it best to interrupt before the two older children came to cuffs. "Peter, did you meet Simon? I'm sure he's delighted to have another young man in the nursery."

"He's just a baby," said Peter dismissively.

"He's our brother," replied Mary, frowning at the newcomer.

"I'll tell you what, girls. Why don't we take Peter outside and show him the stables? I'm sure he would like to see your ponies, wouldn't you, Peter?"

"I suppose so."

"Good, then fetch your cloaks, girls. Jane, you'll look after Simon?"

"Gladly, miss," said the maid. While the children were putting on their wraps, Jane whispered, "That one's going to be a real pleasure to have around."

"I think when they are left to their own devices, they'll work things out," said Eleanor, wincing as she smiled.

Jane cocked her head to one side and asked, "Is that a bruise on your face? What happened?"

"I, uh, ran into a door," she said. "I hoped it wouldn't be noticeable."

"Oh, it's not, really. It was just the face you made when you smiled. It looked like it hurt."

"Just a little. I must learn to be more careful. Are you ready, children?"

"I could take them, miss, if you like," said Jane.

"No, no, I don't mind. Everybody bundled up? Good, then let's go," said Eleanor, shepherding the three children from the room.

Jane remained behind with the baby, who was busily dismantling the buildings his sisters had so carefully built out of blocks of wood. His childish squeals filled the air, and Jane clapped her hands and cheered.

"So this is where all the fun is," said Stephen, leaning on the door frame. Behind him, Sir Michael peered over his shoulder. Jane jumped to her feet, wide-eyed at receiving such lofty visitors in the nursery.

Dipping into a low curtsy, she bobbed up and said, "Beggin' yer pardon, sirs. We were just havin' a bit of fun."

"So I see," said Stephen, entering the room and sitting down on the floor beside his nephew. "And how are you today, Simon?"

Simon answered by climbing onto his uncle's lap and hugging his neck. Looking over the baby's head, Stephen asked, "Where is Miss Webster? I was told she was up in the nursery."

"She's taken the girls and Master Peter for a visit to the stables, sir. They shouldn't be too long."

"That's a shame. I brought her brother up for a visit. Michael, this is Jane, who looks after my nieces so well."

"Her brother?" exclaimed the maid, dipping into another curtsy. "Please do come in, Mr. Webster."

"It's Sir Michael," said Stephen.

"Oh, I do beg yer pardon, Sir Michael."

"Think nothing of it," said the tall, blond-haired man.

Michael grinned as she studied him gravely and pronounced, "You have the look of Miss Webster; I mean, you're tall like her, and have the same hair and eyes."

"His eyes aren't at all the same color," said Stephen from

his vantage point on the floor. "Miss Webster's eyes are violet."

Michael and the maid stood amazed while Stephen continued, speaking to the baby this time, "Isn't that so, Simon? Miss Webster has very pretty violet eyes. A little deeper than lavender, I would judge."

Simon ignored this commentary and began to rearrange his uncle's cravat while Stephen looked up at the maid. "If you have other things to do, Jane, I'll stay with Simon for a little while."

"Sir, he can be quite the handful. I think I should . . ."

Michael, who had even less experience with children, chimed in, "Don't worry, Jane, I'll stay and help."

"If you say so, Sir Michael. I do need to speak to Cook about the children's dinner. I won't be but a minute." Jane slipped quietly out of the room, leaving the two men alone with the baby.

Michael sat down on one of the tables and watched Stephen playing peekaboo with the baby.

"He's got your hair," he said after a moment.

"What? Oh, you mean the white streak. Yes, I noticed that right off. My mother had red hair, too, and the streak of white as well." Stephen began to stack the wooden blocks, laughing when Simon kicked them over.

"Well done, milord," he said, nodding to the little boy. "Now, can you stack them up again?" They stacked them together and, once again, Simon knocked them down with squeals of delight.

"You should think of marrying and setting up your own nursery, Stephen. You're really quite paternal," quipped his friend after watching for several minutes.

"I'd have to find a wife first, and that's the part that just doesn't set well with me. I don't think I could stay with just one woman. I mean, look at me. I've been back in England for six weeks. I've had the Goodbottom in my keeping for four weeks; I've been here for a week of that, and I'm already bored with her. No, I don't think that would be fair to a woman—or to me!"

Simon toddled over to Michael and stared at him for a moment before raising his arms to be picked up. He quickly set about destroying the carefully crafted folds of the newcomer's cravat. Michael laughed good-naturedly and stood up, hefting the baby above his head and then back down; Simon giggled gleefully. Michael stopped, holding the boy close for a moment as he looked down at his friend.

"I know I only just arrived, but I am very observant. The thought occurs to me that perhaps you might not grow tired of having a wife if she had golden hair and violet eyes, eyes a little deeper in color than lavender."

"Devil a bit!" exclaimed Stephen, his nostrils flaring in disdain, his dark brows drawing together in a fierce frown.

Looking down at him from Michael's arms, little Simon shook his finger at his scowling uncle and said solemnly, "You be nice."

The two men roared with laughter, and Michael swung little Simon around his head, setting him back on the ground, where he clamored for more.

Stephen watched as Michael swung the baby up again and said, "Before you get too busy rearranging my life, old friend, perhaps you should see to your own."

Still holding Simon high, Michael said, "You mean Eleanor?"

Stephen nodded, smiling up at his giggling nephew. "It's rather odd, don't you think, that you never even mentioned you had a sister?"

Michael set the boy down again, saying, "I've told you enough about my father for you to know how bad it was for me growing up. Only think how it must have been for Eleanor. And her brother didn't even have enough moral fiber to protect her," he said with bitter self-recrimination. "No wonder she ran away when she saw me; now I have the distinct feeling she is avoiding me."

Jane entered, putting an end to their conversation. Simon reluctantly released his new friend's neck and latched onto his uncle, letting him go only when Stephen promised to return again soon.

* * *

"Where have you been all day, Captain Ransom?" asked Hilda Jones, clamping her hand down on his arm when he entered the drawing room before dinner.

He looked into her pretty face and smiled, curbing his impatience. "I am running the estate now, Miss Jones. I have many things to do every day," he said. Afraid he had been rude, he asked, "What have you been doing?"

"Oh, this and that," she drawled with a bored sigh.

"Are you enjoying spending time with Sailor again?"

"Sailor? Oh, you mean Malcolm," she said, giggling. "I always look around to see who you gentlemen are talking about when you mention Sailor. How did he come by such a droll nickname?"

"He didn't tell you?" asked Stephen, grinning down at her.

"No, I'm afraid not."

"Then I'm certainly not going to reveal the tale," said Stephen, leading her over to the other guests.

After only two nights, the gentlemen had already fallen into the habit of meeting in the drawing room an hour or so before dinner. The ladies usually put in an appearance ten or fifteen minutes before dinner was announced. Stephen looked down and grimaced at Miss Jones, who had her talons in his coat sleeve.

Most of the ladies, he thought dryly. As Sailor had warned him, Hilda meant to find herself a husband while under his care, and Stephen was very much afraid the lady had settled her sights on him.

"Why, I vow I am the luckiest lady in all of England to have such a handsome group of gentlemen all to myself. How fortunate that the other ladies don't know what they are missing," she simpered.

"We are the fortunate ones," said Ensign Ardmore, the youngest officer at the house party.

"La, you are a rogue," she tittered, giving his arm a playful rap with her silk fan. "Now, don't let me interrupt your conversation, gentlemen. You just go on with whatever you were talking about. I assure you, with a brother like Malcolm, I am accustomed to masculine conversation."

She was either a consummate actress or Sailor had been away too long and didn't know his sister at all. Plucking Miss Jones's fingers from his arm, Stephen signaled his friend with a tiny jerk of his head. Together, they wandered away from the others.

"Sailor, your sister is not at all the way you painted her," said Stephen.

Michael joined them and concurred. "She's charming," he pronounced.

"Maybe. I must admit I haven't been around her in years, and I suppose it is possible she has changed, grown up. But I tell you, if you value your freedom, you had best watch your step," said Sailor, shaking his head.

"By the way, she wants to know how you earned your name, Malcolm," said Stephen with a lewd grin.

"Devil take me, you didn't tell her, did you?"

Michael and Stephen laughed at their friend's alarm. "Do you not think she would applaud your accomplishment— bedding more camp followers on that first sail to Spain than anyone else?" Stephen said.

"Ah, those were the days," said Sailor, his gray eyes lighting with mirth. "Now, we're just a dull bunch of ex-soldiers. No more derring-do, my friends!"

"Derring-do?" laughed Sir Michael. "More like tales of derrieres . . . er, good evening, Lady Ransom."

The gentlemen greeted their hostess warmly, and Laura very properly ignored the topic of the conversation she had interrupted.

"Is Eleanor down yet?" she asked Stephen.

"No, not yet."

"I do hope you and Eleanor can patch things up, Sir Michael. I have always considered her like a sister to me, you know," said Laura, laying her hand on Michael's sleeve.

"I'm sure we'll be able to settle things. We have both changed through the years. I hope she can forgive me my youthful transgressions," he replied, covering her hand with his. He looked up to find his sister's gaze on his hand and quickly stepped away from Lady Ransom.

"Eleanor," he said, nodding slightly.

"Good evening, everyone," she said. Turning to Lieutenant Jones, she added, "I do hope you'll forgive my discourtesy yesterday when I didn't greet you properly. And your sister, too."

"Of course, Miss Webster. All is forgiven. I hope you are feeling more the thing," said Sailor Jones. "By Jove, you and Michael really do look alike."

"How . . . kind of you to say so," she replied haltingly.

He blushed a fiery red and stammered, "That is, you are so much prettier than Michael. I mean . . ."

"We know exactly what you mean, Mr. Jones," said Laura, smiling up at him in such a way that his color returned to normal and he was able to laugh at himself.

"There you are, my dear captain," said Hilda Jones, latching onto Stephen's arm again and turning so that she singled him out.

"Hilda, may I introduce you to Miss Webster, Michael's sister?" said Sailor, frowning slightly when she turned and regarded Eleanor with a haughty stare. "Miss Webster, this is my sister," he added dully.

"How do you do, Miss Jones?" said Eleanor.

"Quite well, thank you," said Miss Jones, turning away and pulling Stephen along with her.

He balked at her high-handed treatment, but Punt arrived just then and announced dinner. He had little choice but to escort Miss Jones into the dining room.

Eleanor placed a reluctant hand on her brother's arm.

"Eleanor, we should talk," he said quietly.

"Yes, I know. I'm sorry. I shouldn't have avoided you all day. I simply didn't feel up to it."

"I understand," he began. "And I'll understand if you feel you cannot forgive me."

Eleanor looked up sharply. In more than fifteen years, she had never trusted any man. How could she do so now? And especially this man who had betrayed her all those years ago?

"Why don't we go for a ride in the morning?" she suggested as he seated her at the table.

Leaning over her shoulder, he whispered, "I look forward to it."

As he moved down the room to his own seat, Eleanor watched him go.

Her vision was suddenly blocked by a tall, older woman with steel-gray hair, who leaned around Mr. Ardmore and nodded at her, saying, "He's a fine figure of a man, your brother. He was a fine soldier, too. The company chaplain, don't you know." The woman sat back and attacked the first course, leaving Eleanor to her troubled thoughts.

She had no idea Michael had become a chaplain. The notion astounded her. The more she thought about it, the more outlandish it seemed. Of course, she reminded herself with the usual cynicism she felt toward men, her father had also been a servant of the church. She choked on the fish she was eating.

Mr. Ardmore pounded her back, watching her reddened face with concern until she smiled and assured him that she was fine."

"Do be careful of the bones, Miss Webster," he said, smiling back shyly. "I always chew very slowly when I eat fish of any sort."

"A very wise thing to do," she agreed. "How long were you in the army, Mr. Ardmore?" she asked, thinking he couldn't be more than twenty-five or -six.

"Four years. I know people think I'm just a youth, but I'm almost twenty-five years old," he revealed.

"Really! I had no idea you were such a seasoned veteran."

"Oh, I saw enough action. I was wounded, too, but not fatally," he said.

"No, I can see that," said Eleanor, her eyes lighting in amusement. She wondered if the young man knew how silly he sounded.

"When I was wounded, Mrs. Prentiss took care of me

mostly. The other chaps helped, too, but she made me soup every day and changed my bandages. She thinks we're her sons," he confided.

"Mrs. Prentiss seems to be a remarkable woman. She traveled with her husband all through the Peninsula?"

"Oh, yes. I can't imagine my mother doing such a thing," he said. "Most ladies wouldn't like it at all."

"No, we ladies prefer to leave the wars to you gentlemen," she agreed. "You knew my brother over there?"

"Yes. Sir Michael was right there with us, too. I thought about going into the church myself after I met him, but I don't have enough patience and, uh, dedication. And the way he helped out with the wounded . . . I could never do that. The sight of blood makes me ill," he said.

Eleanor fell silent, and Mr. Ardmore turned to Mrs. Prentiss on his other side, leaving her to her own thoughts. These were worrisome, to say the least. How could she fit together her memories of Michael as a callow youth with this paragon he had evidently become? Had she been harboring resentment and anger all these years against a person who no longer existed?

Her gaze traveled the length of the table to Stephen, who was bending forward and laughing at something Miss Jones said. As if her gaze had drawn him to her, he looked at her, nodded, and returned to his conversation.

Eleanor didn't know where to turn. She was so confused—confused about Michael . . . and about Stephen. Two men she thought she knew; but did she really know anything about either one of them?

She spent the remainder of the time at the table answering politely when spoken to, but otherwise she kept her own counsel. When they reached the drawing room, Eleanor offered to play the pianoforte while the others danced. That way, at least, she didn't have to worry about anyone noticing her bruised cheek.

They moved the furniture against the walls and rolled up the carpets. Eleanor sat down and played the first of many jaunty tunes, relieved to be active and yet separate from the others.

She couldn't be certain how many times Miss Jones snared Stephen as her partner, but she was certain it wouldn't have passed the rules of propriety in London. If Stephen wasn't careful, he would find himself leg-shackled.

Not that she cared one way or the other, of course. Not a bit.

Eleanor rose, stretching her stiff joints as the others said their good nights and made their way to bed. She blew out the candles beside the pianoforte and turned to leave. Stephen was waiting for her in the shadows.

"Might I have a word with you, Miss Webster?" he asked, pointing to an empty sofa.

"Certainly, Captain," she said, stilling her trembling heart and joining him there. "Are you going to critique my playing?" she quipped.

"No, Eleanor, I'm going to ask you a question."

Her heart turned over, but she rolled her eyes at her own thoughts. The man was looking much too sober for her to fool herself into thinking his motives were romantic. Besides, she reminded herself sternly, she didn't want romance!

"Eleanor, I have made inquiries about you, about the way you have handled the funds for Ransom Hall."

Her eyes hardened. She certainly hadn't been prepared for this! "Go on," came her crisp reply.

"I have learned that you have a large account at one of the banks in London, an account that, given your lack of family money, is very difficult to explain," he said, turning and watching her, waiting for that impossible explanation.

"You had no right . . ."

"As the guardian to my nieces and nephew upstairs, I had every right."

She frowned at him as though he were a student who hadn't quite grasped the point of a problem, raising one brow like the good governess she was.

"You said I had an account—one account?"

"Yes, that's right."

"Well, whoever you have doing your spying for you isn't terribly clever. In reality, there are two accounts with my name on them. One of them contains approximately eighty-four pounds. My name is the only name on that account since it is money I have put away myself through the years. The other account has approximately twelve hundred and forty-five pounds. If your spy had investigated thoroughly, he would have noted two things. First of all, money has only been deposited in the account, never withdrawn. Secondly, while I am allowed to oversee these funds, the owner of the account is Lady Ransom, and in the event of her death, her children. And that, I think, is all we have to say to each other, Captain Ransom."

Wounded and reeling, Eleanor held her head high and walked regally out of the room, leaving Captain Stephen Ransom sitting alone on the sofa, free to rake his hand through his dark hair and curse himself for a fool.

Eight

Eleanor rose early the next morning. She had a myriad of tasks to perform before the proposed visit to Chipping Barnet for the market and fair. First and foremost, she had to meet with workers before sending them to the gatekeeper's cottage. The good captain might have decreed that the work be done, but the men had all applied to *her* to confirm the order.

They were waiting for her at eight o'clock in the steward's room. Archer, a tiny old man who had been the head gardener at the Hall for almost fifty years, spoke for his men. He was respectful but firm.

"We don't mind working at the gatekeeper's cottage for you, Miss Webster, but we don't want anything to do with Mr. Lamb."

"I understand, Archer. And I appreciate all of you who are willing to set aside your feelings for the sake of the estate," said Eleanor, calling each man by name, from the youngest to the oldest, for a personal word. "I have informed Mr. Lamb that he is not to interfere with your work in any way."

"That's all well and good, miss, but did Master Stephen tell him, too, meaning no disrespect to you, I'm sure," said Archer.

"I have Master Stephen's support in this," she said firmly, crossing her fingers in the folds of her skirt.

The men began to nod and mumble until Archer held up

his hand. In the silence, the old man stepped closer and looked her boldly in the eye.

He must have been pleased with what he saw, for he nodded and said, "Right. Then it's off to work we go, men."

"Thank you, Archer," said Eleanor, breathing a sigh of relief. Shaw was next, bringing several stable boys with him.

Shaw had also spent his entire life at Ransom Hall, and he wasted no time in the niceties.

"If you say we're to repair the stables at the gatekeeper's cottage, then we'll repair them, miss. And I've got a gelding for Mr. Lamb, just as Master Stephen requested."

"Thank you, Shaw," Eleanor said with a surprised smile. She refrained from questioning Stephen's right to make decisions like this since she agreed with it heartily. "I do hope the horse is, uh, sturdy?"

Shaw grinned, nodding his head. "Oh, he's a sturdy one, all right. Part draft horse, he is, but he's a good 'un," he added soberly. "He won't give Mr. Lamb any reason to resort to th' whip."

"I'm glad. Thank you, Shaw. Let me know if there are any problems."

"No, miss, I reckon that falls more under a man's work. I'll direct any problems to Master Stephen, if you don't mind. He's not one to tolerate nonsense about his livestock."

"Of course. Thank you again."

Shaw led his men outside, making room for a huge man with a horsy face and four younger men of similar size. The room was fairly bulging at the seams as they stood there, bowing their heads slightly under the low ceiling. Despite their intimidating size, Eleanor faced them all politely and without trepidation.

"Good morning, Miss Webster. I'm pleased ye called on me again," said the eldest of the group, his hat in hand.

"There is no one I trust more, Mr. Young. You and your boys are the best builders in the parish, and I appreciate you coming back here."

"You know I'll work for you anytime, miss," said the giant. "But I won't work for that Lamb fellow. He's a liar and a cheat, and I'll make no bones about it."

Eleanor had no wish to delve into past history, but she asked, "You did finally receive full payment for all your efforts the last time, didn't you?"

"Yes, miss, thanks to you."

"Good. Then allow me to give you this on account for the work this time," she said, handing him a thick envelope.

He looked inside and grunted his satisfaction. Looking up, he said, "I'm glad t' know you've figured out how to get around the scoundrel, miss."

She smiled but didn't reply. "When the work is finished, come back and I'll pay you the remainder we agreed on."

"That I will, miss, that I will," he said, settling his cap back on his head and shooing his sons out the door.

Eleanor heaved a sigh of satisfaction and turned, gasping when she discovered the captain watching her from the doorway.

"You really should learn to make a little noise, Captain. It's not polite to always be slipping up on people," she added, taking a deep breath and starting past him.

Stephen caught her arm, and she paused, staring down at his hand with pursed lips.

He released her and said, "Now, what on earth was all that about?"

"You wanted the gatekeeper's cottage fixed; it is being taken care of. Unless you are afraid I will abscond with the money," she couldn't resist adding.

Stephen pulled her back into the steward's room, leading her to the sofa and waiting while she sat down, arranging her skirts with haughty indifference. Finally, he joined her, his head bowed as he formed his apology.

"I do have other duties this morning," she prompted him.

Stephen scowled, all his good intentions fleeing at her preachy tone. "And I have better things to do than waste my time speaking to you, Miss Webster. I have to say good-bye to Beauchamp and his sister, and I . . . well, never mind," he concluded gruffly.

She started to rise, and Stephen pulled her back down, none too gently.

"Wait a minute . . . please," he added when she raised her brow to him. "I wanted to apologize for last night. You're right, of course. Since I arrived, I have been looking for faults with you." He gave her a sideways smile and admitted, "I haven't been able to find any, except perhaps for your temper and your imperious ways.

"Temper! Imper . . . ! Why, of all the . . . What are you laughing at?" she demanded, leaning toward him.

"You see what I mean?" he managed after a moment. Eleanor responded with a sudden smile that caught him off guard. "You're right. I'm a rogue and I apologize for everything. You, Miss Webster, are an absolute paragon. I can find nothing wrong with you, nothing at all."

Eleanor bowed her head, unable to face him in view of these overblown compliments. Without looking at him, she rose and marched across the room, finding her courage in distance.

Turning, she said, "I have arranged for our own men to work in the stables and gardens at the gatekeeper's cottage. The men who just left are from the village, Mr. Young and his sons. They will take care of any structural repairs to the house and stables. I have already paid them half of their wages."

"Is that wise?" he couldn't resist asking. "One usually pays when the work is finished."

"The last time, when your brother ordered the work done, he gave the funds to Lamb to pay them. When Lord Ransom died, Mr. Young applied to Laura—and so, to me—for payment."

"What happened to the original funds?"

"I don't know. It took some time, but I was able to pay Mr. Young out of Laura's pin money."

"I see. Thank you. I will look into the matter of the missing funds. If that is all right with you?" he added. Eleanor favored him with a fleeting smile and turned to go. He stopped her with one last quiet speculation. "I wondered,

Miss Webster, why the deposits on your personal account stopped when my brother died. Now I understand. You paid him out of your own wages."

She didn't know why, but tears sprang to her eyes, and she fled.

Hurrying toward her room to change into her habit for her ride with her brother, she encountered the girls and Peter, heading toward the kitchens, giggling and whispering.

"What are you three up to?" she asked, directing her gaze at Susan, who avoided her eyes by looking at the carpet.

Peter piped up, "We're just going down to see if Cook has anything to eat. Jane was busy and told us she would be along shortly."

Mary and Susan cast their new playmate sidelong glances.

"Very well," said Eleanor. "Only remember, Cook is very busy. You mustn't get in the way." They scampered down the corridor, giggling loudly, and she called, "And don't stray too far. We leave for the fair at eleven o'clock."

"We won't," they replied, disappearing around the corner.

Eleanor shrugged and continued on her way. She opened the door to Laura's sitting room to inquire of her maid if she was awake yet. To her surprise, Laura was wide awake and dressed in a demure pink morning gown, sitting on the sofa with Sailor Jones by her side. When he spied her, he jumped to his feet guiltily.

"Eleanor, my dear, what brings you here so early?" asked Laura, tucking her sketchbook behind her skirts.

"I was just checking to see if you needed me for anything before I go out riding," said Eleanor, adding, "Good morning, Lieutenant."

"Good, uh, morning, Miss Webster," he stammered. His face lit up in a sunny smile and he offered, "Lady Ransom has been showing me her sketchbook of the children. I fancy myself a bit of an artist, and I . . . asked to . . . see them."

The lieutenant was a bright young man; looking from one woman to the other, he could see he had somehow put his foot in it.

Turning to Laura, he said, "Perhaps I should be going,

my lady. We can continue at some other time." He hurried past Eleanor and out the door.

"You needn't look at me so, Eleanor," said Laura, pulling the sketchbook out and smoothing the pages. "He was kind enough to inquire about my artwork last night. . . ."

Chuckling, Eleanor crossed the room. Taking the book from her friend's hands, she teased, "It is also the book with the self-portraits, I see."

Laura snatched the sketchbook back with an angry pout; the expression did not mar her lovely face in any way, reflected Eleanor, who smiled at her former charge indulgently.

"There is nothing wrong with my drawings," said Laura, sounding very much like an angry child.

Eleanor sat down and took the book again, leafing through the familiar pages slowly, stopping to study one or two.

With a fond smile, she returned it to Laura, saying, "No, my dear, there is absolutely nothing wrong with your drawings. They are exceptional, as I have often told you. And the ones of you, though they are a bit unrestrained, are quite lovely."

"Thank you," came the grudging reply.

"I was just surprised you showed them to the lieutenant, whom you barely know. I don't think you ever showed them to Charles, did you?"

Her eyes shining, Laura lifted her head and whispered, "I know, but Sailor is different. He's such a gentleman; he has such a gentle soul."

Eleanor leaned forward and gave Laura a motherly peck on the cheek. "I see nothing wrong with you showing your work to the lieutenant, Laura." She rose, adding, "You will be careful, won't you? Give it time, my dear. Remember, this time you have only yourself to please."

Laura looked up, her heart in her eyes, and said, "I'm afraid it is too late, Ellie. I fear he has already stolen my heart. Please do not say you find me too foolish."

"No, I would never say that, and I hope the lieutenant is

all you ever hoped for and more. He hasn't spoken to you yet, has he?"

Laura blushed a deeper shade of pink and shook her head. Then, looking up again, she said, "But he will, Ellie. I know he will. Don't ask me how, for I can't possibly explain it."

"I hope you may be right," said Eleanor, feeling out of her depth in this conversation. She barely trusted men; she could not fathom giving her heart to one as Laura had done—not once, but now twice.

With a final smile she left the room, hurrying along to her own chamber and changing rapidly into the deep purple habit that always made her feel self-possessed and confident. She would need it to face her brother.

"She's not coming," said Michael when Stephen happened upon him in the stable yard at ten after the hour.

Stephen laughed and said, "What makes you say that? It's a lady's prerogative to be late."

"Eleanor, even as a child, was always prompt. She was damned near perfect," muttered Sir Michael, looking worriedly toward the house. Then his expression cleared, and he smiled as his sister entered the yard.

"A woman's prerogative," whispered Stephen. "Good morning again, Miss Webster. A lovely day for a ride, isn't it?"

"Very nice," she replied curtly. "Were you here to be certain I showed up? Or did you plan to accompany us?"

Stephen threw up his hands and strolled toward the barn.

"Let me help you," said Sir Michael, hurrying forward to throw his sister into the saddle. When he was mounted on his large gray charger, he said, "Lead on. You must know the best places to ride."

Eleanor's mare was fresh and gladly sprang forward, settling into a gentle canter for several minutes before they reached the woods. Eleanor pulled back on the reins to allow her brother to ride alongside her.

"It is foolish to try to converse while riding through the

woods," she said stiffly. "There's a small opening by a stream where we can dismount and converse without interruption."

"That's fine with me," he said, following after her.

Several minutes later, Eleanor drew rein again, kicked her feet free, and leapt to the ground unassisted. Michael did the same. Looping the reins over a low tree branch, they sat down on a large rock that overlooked the stream.

Michael pulled an apple out of his coat pocket. Taking out a small knife, he offered her a slice.

Eleanor shook her head, but she smiled and said, "You remembered."

"I remember a great deal, Ellie, but most of it is painful. We had a terrible childhood, you know," he said, reclining on one elbow on the broad rock.

"We?" she said skeptically. "As I recall it, you were given everything while I worked like a scullery maid."

"Not all the time," he protested.

"No, that's right. After my first suitor showed you and Father that I would be worth more with smooth hands and dressed in pretty gowns, I didn't do as much work around the house."

"Father and I?" he said sharply, sitting up straight and frowning at her. "I was away at school most of the time. How can you put me in the same class as our father?"

"How can I . . ." Eleanor looked up at his familiar face. She had wondered how he could have changed so little in the past fifteen years. Now she understood; Michael had changed, but he had come to look so much like their ne'er-do-well father, she would have recognized him anywhere. That was how she had recognized him that first day, and that was also why the sight of him fairly made her skin crawl.

"What is it?" he demanded when she continued to stare.

Eleanor looked away for a moment before facing him again. "I was just thinking how much like Father you are."

The look of outrage this comment produced made her shrink away from him. He stood up, an ugly sneer on his handsome face; walking several paces away from her, he turned and closed his eyes, the sneer replaced by raw pain.

Through gritted teeth, he ground out, "God help me, I wanted to hit you just now. I have spent years trying to erase every vestige of our father's influence from my life, from me, and one sentence from you, and I . . ."

"I'm sorry, Michael," she said, her heart going out to him. But her own pain was so overwhelming, it was impossible for her to reach out to him, to ease his anguish.

Her voice calm, almost dull, she said, "The last thing you said to me, before you went back to your life in London, was that I ought to marry that old man who had offered to pay off all of your and Father's debts."

"I never did!" he protested weakly, but his tone held no conviction.

"Yes, you did," she said, her expression dark and shuttered.

"But you didn't do that."

"No, though the man tried to force himself on me. I broke a vase over his head. Then I packed my clothes and ran away. My choices were limited, naturally. Any of Father's friends would have turned me over to him immediately, but I remembered Mrs. Thurgood in the next parish. She took me in and wrote false references for me, and I found my position with Laura, who was making her bow in Society."

"You were lucky, no thanks to me."

"I trusted you," she said, tears starting to her eyes.

"I know, and I betrayed you," said her brother, crossing the clearing and sitting by her side again. He touched her shoulder, but he didn't attempt to take her in his arms.

"I know it's too late to make up to you for that time, Ellie, but I am sorry. I've spent years being sorry." She shrugged, and he continued, "I know I wasn't much of a brother. I guess I didn't really know how to be a brother until I had been in the army for a few years. That's where I learned what it means to stand up for your beliefs; I learned about courage and honor. When Father wrote to tell me you had run away with a company of traveling players . . ."

She gasped and exclaimed, "He told you that?"

"Yes, and that's why I never spoke of you to anyone, not

even to Stephen or Sailor. I felt so ashamed that I hadn't lifted a finger to stop him from treating you like a . . ."

"A lightskirt?" she asked.

"I was going to say like a slave. I should have known that wasn't the way it should be, that a man—especially a man of God—didn't treat his own daughter as though she were no more than livestock. But if I showed the slightest sign of weakness, of compassion . . . I just couldn't stand up to his ridicule."

Eleanor took his hand in hers and leaned her head against his shoulder. After a few minutes, she looked up at him and asked, "When did you become a chaplain, Michael?"

"It took a long time for me to grow up," he said. His old smile reasserted itself. "My friends were shocked. But I wanted to make amends. So I spoke to our chaplain, and he helped me."

"You and your friends, you're not like Father and his cronies—I mean, betting on anything and everything and drinking until you forget you're supposed to be gentlemen?"

Michael shook his head and confessed with a rueful smile, "We're not saints, but we respect ladies enough to keep our wicked ways to ourselves. The first few years, before I became a chaplain, we were deuced uncivilized, but even then there was never any harm in our highjinks."

They fell silent, each wrestling with his own demons from the past.

Finally, Michael said, "Let's go back to the house, Ellie, before you catch your death of cold. I would hate to lose you now that I've finally found you again."

"I'm fine," she protested. "I'm not a child, you know."

"I know. You've grown into a lovely lady. Stephen tells me you have been with Lady Ransom since you left home."

"Yes, more than ten years now," she replied as he boosted her onto the mare's back.

"You know, Ellie, you have no need to work anymore. I have been offered a living in a parish south of London. I mean, if you would like to come and live with me . . ."

She was touched by his offer, but she knew she could not

accept. The gulf between them was too wide. She started to tell him so, but he was looking at her, his concern for her evident in his kind expression. She couldn't wound him so.

Smiling, she shook her head, saying, "I couldn't leave the children. They are my family now."

"I understand," he said, swinging up on his horse.

They rode back to Ransom Hall in silence.

When Michael had helped her down again, he said softly, "I hope you can find it in your heart to forgive me, Ellie."

She tried to smile, but the effort was too difficult. Instead, she said, "I will try, Michael. But it will take time, a great deal of time to erase the past."

"You can't erase it, my dear; you can only accept it and move on. But I'll wait. Through the years, I have learned to be patient."

His deep blue eyes met hers with such warmth—and perhaps—with love, thought Eleanor. She wanted to return the warmth, but her experiences barred her from giving him that comfort.

She left him and made her way to the house through the gardens. Forgiving Michael was not going to be easy. It wasn't just that he hadn't protected her from their father— that would have been asking too much of a young man barely twenty years old. Besides, their father had been quite charming and even overpowering when he chose to be. She felt that same magnetism in Michael; there was a look about him which she quite naturally fought against, just as she had tried to fight against her father, with disastrous results.

But Michael was her brother, and the years had changed him. She was touched that he had offered to give her a home. Perhaps, with time, she would be able to see him without feeling that old resentment and helplessness.

Eleanor entered through the kitchens, where Cook was busily preparing a basket for them to take on their outing to the fair in Chipping Barnet. There would be countless vendors selling everything from sweets to roasted suckling pig, but Cook was afraid they would starve before they returned, and no one had the heart to tell her otherwise.

After tasting a bite of cold ham, Eleanor was about to ascend the backstairs when she spied the children coming out of the larder with a cloth bag. They froze, their faces the very picture of guilt.

"What do you have there, Peter?" asked Eleanor.

"Here? Oh, nothing, just, uh . . ."

"They wanted some of my tarts and some fruit and nuts. I told them to help themselves, the poor little mites. They're growing children. You can't expect them to wait all day for their nuncheon," said Cook, shooing them out of her kitchen.

The children ran up the stairs and were out of sight by the time Eleanor reached the first landing. She put their odd behavior from her mind and hurried to her room.

After washing her hands and face, Eleanor slipped into a navy blue carriage dress with long sleeves and a high collar trimmed with red piping. The fluffy clouds floating across the sky that morning promised warmth, but being outside all afternoon would be chilly. She put on her half-boots and allowed Penny to coil her heavy tresses around the crown of her head before putting on the matching bonnet that tied under her chin with red ribbons.

As planned the night before, the dressing bell rang at eleven o'clock to signal that the carriages were at the front door to carry the entire party to Chipping Barton.

Eleanor noted with amusement that Sailor Jones had taken Laura up in his curricle, so she turned to join the children in the big traveling carriage. As the footman helped her inside, she looked into the captain's smiling face.

"Good morning again, Miss Webster," he said. Turning to the children, who sat opposite them, he grinned. "I told you Miss Webster would be joining us. Now you'll have to explain . . ."

"There you are, Captain," gushed Hilda Jones, climbing into the carriage and sitting between Stephen and Eleanor. She settled her skirts with a satisfied sigh and smiled up at him, carefully ignoring the other occupants of the carriage.

"You will promise to remain by my side at the fair, won't you, Captain?" she said, slipping her arm through his. "I vow I have no sense of direction at all, and being in large crowds makes me terribly uneasy."

"Then perhaps you should stay home," said Susan with unusual intensity.

Miss Jones's eyes widened in surprise at the sight of the three children gazing at her with obvious disgust from the opposite seat.

Her lip curling slightly, she intoned, "I thought you children would be kept in the nursery."

"Certainly not," said their uncle, earning the children's undying loyalty. He carefully extracted his arm from Miss Jones's grasp, adding, "Enjoying a fair is something children are especially good at, so I intend to follow them all afternoon. Oh, good, we're on our way." The children cheered and clapped their hands.

Glancing sideways at Miss Jones's rigid profile, Eleanor could not prevent the escape of a little chuckle.

Eyes blazing, Miss Jones turned to her and muttered, "You put him up to this, no doubt."

Meeting her furious glance with a bland rebuttal, Eleanor said, "I assure you, this was all his idea."

"Here now, enough of your secrets," said Stephen. Turning to the children, he snapped his fingers and asked, "Who knows a song we can sing?"

The remainder of the short journey was spent in noisy song and laughter. Miss Jones cringed with each squeal of delight, but the rest of the occupants of the old carriage enjoyed themselves hugely.

When the vehicle stopped, Miss Jones remained quietly seated while everyone else disembarked. Then, extending her hand, she called, "Captain, would you mind?"

Reluctantly, Stephen turned back and helped her descend. She then latched onto his arm again. Rather like a leech, he thought, scowling at Eleanor, who was finding it impossible to disguise her amusement. The children, seeing their boon companion thus snared, danced around Miss Webster as they joined the others.

"There are too many of us to stay together," Lord Reading

announced. "Choose your partners and we'll meet back here in two hours, agreed?"

"Agreed!" they exclaimed.

Eleanor noticed in amusement that Laura and Lieutenant Jones slipped quietly away while the others were still sorting themselves out. Ardmore gazed longingly at Miss Jones, but Norton, a confirmed bachelor, dragged him away. Michael and the major and Mrs. Prentiss announced their intention of finding some ale and sauntered away. Lord and Lady Reading, after determining that their son was being looked after, followed the others.

Miss Jones held on to Stephen's arm with dogged determination as he and the children discussed whether they should begin with having the gypsy tell their fortunes or seeing what were billed as the greatest oddities of the world. When they applied to Eleanor for her opinion, she said she rather thought they should save the fortune-teller until they were ready to go home, since the gypsy might foretell some tragedy that would spoil their afternoon. Giggling, Mary and Peter took her hands and led the way. Stepping around Miss Jones, Susan grasped her uncle's free hand, and they followed.

As the noisy band exited the tent a half hour later, Peter snorted and grumbled, "I don't think that man really had three legs. Did you see how the third one just sort of flopped about when he danced that jig."

"That's because he couldn't control it," said Mary, who had clapped long and loudly for every performance. "That's what the man said, remember?"

"Come now, you can't believe the two-headed dog was real!" said Peter.

"Was, too!" she retorted stubbornly, frowning at her new friend and stamping her foot.

"But, Mary, surely you didn't believe that woman really had horns," scoffed Susan, shaking her head at her gullible little sister.

"Did, too! I saw them!" shouted Mary, tears springing to her dark eyes.

"That's enough! I saw them, too," said Eleanor, putting her arm around Mary and giving the two older children a warning glance.

Susan readily apologized to her sister, but Peter shuffled his feet and turned away with a roll of his eyes.

Stephen put a hand on his shoulder and said quietly, "A gentleman never questions the word of a lady, my boy."

"Oh, all right. I'm sorry, Mary."

"Me, too," she replied, the sun restored to its rightful place in the sky. "What are we going to do next?" she demanded, dancing around in front of them as they began to stroll along the aisle where booths and tents had been erected, offering an exotic variety of foods and goods.

"Are you hungry?" asked Eleanor. "I see Peter still has that sack of goodies Cook gave you."

Mary stopped dancing and stammered, "Oh, no, I don't think . . . that is . . ."

"We would rather buy something here," said Susan. "Isn't that right, Peter?"

"Yes, that's right," he agreed.

Stephen stopped in his tracks, reaching for the cloth bag. "Not me, not if Cookie put some of her tarts in there."

Peter snatched the bag away, opening it so that no one else could see the contents. Looking up, he tied it into a knot and said, "I'm sorry, sir. We ate all the tarts."

"I see," said Stephen, relaying his suspicions to Eleanor with a raised brow.

Taking his cue, Eleanor plucked the bag from Peter's hands and said, "You know, Captain, I don't know if I have enough money for food. Perhaps we should just make do with whatever is left in that bag."

"Gracious sakes!" snapped Miss Jones, grabbing the bag and throwing it back at the boy. "Can we just move along?" she demanded, dragging Stephen down the aisle.

Eleanor and the children shrugged and followed. Standing beside a booth that offered marzipan, Eleanor watched the captain and Miss Jones. She could not hear their conversation, but the lady had evidently found a topic of interest to the captain, for he appeared quite absorbed.

"Don't you want some, Miss Webster?" asked Susan.

"Oh, I'll share a little," she responded, thinking privately that the candy would probably sit like a stone in the pit of her stomach.

"Miss Webster, may I have a word with you?"

She looked up sharply to find Victor Taylor beckoning to her from between two tents. It needed only this to complete the day, she thought.

Taking a coin from her purse and handing it to Susan, she said, "Pay the man, my dear. I'll be back in just a minute. Don't wander off, now."

Eleanor slipped away without anyone the wiser.

"What do you want?" she gritted out.

"I want to talk to you, Miss Webster, and I don't particularly like your attitude," he said.

"I don't care," she replied. "Get on with it."

"Not here," he hissed, looking at the passing crowds. "Come with me."

She resisted, but he had her wrist in a viselike grip, and short of screaming and making a scene, she had no choice. She couldn't fight him, not with Stephen so close. If cornered, Taylor would be only too willing to explain his behavior by revealing Simon's parentage.

He dragged her behind the row of tents, over a little rise and into a ravine. When he finally stopped, Eleanor wrenched her wrist out of his grasp, glaring up at him.

"What is it?" she demanded.

"I have decided that five hundred is not enough. I want a thousand—"

"A thousand? We can't come up with a thousand pounds!" she exclaimed. "A widow doesn't have that kind of money."

"But she can get it. What's more, I want another fifty the first of each month, just to keep a steady income flowing," he said with a charming smile.

"You're nothing but a vile—what?"

He had grabbed her hands and pulled her against his chest.

"Shut your mouth; somebody's coming. Act like you want to be here or else."

"I'd rather die than—"

"Eleanor! What the devil are you doing down there?" called Stephen, leaving Miss Jones at the top of the rise while he hurried down the slope.

Springing away from Taylor, Eleanor raised her hand as if to tidy her hair. Giggling, she trilled, "Please don't scold, Captain. I know I shouldn't have." She paused, throwing what she hoped was an adoring glance at Taylor. In reality, she felt sick with revulsion. "I just couldn't help myself. Allow me to introduce you to Victor Taylor."

"There's no time for that," he said with a curt nod for Taylor. "The children want to have their fortunes told. Good day, sir."

"Good day," said Taylor, calling after her, "You won't forget, will you, my dear?"

Eleanor could feel the tension in Stephen's arm as she allowed him to help her up the slope. A sideways glance told her that he was absolutely furious, past civil speech or reason.

When they reached Miss Jones, she fell into step on Stephen's other side, leaning forward to say coyly, "Well, well, Miss Webster, aren't you the sly puss? Who would have thought you would have an assignation with a handsome beau?"

Grinding her teeth, Eleanor managed to maintain silence. When they reached the row of tents, Stephen released her arm as though it were a snake.

"Where are the children?" she asked.

"They're by the candy booth," he snapped. "Over there. No, wait a minute. We must have come through farther down the aisle," he said, stepping forward and looking one way and then the other.

"There it is," said Eleanor, spying the booth where they had purchased the marzipan and striding toward it.

Stephen caught her up, the breathless Miss Jones still clinging to his arm.

"Where are they?" he demanded.

"I don't know," she said, panic rising in her breast. "I told them to wait right here."

"So did I," he retorted. Eleanor gasped, and he relented, saying, "Don't jump to conclusions. They've just wandered off, probably looking for us. We'll divide the search and meet back here in about five minutes."

Eleanor nodded, and they went their separate ways. Miss Jones never offered to search in a third direction. Meeting back at the candy booth, Stephen shook his head, worry creasing his brow.

"If you hadn't gone off with that bounder . . ." he grumbled.

True panic set in at the mention of Taylor. What if the man had decided kidnapping would pay even better than blackmail?

"I'll never forgive myself if anything has happened to them!" exclaimed Eleanor, unable to keep her calm in the face of her growing alarm.

Stephen shook free of Miss Jones and put his hands on Eleanor's shoulders, saying firmly, "We'll find them."

Eleanor collapsed against his broad chest.

Nine

Her hands on her hips, Miss Jones drawled with awful sarcasm, "How very touching, but perhaps it would be better if we actually did something?"

Reluctantly, Eleanor raised her face, which she had buried in his cravat. Stephen gave her shoulders a final bracing squeeze and set her away from him.

Turning, he said, "Very right, Miss Jones. We will look for your brother and the others and then have a proper search. The children have very likely gone into some tent and have forgotten about the time."

"There's Mr. Norton and Sir Michael," said Miss Jones, pointing down the aisle.

"And the Readings are with them," said Eleanor with a grimace. "They will be so worried."

"Then they should have kept Peter with them," said Stephen.

As it was, when the others joined them, Lord and Lady Reading scoffed at the idea that any mischief had been done to the children.

Giving a cynical snort, Lord Reading said, "If there is any mischief being done, it is very probably our Peter doing it."

Lady Reading had the grace to look remorseful as she seconded her husband, saying, "We really should have warned you—Peter is the most frightful scamp. He is forever hatching some naughty plot."

"Tomfoolery, more like," added Lord Reading.

The clock on the tower at Hadley Highstone began to chime the hour, and suddenly everyone began moving down the aisle of tents and booths, as if in a wave.

"Four o'clock," said Lord Reading, looking thoughtful. "Wasn't there going to be a horse race at four?"

"Yes, but why?" asked Eleanor.

"If I know my boy, he won't miss that race."

"Come on," said Stephen, leading the way. "What is the course like, Eleanor?" he asked.

"It's a circle, beginning and ending at the same spot. There are usually fifteen or twenty horses," she replied, keeping up with his long strides easily. Though she worried about the children, she felt a flash of satisfaction from hearing him call her name . . . and the fact that the petite Miss Jones had fallen behind.

They stopped at the edge of the crowd that had gathered to watch the beginning of the race. Searching the crowd, Lord Reading shouted, "There! Across the road and down a bit."

"I see them!" shouted Stephen.

The curate of Barnet Church held up his hand for silence, and the crowd settled down.

"On my count of three," he roared.

Across the way, Susan's face was scrunched up as if she were waiting for a thunderclap after seeing the lightning. Peter was smiling from ear to ear, his eyes darting from one horse to another. Mary had covered her eyes with her hand and was peeking through her fingers.

"One!"

Stephen bent his head and whispered in Eleanor's ear, "I don't like this."

"Two!"

"Look at Peter's face, and Susan's."

"Three!"

The horses leapt forward, flying away from the starting mark . . . except for five or six, who were plunging and rearing, their hooves flying out at the spectators one moment

and then flashing in the air the next. The crowd scattered,
running over each other to get away.

"Merciful heavens!" exclaimed Miss Jones, crumpling to
the ground.

Stephen and Michael darted through the crazed horses,
scooping up the girls, who stood petrified with fright. Peter
had fallen back to the safety of the trees and was jumping
up and down, chortling like a madman at the spectacle—until his father appeared in front of him.

"What the devil have you done this time?"

The horses had relieved themselves of their riders by this
time and were running down the road after the other racers.
Clutching each other, Eleanor and Lady Reading sighed with
relief. Norton and Ardmore were busy reviving Miss Jones.

The crowd returned to the road to wait for the finish, and
Michael, carrying a weeping Mary, returned to his sister's
side.

"What happened?" Eleanor exclaimed.

"I'm not certain, something about some burrs under the
saddles," said Michael, trying not to laugh.

Norton and Ardmore, staggering with loud guffaws, were
not as easily cowed by Eleanor's glare.

She turned away and watched as Stephen squatted down,
his face close to Susan's as he spoke earnestly to the girl.
She nodded and dashed away tears before throwing her arms
around his neck.

Stephen rose with his niece still in his arms, her long legs
dangling near his knees as he carried her back to the others.

With a stern, "Gentlemen!" he quelled the younger men's
laughter. Putting Susan down, he asked, "Where's Peter?"

"His father is tending to him," said Lady Reading. "Not
that I think it will do any good. Reading would insist on
telling his tales of pranks and jokes in front of the boy. This
is the result."

Her husband and son, the latter walking gingerly, returned
a few minutes later.

Shuffling his feet in the dirt, Peter said, "I'm sorry for

talking Mary and Susan into doing such a stupid thing. And I'm sorry I upset everybody, especially the ladies."

"Yes, well, I hope you have learned a lesson," said his mother.

"And I hope you have been thoroughly thrashed!" snapped Miss Jones. Her remark would have been more effective if her pretty bonnet hadn't been sitting at such an odd angle on her head, making her look as if she had imbibed a little too freely.

Biting her lip so that she did not succumb to foolish giggling, Eleanor looked away and said sensibly, "Shall we go back to the carriages? We have another hour before the others return, but we could leave a message with the grooms."

By consensus, they returned to the carriages, where they found Mr. and Mrs. Prentiss eating ices under the shade of a tree. Laura and Lieutenant Jones were nowhere to be found, but since they had arrived together in his curricle, there was no difficulty leaving one of the grooms to wait for them by this vehicle.

After ascertaining that the only carriage without children was the Prentisses's, Miss Jones took Michael's place in it. Michael, as amenable as ever, rode back with his sister, Stephen, and the girls.

Dinner was a quiet affair. The children were sent directly to the nursery when they arrived home. Eleanor joined them there, giving all three a stern lecture on the dangers of such malicious pranks. Peter looked mulish, but the girls were in tears by the time she finished. Rising, she again accepted their apologies.

"I wonder if I might add a word or two, Miss Webster?"

She pivoted slowly and said calmly, "Certainly, Captain."

"Peter, you may go to your room for the night. Your father has sent word that you're to remain there until morning."

"Yes, sir," he said, giving the girls a sympathetic grimace before he escaped.

Stephen entered the room and sat down between the two

girls. "I know that Peter was the instigator of this act, but I am more concerned with the part you girls had in this fiasco."

"We're very sorry," said Susan.

"Very sorry," echoed her little sister.

"I'm very glad to hear that. As young ladies, it is a difficult role you play in this world. You must be the beacons of good sense and propriety; you mustn't allow yourselves to be swayed from this by some rough-and-tumble boy like Peter. Even when you are grown up, you must be the civilizing influence in our society."

He glanced up to find Eleanor gazing at him, her mouth open and her brows raised in disbelief.

Susan looked from her newest idol to the other and frowned in confusion.

"How very enlightening," Eleanor said, tight-lipped with anger.

"You don't seem to hold the same opinion, Miss Webster," said Stephen, watching her in some amusement.

Eleanor glanced at the girls and curbed her tongue, saying cautiously, "I think there is some merit to your words, Captain, but I think ladies, be they young or old, can only do so much to curb the uncivilized tendencies of men . . . and boys. I think you are setting them a task that would be impossible to fulfill."

The girls' attention swung from Miss Webster to their uncle in anticipation.

"I said it would be difficult, if you will recall, but impossible? I don't think so. Ladies have always been the civilizing force in society."

"So what would you have had them do? Throw him to the ground and sit on him? Or perhaps you wanted them to tattle on their friend?"

"That would have been better than being a party to someone breaking his neck being thrown from his horse or some observer being kicked in the head and killed," rejoined Stephen, rising and stepping toward her, his nieces all but forgotten.

"This is intolerable!" shouted Eleanor, standing toe-to-toe with him, lifting her face to his. "According to you, men can do anything they please with impunity; it is up to women to stop them."

"You are putting words in my mouth. But surely you are not so foolish as to think women have no responsibility. What's more, it is close-minded of you to encourage this sort of promiscuous behavior."

"Promiscuous! What is promiscuous about an eight-year-old devil set on creating havoc?" she demanded, her color high.

"That sort of thing is only the beginning," returned Stephen. "The next thing you know, they'll be sneaking off to illicit assignations with every redheaded scoundrel they meet!"

Eleanor opened her mouth, then thought better of it and snapped it closed. She would not deign to reply to such slander.

Instead, she held out her hand and said haughtily, "Come along, girls. It is time for bed."

Nothing happened, and she peered around the devil's broad shoulders at the empty chairs. Stephen turned, too, biting at his lower lip, his dark, angry eyes transformed in an instant by laughter.

"At least someone had the good sense to leave before this argument degenerated into a contest of idiotic insults," he said quietly, taking her hand and touching it to his lips. He didn't release it as he continued, his voice soft and sensual. "I'm sorry, Eleanor. I hope you can forgive me."

She returned his gentle smile before shaking her head and breaking free of him, turning away.

"I . . . I don't want you to think ill of me, Stephen," she began, her breath catching in her throat when she felt his hand on her shoulder.

"I don't, Eleanor. If you had business with that man, then I'll try to understand."

Again she moved toward the door, turning to face him

this time. She lifted her chin proudly and replied, "It wasn't business, Captain, but I still hope for your understanding."

A muscle twitched in his jaw as he ground his teeth, but he managed a civil, "Of course, Miss Webster. I have no claim on you."

Eleanor dropped her gaze and backed out the door, hurrying away.

Stephen sat down on the low chair and buried his face in his hands, shaking his head dolefully. What the devil was he going to do about Miss Webster? Each time he began to think better of her, he discovered some new compromising information . . . or assignation, he thought, grinding his teeth again.

"Uncle Stephen?"

He looked up slowly and smiled at his niece. "What is it, Susan? Did we frighten you with our foolish argument?"

Susan moved closer, and he put an arm around her, giving her a hug. Looking up, he said, "I believe you've grown since I arrived last week. You'll be passing your mother before we know it."

But his niece put her arms around his neck, kissing his cheek. "I wish you would marry Miss Webster, Uncle. I think she really loves you."

He held her at arm's length, his face set sternly to lecture her on her impertinence.

He was totally disarmed when she continued, "Mama and Papa used to argue like that, but I have never heard Miss Webster shout at anyone. I think she must love you, and maybe you love her just a little, too?"

Stephen chuckled at this. It was too absurd, but what could a child know of such things?

"What I think, Miss Susie Scamp, is that you should go to your room for the night and think about what you did wrong today. Leave Miss Webster's temper out of this . . . and mine, too," he added, kissing the top of her head and sending her off with a gentle swat.

Stephen remained in the nursery, trying to clear his thoughts but finding himself being dragged back time and again to his niece's clear, childish words—that Miss Webster, Eleanor, might possibly have some tender feelings for him. He wouldn't consider love as a possibility, of course. That really was absurd.

As for his feelings, he found the woman haughty, temperamental, possibly dishonest, and entirely too prudish for his taste. What's more, she was self-important and . . . lovely, he confessed. Perhaps she was not the beauty his sister-in-law was, but with that golden hair and those violet eyes, she was very probably the most striking woman he had ever seen, and he had seen many. And that figure! She was slender in all the right places and abundantly blessed with . . .

"Oh, I'm sorry, sir. I didn't know anyone was here," said Jane, the children's maid, raising her handkerchief to mop her tears.

"Here now, what's wrong?" he asked, rising and pulling the distraught maid into the room.

"It's . . . nothing!" she wailed.

Stephen pulled out his own handkerchief and thrust it into her hands, saying, "Now, now, we can't have that. It's been a splendid day, hasn't it? I thought you had leave to go to the fair?"

Her sobs had stopped, with only the occasional sniffle escaping. "Yes, sir, but things didn't go as I planned. There's this fellow . . ."

"Ah, there is always a fellow," he agreed. "So he didn't come up to scratch?"

"Up to scratch?" said the startled maid. "I can't even get him to admit he favors me, but I know he does."

Stephen sat down by her side. Now here was an opportunity not to be missed. He could learn something of the female's point of view from Jane.

"How do you know?" he asked.

"He's always talking to other girls and then watching me to see what my reaction is."

"And what is your reaction?"

"I do just what Miss Webster suggested; I turn my head and pretend I don't care. It serves him right, it does!"

"Miss Webster told you to do that, did she?"

"Yes, sir," said the maid, her sniffles growing in volume.

"Does it seem to be working?" he asked, earning a quizzical frown. "I mean, has your fellow reacted as you hoped?"

"No, he just goes on with his flirting. I don't know what to do."

Taking the maid by her shoulders, Stephen gave her a mischievous grin and said, "I'll tell you what to do, Jane. The next time you see your fellow, you tell him exactly how things are going to be between you, that you're finished with all the nonsense."

"Do you really think I should?" she breathed, her eyes lighting with hope.

"Indeed, yes, but you mustn't stop with that. You must put your arms around his neck and kiss him for all you're worth."

"I couldn't!" Jane exclaimed. "I just couldn't!"

"Suit yourself, Jane, but if you don't show him you mean business," he said, punctuating this comment with a lewd wink, "you'll never get your fellow."

"I'll do it! I'll do it this very night! Thank you, Captain, thank you ever so much!" she breathed, dashing from the room.

To the empty room, Stephen said, "You're welcome, Jane." Then his thoughts returned to Eleanor and her most generous attributes, and a grin split his face. If his advice was good enough for Jane, it should work for him, too.

Whistling, he made his way downstairs to dress for dinner.

It was late when Eleanor entered the drawing room before dinner, and everyone was there already, clustered around young Mr. Ardmore and singing a rousing chorus of "For He's a Jolly Good Fellow."

Mrs. Prentiss spied her and motioned her forward. "Come join us, Miss Webster," she called. Then, her voice low and conspiratorial, she added, "Mr. Ardmore is about to open the gift we bought at the fair today."

"How nice. I had no idea it was your birthday, Mr. Ardmore," she said.

"Yes, he's twenty years old today," said Norton.

"I am not! I'm twenty-five!" said the young man.

"Almost ready for the pasture," said Michael. "Open that one next. It's from Stephen, Sailor, Norton, and me."

"And Beauchamp, too. He was sorry to miss the big event, but I told him you'd write him a letter telling him all about it," said Norton. The men roared with laughter at this, and Mr. Ardmore blushed.

"Go on, open it. It won't bite," said Stephen.

The young man opened the box and paused, his face glowing with emotion.

"Well, show it to the rest of 'em!" said Norton, giving the young man a gentle nudge on the arm.

"You'll not understand, most of you, what this means to me, but I thank you. Thank you very much!" he said, holding up a small knife with a carved ivory handle.

"What does it mean?" Laura asked.

"It means he's really one of us," said Lieutenant Jones. "Each of us has one of these folding knives. We had them made in Toledo, in Spain. Ardmore here was still in leading strings when we were fighting over there."

"Now, be fair," said Stephen. "He was there for the end of it, but he wasn't quite one of us yet."

"Not until Waterloo, where he proved himself ten times over," said Norton, clapping Ardmore on the back and adding, "And now it's official."

"Thank you," said the young man, holding the knife in the air like a trophy.

After a moment, Major Prentiss said, "Well, come along, enough sentimentality, my boy. Open another."

The gift from Lord and Lady Reading was a new pair of gloves for riding. Finally, he picked up the package from Major and Mrs. Prentiss.

The major looked around the group and said broadly, "No children present, are there? Good. Wouldn't do for them to be here for this."

The men groaned. Laura asked, "Why? What's wrong with it?"

Sailor Jones chuckled and gave her hand a squeeze. "Just wait. It's a standing joke with the Prentisses. Watch."

"Now, this is just a little trinket," Mrs. Prentiss announced. "Something we found at the fair today. They were just invented by Sir Something-or-other, a Scotsman. He calls it a kaleidoscope or some such thing."

Ardmore pulled out a long tube that rattled when he lifted it.

Major Prentiss said, "The name means 'beautiful form to see' or some such rubbish. Just hold it up to the light and look in that end, there, my boy."

Mr. Ardmore did as he was instructed. "This is quite extraordinary!" he exclaimed.

"Keep looking," said Mrs. Prentiss.

"Why, it's all sorts of colors . . . and objects . . . and, oh, my!" he breathed, his face turning red while Mr. and Mrs. Prentiss chortled with laughter.

"Let us see!" said Norton, tearing the tube out of Mr. Ardmore's grasp. "By Jove!"

The gentlemen spent the next few minutes passing the kaleidoscope from one eager pair of hands to the next, while Laura and Eleanor looked on with growing bewilderment.

Lady Reading cocked her head at Mrs. Prentiss, who was right in the middle of them, and said, "She's as bad as they are."

"Would you ladies care to see?" called Mrs. Prentiss.

"I suppose so," said Laura, taking the tube and exclaiming at the pretty colors. "Oh, my!" she exclaimed, turning quite pink and handing it to Eleanor.

"I don't think Miss Webster will appreciate it," said Stephen, diving for the instrument.

She pulled it away and said firmly, "If it is suitable for Laura, it is suitable for me. Besides, I must make certain it is civilized enough for the drawing room," she added, giving Stephen a smirk. She knew it sounded stuffy, but she refused to allow him to dictate what she might and might not see.

She turned the tube in her hand as they instructed. Amid the images of flowers and clouds, there suddenly appeared a figure, female in form, and dressed in a see-through shift.

She lowered the tube, her face scarlet. All eyes rested on her. Lifting her nose, she gave a condescending sniff and said, "Boys will always have their toys."

The gentlemen guffawed at this pronouncement and moved away just as Punt entered and announced dinner.

Eleanor quickly accepted Michael's arm, leaving Stephen behind with a little murmur of satisfaction.

"I hope you were not too shocked," he said quietly.

"I was not at all shocked, Michael," she said primly. "Only remember our father's house. You must admit, this pales by comparison. There, one might happen upon the real thing, not just a tiny picture."

Michael ducked his head. There was nothing he could say. His father had had a penchant for ladies of questionable repute, and he wasn't above bringing them home for a visit.

Eleanor was quiet through dinner, which was a noisy affair. More wine flowed than was usual, and Stephen ordered champagne to celebrate Mr. Ardmore's birthday.

Using his knife against the crystal goblet, he signaled for silence from the company.

"Let us all be upstanding." Everyone but Ardmore got to their feet. "I give you Ensign Lucas Ardmore!"

"Here! Here!" they all declared, drinking deeply before sitting down again. Once more, Stephen signaled for quiet, a silly grin on his face.

His gaze riveted on Eleanor, he said, "I have one other announcement. I have decided that I will remain at Ransom Hall for good."

"Oh, Stephen, how wonderful!" said his sister-in-law, raising her glass.

"Here! Here!" seconded the others, once more imbibing deeply.

Stephen sat down again, willing Eleanor to give him some sign that she was pleased by his second announcement. She refused to look at him, and a fierce frown replaced his smile.

Deuced female! He didn't need her blessing to live at the Hall. He'd do as he pleased and the devil take Miss Webster.

By the time the gentlemen joined the ladies in the drawing room, they were decidedly bosky and feeling little restraint about their surroundings. They called for tables, cards, and more champagne, declaring they would give the birthday boy a night to remember.

The other ladies joined the festivities, but Eleanor slipped away, unable to watch the evening degenerate into loutishness. Climbing into her bed, she comforted herself with the knowledge that this was not her father's house and these gentlemen in question would not slide too far into objectionable behavior.

There was a knock on her door, and Eleanor climbed out of bed, putting her ear to the door and whispering, "Who is it?"

"It's me, miss, it's Jane."

She unlocked the door, and the sobbing maid fell into her arms.

"Whatever is the matter?" Eleanor exclaimed, putting her arms around the maid's shaking shoulders and leading her to a chair.

For once, she wished she kept some sort of decanter in her room, but she had to settle for ineffectual pats on Jane's shoulder. She didn't even have a vinaigrette, never having felt the least need for it herself.

"What happened? Did someone upset you?" she asked again, keeping her voice calm.

Jane hiccuped and nodded.

"Who was it?" demanded Eleanor, a martial light in her violet eyes.

"It was . . . it was Mr. Pu . . ." She dissolved into tears again.

"Mr. Prentiss? I cannot credit it!" exclaimed Eleanor.

"No, no, not him, it was Mr. Punt!"

Eleanor sat back in her chair in relief. At least the gathering had not yet degenerated so that innocent maids were being attacked. She shook her head at her own foolishness.

Really, she was making too much of the merriment in the drawing room.

"What happened?" she asked wearily.

"It all started when the captain—"

"Captain Ransom?" she inserted, suddenly finding the maid's tale of more interest.

"Yes. I was crying because Mr. Punt had been flirting with Lucy from Squire Trent's house, and I was looking for you. You always give such good advice, miss."

"Yes, well, how does Captain Ransom figure into this tale?" asked Eleanor.

"He was in the nursery, and he was so nice and all. So I explained what had happened, and he told me I should confess my feelings for Mr. Punt. Then he said I should kiss him."

"Kiss Captain Ransom!" exclaimed Eleanor, jumping to her feet and striding across the floor.

"No, no, miss. You've got it all wrong."

Eleanor took a deep breath and returned to her chair, putting her hand over the maid's. Forcing herself to be calm, she asked, "Then please explain it, Jane."

"The captain said I should kiss Mr. Punt, and I did, only now . . ." She dissolved into noisy sobs again.

Eleanor's patience was fast evaporating, but she comforted the maid once more until her tears had ceased.

"Very calmly now, tell me what Mr. Punt said."

"He said if I was that type of girl, he didn't see any need to be marrying me after all. And then he kissed me back, but it wasn't the kind o' kiss a man gives his wife, if you know what I mean," she said, finishing in a whisper.

"And what did you do?"

"Why, I tore myself away and ran," said the wide-eyed maid. "Now I wonder if I shoulda done that, miss. What do you think?"

"I don't know, Jane. I just don't know, but you must tell him at the first opportunity that you are very much the sort of person a man marries and that you'll settle for nothing less."

"What if he doesn't want to?"

"Then you must find yourself someone who does, Jane. You cannot force Mr. Punt to wed you, but you can make him respect you."

The maid nodded and stood up, thanking Eleanor and leaving the room, her tears cured for the moment.

Eleanor climbed back into bed, determined to forget all about handsome captains and heartbroken maids. All she wanted was the sleep of the just, and she vowed she would find it.

She finally did, just as the first glimmer of dawn began to spread across the eastern sky.

Ten

Stephen rose before the rest of the household, dressing in riding gear and heading to the stables. He found Susan before him, feeding pieces of apple to her new mare.

"Have you decided what to call her?" he asked.

"I think Rosebud is a pretty name," she said. Looking him up and down, she asked, "Are you going riding, Uncle?"

"Yes. Would you care to accompany me?"

She nodded and said, "I told Jane I was coming down here and that I might be going for a ride."

"And if I hadn't come along?" he asked.

"I thought someone else might, or I could even take a groom with me," she replied in her most grown-up manner.

"I'm glad you're enjoying riding again, Susan," he said, throwing the saddle on the mare's back.

"Good morning, Miss Susan, *Capitán*," called Monkey as he led Troubadour past them and into the yard.

"Good morning, Monkey," she replied, walking out to join him while Stephen finished with her mare.

"So you're going for a ride, too," he said, winking at the child. "Good. Rosebud was telling me only last night that she was very hurt that you went to the fair without her."

"She was?" asked Susan, laughing at his foolishness.

"You think she doesn't talk to me?" he demanded with mock indignation. He crooked his finger and motioned her forward; looking from side to side, he leaned closer and said, "They all talk to me."

"Even Troubadour?" she asked, her dark eyes shining.

"What? What's that you say?" he demanded, bending down and putting his ear near the big gelding's mouth. "Yes, yes, I know. Don't worry, my friend. I will try to teach her the language so that she, too, may hear your words."

"Help her up, Monkey. We need to be going," said Stephen, taking the gelding's reins.

"*Sí, Capitán,*" said the groom with a snappy salute. He threw Susan onto the mare's back, and she swung her leg over, picking up the reins.

"Where are we going?" she asked.

"I wanted to speak to Faraday and then our neighbor, Miller, if there is time. If you get tired, just let me know, and we'll come back home."

When they arrived at the Faraday farm, the very pregnant Mrs. Faraday invited them in for a cup of tea, telling them that her husband was working outside somewhere.

"Susan, why don't you wait here? I'll see if I can find Mr. Faraday."

"All right," she said, turning to their hostess. "Can you show me how to knit a blanket like the one you made for the baby, Mrs. Faraday?"

Stephen turned Troubadour around and headed across the meadow toward the fields. He had no trouble spotting Faraday, who was busy flinging debris out of the small ditch that needed widening for drainage.

When he dismounted, Faraday paused in his labor, wiping his brow and squinting into the morning sun.

"Good morning, Faraday," called Stephen.

"Captain Ransom," he said, picking up his ax again and taking a swing at a large tree stump.

"You might find it easier to remove that if you used a rope and a draft horse," offered Stephen.

Faraday rested the ax against his leg, spat on his hands, and returned to his work.

"Just trying to be neighborly," said Stephen.

This time Faraday climbed out of the ditch and stood glaring at the intruder.

"Did you want something, Captain Ransom, or did you just come by to watch an honest man's labor?"

Recalling the bailiff's evaluation of Faraday's temper, Stephen said, "I wanted a little information, that's all, but I'd be happy to help you with that stump, too."

"You going to tie a rope to that big horse of yours?" asked the farmer.

Stephen swung his leg over and hopped to the ground before turning his sardonic scowl on the farmer. "You know, Faraday, it's a foolish man who needs help and then bites the hand of the person offering it." Shoving past Faraday, Stephen picked up the ax and heaved it with a mighty blow, splitting the stump in half.

Faraday laughed and said, "Remind me of that if I should ever again try to pick a fight with you, Ransom."

"I will," said Stephen with an answering smile.

"Of course, you know I had almost split it myself. That's what made it so easy for you," said the farmer, taking the ax back, running his finger along the blade, and shaking his head.

"Needs sharpening," he muttered. Looking up, he asked, "What did you want, Ransom?"

"Well, now I have two questions for you. First off, why not use a horse or an ox on this job?"

"That's simple enough. I don't have either one."

"I see," he replied, though he didn't actually understand. By all accounts, Faraday, though a tenant, was prosperous enough. "The other thing is, why were you and Miss Webster smiling at each other like you had some secret?"

The man cocked his head to one side and studied Stephen for a moment before replying cautiously, "Why do you care? I mean, are you worried because you think I'm cheating you or the estate, or is it because you fancy Miss Webster?"

"What if I told you it was both?"

"Then I'd be really tempted to split your head with this ax for insulting Miss Webster . . . on both counts."

Stephen knew he was very close to blows with this man, but that wouldn't solve anything. To defuse the situation, he smiled, saying softly, "It's very tempting to let you try, Faraday, but I think your response tells me what I want to know."

Faraday took a step back, relaxing his stance. "Look, Ransom, I have an understanding with Miss Webster about this ditch and my livestock. I did a foolish thing a year ago; I lost almost everything, including my wife, betting on a cock fight. I was so sure my rooster . . . but I was wrong. My wife went home to her father, refused to even speak to me. Miss Webster, she helped me patch things up."

"A remarkable woman, Miss Webster," murmured Stephen.

"That she is. She wanted to help me get my livestock back, but she couldn't just then. She had given Lamb the money to have this ditch widened, but he never got around to it." Faraday paused to allow this bit of information to sink in. Stephen nodded, and he continued, "Miss Webster said she would pay me in livestock this coming spring if I would do the work. I was only too happy to take her up on the offer."

"So that's why you don't have a horse or an ox yet. Couldn't you have borrowed one?"

Faraday looked uncomfortable and admitted reluctantly, "My mistress thought it would probably be a good lesson for me if I did the work without them." Waving his hand along the ditch, he grinned and added, "She's right. I'll not soon forget this!"

Stephen held out his hand; Faraday grasped it, giving it a hearty shake.

"I'll let you get back to your work, Mr. Faraday," he said. After mounting, he looked down and asked, "If some of the men from the Hall happened along this afternoon to lend you a hand, would you be offended?"

Christian Faraday shaded his eyes with his hands as he looked up at Stephen, studying him for a moment before shaking his head and replying, "I wouldn't want you to think I'm a foolish man for turning down the help I obviously need. Thank you, Captain Ransom."

"You're welcome. Good day," he called, turning the big

gelding and heading back toward the farmer's cottage, where he collected Susan and they continued on their way.

The visit to the Millers' farm was a little different. He'd inherited the farm from his father and worked it with the help of his three sons. Each boy was grown and married and had provided him with numerous grandchildren, all girls.

Several of the smaller girls were helping their grandmother churn butter when Stephen and Susan arrived. They greeted Susan like an old friend, and she was soon helping the other girls with their chore.

Mr. Miller took Stephen into his office, providing him with a large glass of ale, saying proudly, "Make it myself. It's sort of famous around here, you know. I supply the public house in Church End, as well as several others in Chipping Barnet."

Stephen took a long, appreciative pull on his glass and said, "No wonder you are so prosperous, Mr. Miller."

"Thank you, Captain," he replied. "If you don't mind my asking, have you sold out yet? Or are you going back?"

"No, I don't expect to go back to the army; I just haven't sold out yet. Living so close to London, I may do some work for the Home Office eventually, but right now I'm trying to make sense of my nephew's estate."

"I had heard that you were the little viscount's guardian. I'm glad you're taking an interest in the place. It's gone downhill since your father's day, I'm afraid."

"You mean since my brother died," said Stephen, watching the man's reaction over the top of his glass.

Miller shifted uncomfortably in his chair, finally shaking his head and saying, "Not so much as it did the last few years he was alive. I'm not one to speak ill of the dead, but Lord Ransom, your brother Charles, was not much of a manager where the estate was concerned. Maybe he was just too trusting. As the years passed, he let Lamb take over all aspects of the estate and never checked up on him."

"Lamb again," muttered Stephen, draining his glass and setting it down on the table. He stood up and shook his host's hand, saying, "Thank you, Mr. Miller. I appreciate your candor."

"You're welcome, Captain. If there's anything I can do to help . . . but I guess you don't need me. You've got Miss Webster to sort things out for you," he added, as though that clarified everything.

Stephen collected his niece, and they headed back home. He left Susan at the stables, where Monkey was regaling her with tales of magic. He passed Peter and Mary in the garden and sent them along to the stables. Monkey had been getting a little too lax since they came home; entertaining three children would keep him busy—and happy. It was obvious the groom adored all the children, but especially little Mary. Perhaps she reminded him of the sister he had lost so many years before.

His head was swimming with all he had learned about Eleanor Webster. He was already taken with her, but now he was in awe of her as well. She was about the closest thing he had ever known to perfection, he thought, whistling as he headed for the stairs. There was just one other thing vexing him, but in his present sunny mood, he was certain that would soon be explained away, too.

Spying the butler in the hall, he asked, "Pum, is your mistress down yet?"

"Lady Ransom has not come down, sir, but she had her breakfast sent up an hour ago."

"Thank you," he said, taking the steps two at a time.

With a jaunty rap on the door, Stephen waited for his sister-in-law to open it. He could hear movements and voices within, but still she didn't open it.

"Laura, it's Stephen. May I come in?"

"Just a moment," she called. Finally she opened the door and allowed him to enter.

"I see I'm not the only early caller," he said, studying his friend Lieutenant Jones lounging casually on the sofa.

"Good morning, Stephen, old man," he said, looking down and tucking in a corner of his shirttail.

"Hmm," muttered Stephen, following his sister-in-law and sitting down on a lemon-yellow chair. Laura gave him a brittle smile, and he chuckled.

"What is it?" she inquired with wide eyes.

"Nothing, my dear. Nothing at all, only . . . never mind."

"No, Stephen, if you have something to say, then say it," growled Sailor, sitting forward and frowning at his friend.

"I see no reason to state the obvious," drawled Stephen, extending a languid hand and pulling his sister-in-law's lace collar out of the neck of her gown.

She gasped, blushing furiously, but Sailor stood up and stepped between her and his friend. "That was not well done of you, Stephen."

Stephen leaned over so he could see Laura again and said, "Would you please tell your beau to sit down and behave. I have no intention of either calling him out or accepting a challenge. If you and the good lieutenant have forged some sort of understanding or friendship, then I will be the first to wish you happy."

Looking sheepish, Sailor sat down on the sofa beside Laura and took her hand in his. "We were going to wait before we told anyone."

"Splendid," said Stephen. With a little laugh, he said, "You might want to reconsider that. If I know about you two, then others probably do, too."

"He's right, my dear," said Sailor, lifting her hand to his lips. "I know you wanted to wait until we had become better acquainted, but . . ."

"Oh, I don't know. It is all so sudden," said Laura. "I wish I could speak to Eleanor about it, but she will think me the veriest goosecap!"

"Why?" asked Stephen.

"Eleanor doesn't really believe in love, certainly not in love at first sight!" exclaimed Laura.

"I . . . I see," he said pensively.

"Stephen, was there something you wanted to say to me?"

"What? Well, yes, but it concerns the estate, and . . ."

"Say no more. I can tell when I'm not needed," said Sailor, rising and walking toward the door.

"Oh, don't say that!" cried Laura. Running after him, she took his hand and held it to her cheek.

Stephen made a choking noise and studied his boots while the lovers said farewell.

Laura, looking radiant, bounced back to the sofa and resumed her seat before asking dreamily, "Now, what did you want to know, Stephen? But remember, if it is estate business, you must apply to Eleanor."

"Yes, I know," he replied, suddenly reluctant to put the question before her. He wasn't sure he wanted to know the truth.

"Do you know a man called Taylor?"

"Taylor?" she echoed vaguely.

"Come now, Laura, you have to know the man; you sold him that piece of land a few months ago."

"Oh, yes, Mr. Taylor. I couldn't place him for a moment."

"Are you all right?" he demanded, taking her hand. "You've gone pasty white. Are you feeling faint?"

Laura made an effort to regain her composure, taking deep, steadying breaths until she could resume normal conversation.

"I'm fine, now. I think I have been enjoying myself too much. We are accustomed to a much quieter way of life here at the Hall," she said, feeling stronger with each word that took them farther away from the topic of Victor Taylor.

"I know, but I appreciate how you have made my friends feel welcome."

"Oh, no, Stephen, I didn't mean to imply that it was any trouble. Why, if you hadn't invited them, I would never have met Lieutenant Jones," she finished with a sweet smile.

"Yes, yes, but if we could return to the problem of Taylor . . ."

"If you want to know why I agreed to sell the land, you must ask Eleanor, Stephen. She makes all such decisions," added Laura, throwing her friend to the wolves without compunction.

"Do you think Eleanor's decision might have been flavored by, uh, more personal motives?" he asked, growing more miserable by the second.

"Whatever do you mean?" she gasped.

Stephen frowned and said dismally, "So it's true. When I saw them together at the fair yesterday, I hoped . . . but I suppose that's why she couldn't explain away their assignation. There really is something going on between them."

"Assignation? What assignation?" demanded Laura.

"I told you; I caught them together yesterday."

"Perhaps you are right about Eleanor and . . ." She couldn't say it, not even to save herself.

Stephen rose, saying slowly, "A shame. I had hoped . . . Thank you, Laura."

He made his way to the door, pausing when Laura said, "Stephen, perhaps you should ask her again."

"Perhaps," he said, but he shook his head.

After leaving Laura, he climbed the stairs to the next floor and entered the nursery, where Simon's nursemaid was feeding him.

"I'll do that," said Stephen, taking the maid's place. Smiling, she moved to the other side of the room and began folding clothes.

"Unc Stephem," said the tot, climbing into his lap and hugging his neck.

"That's right, my boy. Uncle Stephen. Uncle Cawker, more like," muttered his uncle.

"Cawker," he parroted. "Unc Cawker."

"That's right. Here, what do you have here? A little meat pie, eh? Want another bite? No?"

Simon climbed down and toddled over to the shelf, picking up a carved wooden horse and bringing it back to his uncle.

"Now that's a fine-looking steed you have there. Reminds me of my Troubadour."

"Horse," said the boy, placing his treasure in Stephen's lap.

"Yes, horse. I have it; would you like to go see the horses?"

For answer, Simon put up his arms, gurgling with laughter when his uncle swung him onto his shoulders and galloped out of the nursery, Simon's nursemaid following at a more respectable pace.

* * *

Stephen spent the next hour leading Simon around the paddock on top of Mary's gentle pony, Mr. Applegate. The quiet of the yard was broken by Simon's baby squeals and the older children's shrieks of laughter as they played hide-and-go-seek with Monkey in the hayloft.

This was what it was all about, he told himself, leading Mr. Applegate around for the tenth time. He had come home to take care of his brother's children, to be a father to them, and he could certainly do that without being wed. He hadn't been looking for a wife when he came home, he reminded himself yet again.

"Unc Steph-em," called Simon, squirming around on the saddle and rubbing his eyes.

He stopped the pony and held the boy in his arms. Simon squeezed his neck as tight as he could and then lay his head on Stephen's shoulder.

"Poor little mite," said the nursemaid, picking her way daintily across the paddock. "It's time for his nap."

Kissing the top of his nephew's red head, Stephen handed Simon over to his nurse. Then he returned to the house, having decided to confront Eleanor about Victor Taylor and the sale of that land.

Perhaps Eleanor had formed a tendre for Taylor, but the sale had been months ago, and nothing had come of it yet. There might still be a chance.

Eleanor awoke from a deep sleep, wondering why someone was shaking her. Refusing to open her eyes, she fell back against the soft mattress.

"Eleanor, please, you must wake up!"

"Oh, it's you," she mumbled, blinking several times before raising up on one elbow and wiping the sleep from her eyes with her other hand. "What do you want, Laura? What time is it?"

"It's one o'clock in the afternoon!" she exclaimed. "I thought you went to sleep early last night. Here, have some tea," she added, pushing a cup of the tepid liquid into her friend's hands.

Eleanor placed the cup on the bedside table and struggled into a sitting position.

She shook her head wearily and asked, "What is wrong now, Laura?"

"Well you might ask!" Laura exclaimed, bouncing onto the foot of the bed. "Stephen came to see me earlier. He wanted to know why you sold that land to Victor Taylor."

"What did you tell him?" demanded Eleanor, catching some of Laura's urgency.

"I told him that he should ask you. I'm sorry, but I didn't know what else to say."

"That's all right. We knew it would come to that. I'm going to say that we needed the money to set things straight around the house after Charles died."

"He won't believe that," said Laura, averting her eyes.

Eleanor grabbed Laura's wrist and forced her to look up. "Why not?"

"Oh, Ellie, I let him believe that you are in love with Taylor, that you acted out of love."

"You mean you have allowed your brother-in-law, the guardian of your three children, to believe that I, their governess and your companion, have sold Simon's inheritance out from under you for love?" demanded Eleanor, bolting out of bed and hurrying to her dressing room. She had never been so furious with Laura.

Laura followed on her heels, wailing, "I didn't know what else to say! He had formed the idea himself. . . ."

Eleanor whirled to face her. "How could he think . . ."

"He said something about seeing you together at the fair; I didn't understand it. I mean, surely you didn't meet Taylor in some clandestine . . ."

"Yes, I did, but it was broad daylight, for heaven's sake. You needn't look so shocked, Laura. If it weren't for you . . ."

Eleanor closed her eyes and took a deep breath. When she opened then, Laura was staring miserably at her, her face ashen. Eleanor put her arm around her and said resolutely, "There now, we'll come about; you just wait and see. I'll fob Stephen off with some tale of love lost. You're not to worry," she added, turning Laura to face her, bowing heads so that their foreheads touched.

"No more worrying about it, you promise?" asked Eleanor.

"I promise," whispered Laura.

Eleanor straightened, saying airily, "I can't believe what a slugabed I was today. Aren't we going to gather the greenery for Christmas this afternoon? We will have to hurry up and get organized if we're to finish before dark. Now run along, sweeting. I have to get dressed, and I have a hundred things to do before our outing."

When Laura was gone, Eleanor sank against the wall, closing her eyes and shutting out all thought. She opened her eyes, looking around the room at all her clothes, wondering what she would do if . . .

A glimmer of a smile played across her face as she recalled her favorite response to that childish supposition. "We don't play the *what if* game in this house," she could almost hear herself saying.

Penny bustled into the room, picking up her wrapper and slippers and gathering up her clothes for the afternoon.

"I knew you had to be tired, miss, to be sleepin' so late. I told all of 'em to just let you be, I did."

"Thank you, Penny. I needed the sleep, I think."

Penny sat her down in front of the mirror, clucking like a mother hen. "It looks t' me like you could use some more sleep."

"I'll be fine. I'm not wide-awake yet," lied Eleanor.

When she was dressed, she sailed downstairs to the kitchens first to be certain all was well for the night's dinner. Then she headed toward the front entrance, where people were throwing on coats and scarves, laughing and chatting.

"Does everyone have a partner?" asked Lieutenant Jones, taking charge for Laura. "And every couple has a sheet to carry the greenery?"

"I don't, Malcolm," said Miss Jones, her whiny voice grating on her brother's ears. "Where is Captain Ransom? He should be my partner."

"I haven't seen him. We'll have to go without him."

"But, Malcolm . . ." she began.

"Come with us, Miss Jones. We'd love to have your company," said Mr. Ardmore, offering his arm, which she grudgingly accepted.

There was a general burble of agreement, and Punt threw open the front door. They took their laughter and merriment with them, leaving silence behind. Eleanor put her hand on the balustrade to climb the stairs.

"I don't have a partner," came the deep voice from the top of the stairs.

"Stephen," she whispered, watching his approach. He was looking devilishly handsome in his black riding coat.

He sauntered down the steps to her side. "I was hoping you would be my partner," he said quietly.

Eleanor realized she hadn't taken a breath since he had first spoken, and she forced herself to inhale, slowly and evenly. It wasn't easy. His subtle cologne made her senses reel, or was that simply the effect his voice now had on her?

"Well? I promise I shan't bite," he said, and she looked up to his endearing smile.

She smiled back, her heart beating with an emotion long ago forgotten. Memories from the past floated back, too, but she ignored them, taking his hand in hers. She would enjoy this day, this moment, and forget everything else.

Looking up at her devil, the very proper Miss Webster said, "Just let me fetch my cloak and bonnet."

"Can you reach the mistletoe?" shouted Mr. Norton to his friend in the tree. Turning to Miss Jones, he gave a broad wink and said, "We don't want to go back without mistletoe."

She rolled her eyes and yawned.

"Halloo!" called the major and Mrs. Prentiss, spying Norton and Miss Jones and strolling toward them.

"Where's Mr. Ardmore? I thought he was with you," said Mrs. Prentiss.

Miss Jones sighed in disgust and said, "He's in that tree."

"Oh, good boy; he's going for the mistletoe, m' dear," said the major to his wife. "We'll have a jolly good time tonight."

"You're almost there!" called Norton.

"I'm going back to the house," announced Hilda Jones, walking toward the trees.

"Whoaaaa!" screamed Mr. Ardmore, crashing through the branches on his way to the ground.

"Ahhhh!" screamed Miss Jones, kicking her feet and shouting as he knocked her down, landing on top of her. "Get him off me! Get him off me!"

"So sorry, Miss Jo . . ." Mr. Ardmore slipped into unconsciousness while the rest of the party clustered around him.

"Bless him, dear boy, he's still clutching the mistletoe!" cried Mrs. Prentiss as her husband rolled Ardmore off Miss Jones and onto his back. "Be careful, Major. Has he broken anything, do you think?"

"What can I do to help?" asked Norton.

"I need help, too," snapped Miss Jones, sitting on the ground with her hands on her hips.

"Go and help her, Norton," commanded Major Prentiss.

"You go. I'm not in the army anymore," he replied.

Mr. Ardmore, regaining consciousness momentarily, tried to rise, saying weakly, "I'll go," before swooning once again.

Just then, Laura and her lieutenant arrived, along with Lord and Lady Reading. The children danced up, dragging Sir Michael with them.

After removing his greatcoat and putting two large branches through it, Norton and Michael gently placed Mr. Ardmore on his makeshift stretcher. He and Michael carried one end while Lord Reading and the major managed the other end. Mrs. Prentiss and Lady Reading positioned themselves on either side to make certain the "poor boy" didn't fall off. The children, dragging all the sheets full of greenery, led the way. Bedraggled and whining, Miss Jones limped along behind, leaning heavily on Laura and her brother.

* * *

Eleanor and Stephen finally gave up the pretense of gathering greenery. By mutual consent, they avoided the topic that was foremost in both of their minds; Victor Taylor stood firmly between them, but they would ignore him for the moment. Instead, they discussed schooldays, books they had read, and plays they had seen—though that topic was limited, since neither of them had spent much time in Society.

Finally, Stephen said, "I rode over to Faraday's farm this morning. He was working on that drainage ditch. Quite a time he was having with it, too."

"How is his wife? She is hoping to have a Christmas baby, you know."

"No, I didn't know, but she hasn't had it yet. Susan was with me, and she visited with Mrs. Faraday while I talked to her husband."

"Susan rode with you? Oh, I am glad."

"Yes, so was I. I think she's going to be all right."

"I hope so. She used to enjoy riding on Charles's horse. Now Mary, she adores anything with four legs, but especially horses. She has a collection of wooden horses Mr. Shaw carved for her."

Stephen nodded. "I saw one of them. Simon was playing with it."

Suddenly, he put his hand on her arm to stop her progress. Looking down with smiling eyes, he asked, "Eleanor, are you trying to avoid talking about that arrangement you made with Faraday?"

"He told you?" she asked. When he nodded, she said, "He wasn't supposed to tell anyone. That was supposed to be between me, him, and his wife."

"And now me," he said, taking her hand and placing it on his arm again as they continued their stroll.

"I also spoke to Miller."

"How are the Millers? You know, Laura invited them to the ball tomorrow night. I know some people may think they are not quite gentrified enough, but they are such dear people."

"I agree; they are the salt of the earth," he said, laughter in his voice. "Miller also verified what you and others have said about Lamb. I plan to give him the sack."

"I cannot say that I will be sorry to see the last of him."

"I don't understand why you kept him on," commented Stephen.

"According to Mr. Baxter, the solicitor, I had no right to make such a decision. He said he was the only one who could do so, until you—Simon's trustee—returned."

"I should look into that. I suspect Baxter has taken a little too much on himself where the estate is concerned, but I might be wrong. He did a good job of handling my affairs while I was gone."

Stephen stopped again, a thoughtful frown on his face. "My grandfather, who died just before Charles, left me his townhouse. It's been empty for the past two years. Baxter tells me it needs a great deal of work before it can be sold or leased. He wants me to come to London to inspect it."

"When will you go?" she asked.

With a self-deprecating snort, he said, "I don't know that I shall. I know that a wise man should attend to his own affairs; it's never prudent to allow someone else to make such decisions . . ."

"But?" said Eleanor, giving his arm a comforting squeeze.

Stephen put his other hand on top of hers, and they continued their stroll through the barren woods, their sides touching from time to time.

"I confess that the thought of setting foot in that house again . . . well, it's difficult, to say the least. I remember the first time I saw it; it was dusk and there was a deal of fog. We drove up and got out of the carriage. I looked up. The front door was very wide and painted red. There were two tall bay windows on either side of it with candlelight shining through. I tugged on my mother's skirts and told her it looked like a wolf. I didn't even want to go inside, but she ignored me and told my nursemaid to bring me along."

"How old were you?"

"Perhaps four. Then I met my grandfather and found out he was the wolf, not the house."

"If you would like some company, I could go with you," said Eleanor, wondering at her own temerity.

Stephen patted her hand again, nodding solemnly.

"I would like that," he said. "Perhaps the day after the ball. I need to do some shopping for the children for Boxing Day."

"Good; then it's settled," said Eleanor. Suddenly, she didn't care if she was opening herself up to heartbreak. She would do as she pleased, and it pleased her to think that she might help this man by her side lay to rest the ghosts in his past.

Eleanor knew the topic she dreaded was at hand. She shivered as a strong wind whipped her cloak open. Stephen stopped and pulled it closed, his hands resting lightly on the heavy wool cloth at her waist.

"I could stay here, like this, forever," he said softly.

Eleanor willed herself not to cry. She would not spoil this moment with tears. Instead, she lifted her face to his, watching in wonder as his lips descended to hers, their warmth spreading through her body like a warm, cozy fire.

He raised his head, and they turned back toward Ransom Hall.

Though her hand was still tucked into the crook of his arm, the warmth had fled, leaving behind cold ashes. The time had come, he thought. He had to know the truth.

"Why did you sell the land to Taylor?"

"I can't tell you, Stephen. It is not my tale to tell."

He stopped, but this time he didn't turn to face her. His voice hollow, he asked, "Do you love him?"

"Love him?" Somehow she managed to keep her tone light and neutral, although the words made her stomach roil with bile. "No, I don't."

"Then why?" he demanded, turning to her again and taking her hands in his. The pain in his eyes spoke to her in a way words never could.

"I'm sorry, Stephen. I can't tell you. You'll just have to trust me. Can you do that?" she asked, her self-control and her heart near to breaking.

"I don't know, Eleanor. I want to."

"Then I guess I'll have to settle for that right now," she said sadly.

They fell into step side by side, not touching, not speaking all the way back to the house. Darkness was falling as they passed through the gardens and entered the house through the morning room.

"What in the world is all that about?" demanded Stephen as he opened the French doors and a high-pitched wailing assailed his ears.

"It sounds like someone in pain!" exclaimed Eleanor, hurrying inside and coming to an abrupt stop as she took in the chaotic scene before her.

Stephen put his hand on her shoulder, peering over it. Chattering like magpies, Laura, Mrs. Prentiss, and Lady Reading were standing over Mr. Ardmore, who lay on the sofa, his face chalky and his eyes glazed. Sailor was pouring a measure of brandy while the rest of the gentlemen instructed him on the proper amount. Everyone was ignoring Miss Jones.

"What the devil is going on?" Stephen asked loudly, his voice cutting through the confusion so that everyone who was talking stopped, and the only remaining sound was coming from Miss Jones, who was, curiously enough, sitting on the floor.

Stephen stepped around Eleanor and singled out the source of the noise, saying, "Must you persist with that caterwauling?"

This brought a perfect silence to the small drawing room for a moment. Then Miss Jones fastened her malevolent gaze on Eleanor and spat out, "You! If you hadn't taken the best man for yourself, none of this would have happened!" She drummed her heels on the floor for emphasis.

"Hilda! Apologize at once!" said Lieutenant Jones.

"I will not! It's true! The captain should have been my escort today, not hers! And only look!" she added, giving a snort of satisfaction when everyone did so. "They didn't even bother to gather any greenery. I bet they were out in the woods using that sheet for something else!"

Stephen turned to Eleanor and said quietly, "It would be best if you left." She nodded and fled the room. He approached the viperish female on the floor, extending his hand to help her rise.

With a smirk of victory, the petite Miss Jones rose; Stephen lowered his head until his lips were close to her shell-like ear.

He murmured softly, "If you do not retract your slanderous statements, I will turn you over my knee and spank you like the spoiled brat you are. If you do as I say, all will be forgiven. Understood?"

Wide-eyed, she nodded. Turning to the others, who had now forgotten all about poor Mr. Ardmore reclining on the sofa, Miss Jones said, "I do hope you will forget my fit of temper. I was wrong, of course, to make up such a tale."

"Very nicely said," murmured Stephen.

"If you'll excuse me . . . ?" she replied, leaving the room.

When she was gone, Stephen turned back to his friends and asked, "Now, who is going to tell me what happened?"

After Miss Jones's outburst, Eleanor hurried to her room. She was not afraid that anyone would believe the young woman's childish accusations, but she felt keenly that some of Miss Jones's fit of pique was warranted. Sitting in front of her mirror, she whispered hoarsely, "Who am I to take Stephen away from his guests?"

At best, she told herself, she was a hostess of the house party and should have placed the pleasure and comfort of their guests above her own enjoyment.

But how could she have denied Stephen anything when he smiled at her?

There was a quiet knock on her door, and she sprang out

of her chair to answer it, opening it only slightly. Miss Jones pushed it wide and stepped inside, closing it quietly.

"May I be of service?" Eleanor asked coldly.

Leaning against the door, Miss Jones looked her up and down, her eyes narrowed.

"I thought it best if I tell you plainly, Miss Webster, I intend to have the captain. You may be his doxy, but I'll be the one he meets at the altar. You would do well to remember that." With a sneering smile, she slipped out the door.

His doxy! Was that what they all thought? Oh, she was a fool to get entangled with such a rake! Why had she forgotten all those hard-earned lessons in her father's house?

There was another quiet knock on the door, and she threw it open to confront her accuser.

Stephen stepped back, surprised by her wild-eyed look.

"Eleanor, what's wrong? After you left, Miss Jones apologized for her behavior, her false accusations. She was distraught, not that she has any reason to expect special attentions from me. I only hope her nonsense didn't upset you."

Eleanor shook her head. He couldn't begin to guess at Miss Jones's expectations, but she had no right to reveal them to him.

Instead, she said briskly, "Not at all, Captain."

Stephen frowned at the title, but he said, "Good. Let's try to set aside our differences until after tomorrow, Eleanor. It's the Christmas ball, and I have a mind to waltz with you. Will you save me a waltz?"

Eleanor looked into his dark, smiling eyes and nodded, her heart beginning to sing. He took her hand and lifted it to his lips before turning and leaving her alone again.

Eleanor closed the door, sagging against it, trembling; she wouldn't hazard a guess as to whether it was with pleasure or despair.

Eleven

By keeping very busy, Eleanor managed to keep her feet grounded as she floated through the next day. All of the servants and Laura proved very helpful in this, since they directed every question, every problem to her. But Eleanor didn't mind, dealing calmly with every mundane last-minute detail before their guests began arriving.

Around four o'clock, as she paused to catch her breath near the back hall, the door to the study opened with a crash. Eleanor shrank against the wall as the bailiff stormed past her, his large, round face puce with fury.

Stephen appeared in the doorway, his own expression taut with anger. When he spied Eleanor, his face softened to a gentle smile.

"Still saving that waltz for me?" he asked.

"The very first one, St. George," she replied.

"St. George?"

"Remember? St. George the dragonslayer," she responded, cocking her head in the direction Lamb had just taken.

Stephen walked toward her, and her pulse began to quicken.

"Alas," he said with mock dramatics, "I cannot be St. George. Knights always carry their lady's scarf or glove into battle, and I have none."

Eleanor chuckled and reached into her pocket, pulling out a pencil stub, a small leather notebook, and a pearl button she had found on the floor.

"I'm afraid I don't have anything worthy of you, Sir Knight."

"You've forgotten that ribbon in your hair," he said with a mischievous grin, reaching up and giving the bow a gentle tug. Holding up his prize, he touched it to his lips and said, "As I fight the dragon, it will remind me of you, fair maiden, for it is the color of your eyes."

Eleanor's laughter filled the narrow hallway, and Stephen put one arm at her waist, took her other hand, and waltzed her toward the front of the house. There, under Punt's shocked gaze, he released her, delivering a courtly bow, which she answered with a last giggle and a deep curtsy. Whistling an off-key tune, he opened the door to the billiard room, his entrance greeted by a chorus of masculine voices.

Left alone with the butler, Eleanor started back down the narrow hall, pausing after just a few steps. Frowning, she pulled out the small notebook to jog her memory before continuing on her errand, humming that same off-key tune.

Looking at her reflection in the full length cheval glass, Eleanor was glad she had allowed Laura to talk her into having a new ball gown made up by the talented seamstress in Chipping Barnet. It was a deep purple, very dignified and cut simply, as befitted her stature. The neckline was deceptively cut to appear fashionably low, but it boasted a narrow ruching of silk ribbon, the same shade as the gown, that hid some of her charms.

"The mistress sent this amethyst necklace for you, miss, but I think it might be too much. It's that old-looking gold, not shiny at all. I think pearls would be more suitable," added Penny, setting the necklace aside.

Eleanor turned and picked up the amethyst necklace, holding it up to her neck. It was dark and heavy, but the reflection off the stone was breathtaking.

"I think I will wear this, Penny," she said.

The maid fastened it around her neck and stepped back to gauge the effect, her lips rounding in surprise. "You do look a treat in that, miss. I suppose it takes someone with your figure to carry it off. And here are the earrings to match," she added, putting them on Eleanor and nodding in satisfaction.

"Thank you, Penny. I feel like a queen."

The maid chuckled and agreed. "And th' mistress, she's the fairy princess, dressed all in white with that green sash and her emeralds."

"Have the girls had their dinner yet? I promised they could come and see us before we go down to dinner."

"I'll send for them," said Penny, giving her mistress's hair a final pat before she hurried toward the door.

"Send them to their mother's chamber. I'm going to join her there," said Eleanor.

"Yes, miss," said Penny, leaving the door open.

A moment later, Eleanor whirled around at the sound of Stephen's voice. "I can now die a happy man. Or perhaps I have, and this is heaven," he added outrageously as he stepped farther into the room, holding one hand behind his back.

"The devil in heaven? I don't think that's possible," she said, smiling at him.

"The devil? Is that what you think of me?" he asked, clearly puzzled and perhaps a little hurt.

Eleanor shook her head as she approached him. The light in her eyes restored his smile, but she explained, "I thought perhaps you might be the devil—when you first arrived. But now I know better, Sir Knight."

He lifted her hand to his lips for a chaste kiss, his eyes shining with amusement and pleasure. "Perhaps you should have something to remind you, a token of your own. But what can I give you, fair maiden?" he asked, pulling her ribbon from his coat pocket and kissing it.

"I know; since I robbed you of your ribbon," he continued, "I'll give you something else for your hair." The hand he had been keeping behind his back all this time appeared, holding a box wrapped with a red ribbon.

"What is it?" Eleanor asked even as she took it and opened it. "How beautiful," she breathed.

Stephen took the delicate bunch of violets from the box,

holding it up to her hair. Feeling self-conscious, he said gruffly, "I thought your maid could fix them in your hair."

"I'm sure she can," said Eleanor. "How thoughtful! And so rare at this time of year. However did you find them?"

"I rode into London this morning. I knew that some of the vendors had hothouse flowers. I was very lucky," he added.

"So was I," said Eleanor.

"Oh, how pretty, Miss Webster!" exclaimed Mary, darting into the room. "You, too, Uncle Stephen," she added.

"Yes, he is quite handsome tonight, I agree," said Eleanor.

"Quite," agreed Susan, entering at a more demure pace. "That's a pretty necklace, Miss Webster."

"It is your mother's."

"I have never seen her wear it," said Susan.

"No, she doesn't really care for the color or style, but we thought it complemented this gown."

"Oh, it does. It's ever so pretty, and so are you, miss," chimed in little Mary. "Isn't she, Uncle?"

"She is indeed," murmured Stephen before detecting his nieces' speculative gazes. Clearing his throat, he said, "And you two are quite pretty, too. New gowns?"

"Yes, Mama had them made just for the ball. Can we go see Mama now?" asked Mary.

"Yes, of course. Come along," said Eleanor, taking Mary's hand.

"Are you coming, Uncle Stephen?" asked Susan.

With a secret smile for Eleanor, he said, "No, I have done what I wished to do. You ladies run ahead. I'll go downstairs, but I will see you at the ball," he added with a wink for his nieces.

The dining room at Ransom Hall was filled to capacity for the elaborate dinner that evening. Squire Trent and his wife, along with their three daughters, were the first to arrive. Next came the physician, Mr. Powell, with his sister Mrs. Evans, an outspoken widow whose son was a favorite in the nursery. Their other close neighbors, Lord and Lady

Burns, arrived with their son and his new wife. Finally, the vicar and his wife arrived, bringing their three young daughters and only son. In the nursery, the girls were having their own party, and Simon, who rarely had other boys to play with, ran from one to the other, babbling in his baby talk and clapping his hands.

Eleanor floated through the evening, speaking when necessary but for the most part caught up in her own world of dreams and possibilities. She recalled each look, each touch, that she and Stephen had shared. She refused to allow herself to think the impossible—that he wanted to marry her, that he loved her—or that she loved him, she told herself sharply.

No, she wouldn't allow herself to go so far, but the warmth of the looks Stephen was sending her way down the length of the long table fueled such wild speculations, despite her resolution. Just as she was reminding herself that she hadn't cared for a man since the age of seventeen, when young Henry had asked for her hand, just then she would look up to find him smiling at her. And then, as she warned her treacherous heart that men didn't fall in love with spinsters of thirty-four, he would catch her eye and wink, causing her rusty heart to spin like a top.

It was an early dinner and ended by eight o'clock, when the other guests began to arrive. Eleanor was caught up in greeting their new guests and helping Laura introduce the members of the house party. She was still occupied with her hostess duties when the musicians, hired from Chipping Barnet, struck up the first tune, a lively country reel. Out of the corner of her eye, she saw Stephen lead Hilda Jones onto the floor. Her happiness dimmed slightly, but it wasn't the waltz—*her* waltz.

"Yes, good evening, Mr. Taylor," she heard Laura say weakly, and turned around to deflect the bounder's attention from her friend.

"Good evening, Lady Ransom. May I say how very beautiful you look this evening," he said, bowing low before Laura, who threw Eleanor a look of sheer panic.

"What a flatterer you are, Mr. Taylor," cooed Eleanor,

linking arms with the horrid villain and leading him away from the entrance to the ballroom.

He sneered at her and said, "Do you have the money?"

Smiling and nodding at Mr. Miller, Eleanor whispered, "Not yet. I'll have it for you by tomorrow night."

"You said you would have it tonight," he growled.

She dropped his arm and turned to face him, lifting her fan and waving it languidly in front of her face to prevent any passerby from studying her expression closely.

"If you cannot wait until tomorrow, Mr. Taylor, then we are at *point non plus*. I told you we would get the money when I go to London. I go tomorrow. Will you wait, or will you end the game at this? You'll get no more, remember, if you tell your tale."

"I'll wait, missy, but not too long. I'll come see you tomorrow night at midnight."

Eleanor shook her head in disgust and said, "Not tomorrow night at midnight, you clunch. We will be at the midnight service. And after that, there is the Christmas dinner."

"Then when?"

"I don't know. Let me think and I'll tell you before you leave tonight," said Eleanor, growing weary.

"Don't try to pull any tricks," he snapped.

"I wouldn't dream of it," she said, favoring him with one last smile for the benefit of any interested observers before moving away. Eleanor shrank against the pillar, wishing suddenly she were invisible.

Stephen slipped up behind her and put his hand on her shoulder, causing her to jump. "It's only me," he said, watching her. "What is Taylor doing here?"

"Stephen, I told you before that I was not prepared to discuss Mr. Taylor."

"I know, my dear, but only a fool would think you invited the man because of friendship," he said.

"Stephen, I . . ."

His eyes hooded, he twisted an errant curl beside her ear and drawled sensuously, "My dear girl, you are wasting your breath. When you call me Stephen like that, I have trouble hearing anything else you have to say. The flowers are beautiful in your hair—though I expected nothing less."

Eleanor smiled shyly and thanked him for the compliment.

Just then, the musicians struck up a waltz, and he grinned down at her and said, "My dance, I believe," before leading her into the middle of the ballroom.

He held her just as he ought, not too close, but with a grace that guided them through the steps of the dance smoothly. Eleanor smiled and laughed, pretending that no one stood between them and happiness. She knew she was in danger of losing her heart completely to this man, but she simply didn't care.

"We have spies in the gallery," said Stephen, looking up at the balcony that ran the length of the ballroom.

The children were standing at the rail, watching the dancers as they spun around the floor. Eleanor waved to them, and they waved back.

"Poor Simon, he gets left out of everything," said Stephen.

"He is probably fast asleep at this hour, as the others should be also. It's almost ten o'clock, you know. They should all be in bed," said Eleanor.

"If you think I am going to let you go while the music is still playing, Miss Webster, you are very much mistaken," he said, going into a dizzying spin.

When they slowed again, Eleanor looked up at the girls, who were laughing and clapping their hands. As the music stopped, she made a signal to Jane, before thanking Stephen for their waltz.

"And I thank you, fair maiden," he said, bowing slightly. "But I see that you must go back to your tower. Would you care for some company?"

Eleanor was very tempted, but she knew his presence in the nursery would only serve to excite the children, and they were excited enough just to have their friends staying the night.

Laura rushed up to them, her face flushed, and announced, "Mrs. Faraday is having her baby and they can't find the midwife. Have you seen Mr. Powell?"

"I'll find him," offered Stephen, hurrying away.

"Oh, dear, I know she can't help doing this in the middle of our ball, but I do wish she had waited," moaned Laura.

"Laura!" exclaimed Sailor Jones, who had joined them in time to hear the end of the conversation.

"I know, Malcolm, it is terrible to even think such a thing, much less express it."

"I'll get my cloak and go with him," said Eleanor.

"Oh, no, you mustn't do that, Eleanor! I mean, she will want someone with her who has had children. Besides which, I need you here."

"I may not have had any children, but I was present at the birth of all three of yours," said Eleanor dryly.

"Yes, yes, I know. Oh, I don't know what I am saying! Please, dear Ellie, forgive me."

"Of course, but there is no need to take on so, Laura. Would you be so good as to fetch her some champagne, Lieutenant?"

"Gladly, Miss Webster," he said.

"I agree," said the physician, when Laura told him of her concern. Turning to his sister, he added, "Judith, here, will assist me. She has done so on numerous occasions and knows just what to do."

"There! That settles it! Then you may stay here and help me, Eleanor," said Laura.

Eleanor hesitated still, but Mr. Powell said, "I would love to have your help, Miss Webster, but I think your first duty is here with Lady Ransom." He smiled at her warmly and asked, "Would it be too much of an imposition if my nephew stayed the night?"

"Not at all," she replied. "He can share with Peter, Lord Reading's son."

"Oh, thank you, Miss Webster," said Mrs. Evans, smiling at each of them in turn. "I saw Robbie on the balcony a moment ago. I will just run upstairs and tell him what's going on."

"I'll go with you, Mrs. Evans. I want to tuck the children in myself," said Eleanor.

The physician said, "I'll collect your cloak, Judith, and meet you at the front door."

Stephen watched them go, wishing he could think up some excuse that would require his presence in the nursery. Stepping into the hall, his eyes narrowed when he saw a third figure climbing the stairs several steps behind the two women.

"I do hope I didn't upset Miss Webster by turning down her offer of assistance," said Mr. Powell, appearing at his elbow. His tone turning wistful, he murmured, "She is a fine lady."

"Yes, quite extraordinary," said Stephen. "Good night, Mr. Powell. Please give the Faradays my congratulations when you see them."

"Good night," replied the physician, watching the captain climb the stairs.

Eleanor and Mrs. Evans helped the maids herd their charges back to their various bedchambers. There were five girls sleeping in one chamber, though judging from the amount of giggling going on, very little sleep would take place. The boys, Peter, Robbie, and Ronald, the vicar's only son, were in the next chamber. Mrs. Evans said good night to Robbie and hurried away to join her brother. Eleanor said good night to the boys and crossed the hall to the maid's room, making certain the visiting nursemaids were also comfortable on their cots.

Finally, Eleanor closed the door and started down the hall, stifling a scream when someone stepped out of the shadows.

"Have you thought about when and where, Miss Webster?"

"Oh, it's you," she said, grimacing at Victor Taylor. "What are you doing up here?" she demanded, glancing around the empty hallway.

"I was just looking in on the children—well, on one of them," he said with a significant smile.

Eleanor gasped, but she managed to control her fear and say tersely, "Tomorrow night, at dusk, in the garden, the southwest corner. There's a rose arbor. Wait behind it so no one looking out a window from one of the upper floors can see you."

"I'll be there. Don't you forget."

He disappeared, and Eleanor leaned against the wall, thankful for its support. The door to the boys' chamber opened fully, and Stephen stepped into the hall. She was grateful for the shadows that disguised her fear.

"Fair maiden, I have come to take you back to the ball," he intoned with a gallant bow.

Eleanor took his arm as she pushed off the wall.

"You're trembling," he said. "Is anything the matter?"

"No," she whispered. A little stronger, she added, "It's just a little cold in these corridors. A glass of champagne wouldn't come amiss, Sir Knight."

"Your wish is my command," he said.

To Eleanor's surprise, he escorted her down the stairs with military quickness, when they might have lingered in the darkened hall. It was almost as if he was chasing someone, she worried.

As they reached the first floor near the front door, he gave her a little push toward the ballroom, saying formally, "I'll be there in a moment, Miss Webster," for the sake of the butler and footmen near the front door.

When she was gone, Stephen approached Punt and asked quietly, "Did Mr. Taylor just leave?"

"Yes, sir. It was most peculiar. He came down those stairs not two minutes ago, just like you and Miss Webster did. I know it wasn't my place, but I asked him what he was doing up there."

"And his response?" asked Stephen, his dark eyes as cold as ice.

"He said something about looking for the card room and getting turned around. I told him there wasn't a card room, that this was a ball, and he took his coat and left. Good riddance to the fellow, I say."

"Thank you, Punt. If Mr. Taylor should show up again, let me know before you tell anyone else, please."

"Certainly, sir. Happy to oblige," said the butler.

Stephen returned to the ballroom, his eyes immediately seeking Eleanor. He found her on the dance floor, performing the quadrille with Michael as if nothing had happened. He hadn't been able to hear her whispered exchange with Taylor, but he had seen the result. She hadn't been trembling from the cold, but from anger or fear. He admired her integrity, but he couldn't help wishing she would confide in him.

Backing up to the wall, Stephen was free to study her without anyone knowing it. All through dinner, he had felt very keenly the constraints of dining table etiquette. He had limited his conversation to the ladies on his left and right, but his mind—and quite often his gaze—had been halfway down the table. He wondered if she felt the same thrill shoot through her as he did when their eyes chanced to meet.

Stephen shook his head; two weeks ago he would have considered such thoughts beneath him, the stuff of young men's bad poetry—mooncalf love. Now . . . now he was counting the minutes until the musicians would stop playing so he could speak to her again.

The squire's oldest daughter strolled past, giving him a bold look, but he ignored her open invitation and craned his head to keep Eleanor in view. Puckering her lips in a childish pout, the girl moved on. She was just an infant, probably no more than eighteen. His gaze settled on Eleanor again, a satisfied expression on his face; that was what he wanted, not some chit just out of the schoolroom.

"I wouldn't have picked her out for you, my boy," said Mrs. Prentiss. "If any female could lead you to the altar, I thought it would be one of those mindless little ninnies you could twist and mold as you saw fit."

Stephen never took his eyes off Eleanor, but his smile widened and he shook his head. "That shows how little you know of me, Mrs. Prentiss. I never entertained such a notion. Of course, I never thought I'd want to get leg-shackled with anybody." He turned and gave her leathery cheek a quick kiss. "After all, the best lady was already taken."

"You are a rogue!" she chortled, slapping his arm with

her fan. Lowering her voice, she said in her hoarse whisper, "When will you ask her?"

"I'm not certain, and don't you go telling anyone about this. I don't want someone else asking her to wed me!"

Again she laughed, promising, "Mum's the word."

When the music ended, Stephen hurried forward, but Norton was before him, asking for the next dance. When he arrived, Eleanor was accepting the other man's invitation. The musicians struck up another waltz and she grimaced, her eyes seeking his. With a little shrug of her slender shoulders, she allowed Norton to lead her away.

"There you are, Captain," said Hilda Jones, grasping his arm and looking from him to the dance floor twice before he finally succumbed and asked her to dance.

"I would love to," she said, putting on her demure look.

When they had executed two dazzling turns, and she had stepped on his foot three times, she said, "I'm afraid this waltz is just beyond me."

Stephen reminded himself that this was his friend's sister and, as such, deserved a pleasant conversation. "I don't see why. You were splendid in the country reel."

Miss Jones gave a delicate shudder and said, "I just can't get accustomed to being in a man's embrace. Some ladies, like that Miss Webster you were waltzing with earlier, have no trouble being so intimate, but I find it scandalous."

Stephen glared at her. How dare the chit insult Eleanor!

"Ouch!" he growled when she stepped on his toes again.

"Please forgive me, Captain."

Either she was lying or she really was a terrible prude, and Stephen decided it might be the latter. That would account for her grace while performing other dances and her obvious lack of grace when performing the waltz.

"Would you rather sit out the waltz, Miss Jones?" he asked politely.

"Oh, yes, thank you," she said, allowing him to maneuver toward the edge of the ballroom, where they finally stopped waltzing and began looking for chairs.

Her color high, Miss Jones breathed, "I know it is quite

cold outside, but I am about to faint from the heat in here. There are just so many people," she said with a die-away sigh.

"Perhaps a few minutes on the terrace would serve to cool you off," said Stephen, ushering her toward the French doors.

When they were outside, Miss Jones pulled her silk shawl around her shoulders and shivered.

"We should go back in," he said, but she walked farther away from the house. Hesitating a moment, Stephen followed. The terrace was empty; no one else was foolish enough to brave the cold December air.

Touching her elbow, Stephen suggested, "The music has stopped, so you can find someone for the next set. Really, Miss Jones, you shouldn't have come outside. It's much too cold."

"Not if you will take me in your arms!" she said coyly, throwing her arms around his neck, realizing he was too tall and settling for his waist.

"What the deuce? Stop that!" he demanded, trying to loosen her grasp and having little success. Capturing both her hands, he gazed down at the petite beauty and said firmly, "I feel certain you will think better of this in a little while, Miss Jones. You are a beautiful young lady, but you can't have considered properly."

"But I *have* considered," she declared dramatically, drawing her hands away and holding one to her brow as she gazed at him soulfully. "I have only now found my mind—and my heart!"

"I am sorry if you are telling the truth. You are my friend's sister, and I would not hurt you for his sake, but I cannot . . ."

"Oh, do not continue!" she snapped, stamping her foot. "You are like all the others!"

"There you are, Miss Jones," called Eleanor, trying not to laugh when the lady in question bounded away from Stephen and glared at her ferociously. Eleanor added, "Your brother was just looking for you; I believe it was quite urgent."

Miss Jones threw out her chest and stalked past Eleanor. At the door to the ballroom, she snarled, "If you dare tell anyone about this, Miss Webster, I will have your job!"

Stephen took a step toward Miss Jones, and she fled.

"Is that any way for a handsome knight to act with an innocent maid?" teased Eleanor, not feeling the cold in the least as she looked up at him.

Stephen was still shaken by his ordeal and vowed, "I swear I have done nothing to encourage her, Eleanor. Nothing at all."

Eleanor chuckled and said, "Let's go inside. You can tell me all about it."

As they walked toward the house, Stephen declared stoutly, "Of all the queer starts! I don't know what got into her. I'm afraid Sailor's sister must be all about in the head."

"Oh, I don't think so. She contrived to get you out here alone, didn't she?"

"Yes, but to what purpose? She can't think that I returned her feelings."

"I think it is because she disgraced herself so badly yesterday when everyone was gathering the Christmas greenery. She realizes now she has managed to set up the backs of almost all the eligible gentlemen here at the Hall."

"Including me," he said.

"Yes, and Mr. Ardmore, though I don't think she is the least interested in him," said Eleanor, giving his arm a sympathetic squeeze as she teased, "If I were you, I wouldn't allow myself to be alone with her. She might try to compromise you."

Stephen shuddered. Trying to regain his balance, he said lightly, "Never mind her. What about you, my dear? Wouldn't you care to compromise me?"

The question caught Eleanor by surprise, sending her spiraling into the past. She knew it was Stephen speaking, but the words and tone reminded her so forcefully of the so-called gentlemen who had visited the vicarage and thought it perfectly splendid sport to flirt offensively with their host's daughter. They had been harmless enough and had never touched her, but their innuendos and laughter had robbed her of the desire to flirt, albeit an innocent flirtation.

Eleanor fought to return to the present, pasting a false smile on her face.

But her violet eyes could not tell a lie, and Stephen whispered urgently, "Eleanor, what is it, my love? If I have said anything to upset you . . ."

"No, no, it's not that. What you said just now, the way you said it . . . I'm sorry, Stephen, but it was like stepping back in time. I'm fine now," she added in her usual sensible tone.

From the dark recesses of her mind, a voice was demanding how she could ever have believed that she could fall in love with a man like Stephen, or that he could love her. He was so handsome, so virile, so much like her father and his friends. Panic rose in her eyes, and she pushed away from him.

Stephen took her hands and wouldn't let her go, saying calmly, "No, I'm sorry, my sweet. I didn't mean to upset you. I thought it was more of our little jest, fair maiden."

"I know, Stephen, and I hate myself for being so silly. It's just so difficult to believe that, after all these years, I have finally found . . ."

Her blush has hidden by the dark night, but again Stephen seemed to sense her every fear, her every need. He drew her close and lifted her hands to his lips, kissing her fingertips.

"Eleanor, I want to ask you something. I . . ." He paused as she closed her eyes and shook her head. His heart near to breaking, he asked, "You don't want me to speak?"

Again Eleanor shook her head, and he dropped her hands. Opening the door to the ballroom, she saw the raw pain in his dark eyes and put a hand on his sleeve to restrain him.

"Not yet, Stephen," she whispered, answering his questioning eyes with a smile.

"I have never been a patient man, Eleanor," he replied softly, "but for you, my dear, I will wait."

Twelve

Eleanor felt that all eyes were watching as she preceded Stephen into the ballroom. Heads turned, but no one appeared terribly shocked, she noted with relief. Several of the older ladies even smiled at them indulgently.

The guests began to drift toward the dining room, and Stephen offered his arm, saying, "Evidently we missed the announcement of supper. May I have the pleasure of your company, fair maiden?"

Eleanor declined reluctantly. "I really must go to the kitchens and be certain all is well."

"Shall I accompany you?" he asked. "I know a thing or two about cooking—well, I can spoon up a sauce or something."

"No, no, you must help Laura preside over the buffet supper." He groaned, and Eleanor added, "Everyone must do his part, and your part this evening is to play host to Laura's hostess."

"I think Sailor has been doing a fair job of it. I daresay they won't even miss me. We could slip out and . . . I know. To the dining room!" he said, leaving her to make her way to the kitchens, where Cook was about to strangle one of the girls hired from the village.

"Now, now, there's no harm done," said Eleanor, sailing into the fray. "Pick up the silverware, Patsy; rinse it and dry it. Now, what can I do to help, Cook?"

* * *

It was after two o'clock when the ball finally drew to a close. The younger gentlemen of the house party declared it was still too early to contemplate retiring, and they headed for the billiard room.

Wearily, Eleanor climbed the stairs with Laura, bidding her good night at her door. Laura continued on to her own chamber, and Eleanor glanced down the hall, seeing Stephen at the corner watching her with a little smile playing on his lips.

"Good night, fair maiden. Until tomorrow at nine o'clock?"

"If you think you can rise that early, Sir Knight," she teased.

"I will be ready and waiting. Where shall we meet?"

"In the breakfast room?"

"No, too public. I don't want anyone else asking to come with us. Let's meet in the stables. I have told Monkey to have the curricle ready by nine. We'll be away before the rest are any the wiser."

"Perhaps they want to come along," said Eleanor.

"Then they must make their own arrangements," said Stephen warmly. "Just as you and I have done. Good night, my . . . Miss Webster," he finished as Miss Jones scurried past them, heading for her room down the hall.

"Good night, my captain," Eleanor replied as soon as Miss Jones had closed her door.

Stephen entered his room and dismissed Corbin, who had a tendency to fuss over him. After removing his clothes and putting on a dressing gown, he began to search through the drawers of the dresser and the small desk that sat in the corner.

With a grunt of satisfaction, he pulled out the small pistol he had carried throughout the Peninsular campaign and in Belgium. He set about cleaning it and loading it, whistling softly as he worked.

He wasn't certain he would need the weapon, but he intended to be prepared. He hadn't been able to hear Eleanor's conversation with Taylor, but the way she had jumped when he appeared told its own tale. Taylor had some stranglehold on Eleanor and Stephen needed to be prepared for anything.

Stephen put the pistol on the dresser and climbed onto the bed, sitting up against the headboard and closing his eyes. He knew he wouldn't sleep well. On the one hand, his heart was singing, thrilled with Eleanor's "not yet"; she hadn't said no, though he knew she had been close to running away. But he had seen the pain in her eyes; it had been a near thing.

His fists clenched, itching to come to blows with a father so set on his own pleasure that he thought nothing of exposing his innocent, impressionable daughter to such an unwholesome atmosphere. His own childhood had been bad enough, but his mother had cared for her sons; she just hadn't been able to tolerate living the life of a country squire's wife. As for his kind, bumbling father, he had given his sons the same unconditional love he offered his wife until he died of a broken heart.

But through the years, Michael had revealed intimate details of his father's antics; he had been a man driven by lust—lust for riding, gaming, and wenching. No wonder Eleanor had never wed. Why would she do so, when she thought it would provide little comfort and a great deal of pain?

Stephen swung his feet off the bed and stood up. He fought the overwhelming desire to go to Eleanor's room and hold her in his arms. Grinning at his own foolishness, he sat down again. When had his purpose in life changed? When had he decided that he couldn't live another day without knowing that she was his? He had seen men lose their heads and their lives for love and passion. He had never expected, had never even wanted, to experience such a deep, powerful love.

Until he had looked into those violet eyes, he had been quite content to muddle along with his pleasure-seeking ways, fulfilling his needs—both physical and emotional—through the comradeship of war and in the arms of the easy women who entered his world. But now, everything hinged on Eleanor's answer to a single question.

He would have to be careful, he realized, frowning as he blew out the last candle and slipped under the counterpane. She was as skittish as a colt. For someone as sensible as Eleanor, his offer would need to be sensible, too. He would have to curb his passion and desires or he might frighten her, and he certainly didn't wish to do that.

All he wanted was a yes—a sweet, simple yes.

Monkey had the curricle and horses ready and waiting at nine o'clock when Eleanor arrived at the stables the next morning. Stephen's face lit up when he saw her, and he gave her that special smile that always lifted her heart.

Eleanor wore a close-fitting wool carriage dress, deep red in color and trimmed with black braid. Her matching bonnet covered her golden curls completely, although Penny had pulled several strands loose to frame her face with short curls.

Stephen thought she had never looked more bewitching. Of course, he had to admit, he thought that every time he saw her.

"Captain, do you think we might stop by the Faraday farm first? I want to make sure everything went well, and I have a present for the baby."

"A very good idea. We must do all we can to encourage our good tenants." Holding out his hand to help her climb up, Stephen added, "Shall we dispense with Monkey's services today? After all, it is an open carriage."

"But who will hold the horses, *Capitán?*" complained the groom.

"There are always willing lads about," said Stephen.

"Strangers to look after my cattle," grumbled Monkey, turning to Eleanor and pleading, "Please, miss, cannot you tell him?"

"I'm sorry. When your captain has made up his mind, there is nothing else to be said," replied Eleanor.

"Yes, he is that stubborn," said Monkey, standing away from the horses' heads as Stephen released the brake, sending the pair forward, around the house, and down the long, tree-lined drive.

"You are looking very fetching this morning, Miss Webster. Is that a new bonnet?" he asked, glancing down at Eleanor in admiration.

"Not at all," she said, giving a lighthearted laugh. "I have had it for ages."

"Well, it suits you," he said, smiling as the wind ruffled the curls framing her face.

They arrived a few minutes later at the Faradays' cottage. Mr. Powell's carriage stood against the small barn, and his horse whickered to them from the paddock.

"I hope everything is all right!" exclaimed Eleanor, climbing down and hurrying toward the house.

The door opened just as she raised her hand to knock.

"Miss Webster, Captain, good morning! Come and see the latest addition," said the physician.

Eleanor entered the small, neat room where Mrs. Faraday lay on a bed with pure white linen.

"Come and see my son," she said softly, turning the tiny bundle beside her so they might have a better view.

"He is beautiful," breathed Eleanor. Handing the gift she had brought to Mrs. Faraday, she asked, "May I hold him?"

"Of course," said the new mother.

Faraday offered Stephen a mug of ale, lifting his own and saying, "To the ladies!"

"To the ladies," echoed Stephen, watching Eleanor as she tenderly kissed the baby's pink cheek. As she gazed at him, her face was transformed by a luminous smile that made Stephen ache for something he didn't even know had been missing.

With a sigh, Eleanor returned the baby to his mother.

"We really should be going. I'll stop by tomorrow to see if there's anything I can do to help," she promised.

They were both pensive as Stephen returned to the main

road. Finally, he asked, "What shall we do first when we arrive?"

"I have some shopping I must do," said Eleanor, feeling her spirits sag at the thought of the amethyst necklace and ruby ring in her reticule. Still, it would be good to have that distasteful task behind her. Then she could enjoy the remainder of the day with Stephen.

"Very well, then shopping will be the first order of the day. And afterward we will visit the house," he said, his own spirits turning downward.

Eleanor took her hand out of the fur muff in her lap and touched his gloved hands. Stephen smiled, his eyes still on the road before them.

"Tell me more about the house, Stephen. I know you were frightened when you first saw it, but after living there for a time, did you come to accept it?"

He considered this for a moment before saying finally, "No, but not because of the house. It was my grandfather; I despised him, and feared him, too. He was a cruel man who took pleasure in taunting me and Charles, telling us what a weak man our father had been."

"Charles mentioned once that he lived with his grandfather."

"Yes, our mother's father. He was devoted to her; very possibly, she was the only thing on this earth he ever loved. Ironically, I think that is what led to her destruction. I didn't understand it at the time."

Eleanor put her arm through his, her side touching his, providing both warmth and comfort.

"You needn't tell me if you don't want to," she said gently.

He put his hand over hers, allowing the horses to slow slightly as he said bleakly, "The first time my mother ran away, it was with a footman. My father forgave her and took her back in. The next time, it was our tutor. Charles was away at school by then, but I was still at home. My father took her back again, but he was a broken man. When I went away to school, I think things grew worse. When we would come home on holiday, we would overhear the servants' gossip."

"How terrible for a little boy."

"When our father died, Charles and I were both at school. Mother ran away again, and when the term was over, we were sent to live with my grandfather. I had met him only the one time when Mother had taken me to visit.

"The most shocking thing about my grandfather was that he had the kindest face. His hair was stark white and his eyes were a bright blue. He looked like an angel, but he hated me. He tolerated Charles; I never knew why I was singled out."

"I'm sorry, Stephen," she said, laying her head on his shoulder.

He couldn't see her face because of her bonnet, but this gentle act of trust filled his heart with pleasure. Forget all the other women he had ever met; to have Eleanor's head resting on his shoulder was worth more than life itself.

The journey to London took little more than an hour, and the time passed too quickly for Eleanor, who was in a quandary. How could she tell Stephen she had to be alone to conduct her shopping? She had come to no solution when the houses began to be spaced closer together, and all too soon, they were heading up Bond Street.

"Where did you wish to go first?" he asked.

"I don't know, precisely. What about you?"

"I want to find some presents for the children," he responded. "And then something for Laura. You'll help me with that, I hope."

"Of course. I have a few small commissions to take care of here, but I would like to look at some jewelry, on Laura's behalf," she added quickly. "There's a small shop we have dealt with before, on Henrietta Street."

"Then we can begin there," he said.

"No; that is . . ." she said, thinking quickly and smiling at him, "I would prefer to do that by myself."

"Very well," said Stephen, frowning slightly. But he shook off his uneasy feelings and turned down the next side street.

"Here we are," said Eleanor, forcing another smile to her lips as she descended into misery. When he had helped her down, she suggested brightly, "Why don't you try that shop over there for the girls' presents? They have pretty dolls from Paris."

"Then I'll come back for you in fifteen minutes," said Stephen, flipping a coin to one of the boys who hurried forward to watch the horses.

"That will be fine," said Eleanor, scurrying into the small jeweler's shop.

"May I help you, madam?" asked the jeweler, who served behind the counter as well. "It's Miss Webster, isn't it?"

Eleanor glanced over her shoulder and breathed a sigh of relief. Stephen was out of sight.

Opening her reticule, she said, "Yes, I would like to sell the jewels out of these two pieces and replace them with paste."

"I see," he said, looking sharply at her.

"Can you manage that?" she asked, enduring his scrutiny with a haughty stare as he studied her thoughtfully.

The last time, she and Laura had come together. She hoped her gown was rich enough that he would think the necklace and ring belonged to her. Finally, he picked up the necklace, looking at her over his jeweler's glass and nodding in satisfaction.

They agreed on a price, and a time when he would have them ready that afternoon. With a sigh of relief, Eleanor turned to go. There was Stephen, watching her, his face closed and impassive.

"Are you finished?" he asked.

"Yes," she replied, blinking and looking away. Somehow she had to find a way to end Victor Taylor's perfidy. Laura could not go on paying indefinitely. He helped her into the curricle. She glanced at Stephen's rigid profile and wondered if she dared confide in him.

No, she thought. For Simon's sake, she couldn't take the chance.

"Did you find dolls for the girls?" she asked.

"No. I couldn't decide, so I came back to get you," he said, taking his eyes off the road for a moment and delivering a speaking glance at her.

Eleanor shrank from him as if hit by a physical blow. The worst part was, she felt she deserved his repugnance.

"Do you want to try another shop?" she asked timidly.

"No, I thought we would get all the unpleasant errands out of the way first," he said, his voice cold. "I must stop at Mr. Baxter's office and get the key to my grandfather's house. Then we'll go to the house."

Eleanor remained silent as they entered the city and stopped in front of the solicitor's office. One of the clerks came down the steps and took charge of the horses and curricle.

"Shall I wait here?" she asked.

"If you wish," came the curt reply.

In a sea of misery, Eleanor waited while Stephen entered the abhorrent solicitor's office. After several moments, Mr. Baxter appeared, opening the door personally for his client and giving him an obsequious little bow.

Then he spied Eleanor and exclaimed, "You've got the Webster woman with you?"

"Yes, she was kind enough to accompany me to my grandfather's house," he said, his irritation with the solicitor making him forget his distrust of Eleanor for the moment.

"Are you sure that's wise, Captain? I mean, surely someone else . . . anyone else . . ."

Stephen looked the man up and down, his nostrils flaring with distaste. Setting aside his confusion over Eleanor's actions, he said sharply, "Perhaps I should warn you, Baxter, to be very careful what you say of Miss Webster. I hold her in the highest regard."

He felt a flash of grim satisfaction when he saw Eleanor's mouth drop open, wider even than the solicitor's, who followed Stephen down the steps as fast as his short little legs could carry him.

Stephen was already in the curricle when Baxter reached it, bowing low to Eleanor and cackling his congratulations.

"That's enough," said Stephen, putting an end to the toadying little man. "Stand away from their heads!" he told the clerk.

Soon they were bowling down the street, heading toward a once fashionable neighborhood near Berkley Street. When Stephen stopped the curricle, he looked around for someone to hold the horses, but there was no one around the quiet street. With a grimace, he put on the brake and hopped to the ground, tying the ribbons to a rickety fence post.

Looking up at Eleanor, who was still too shocked for action, he asked sharply, "Are you going to get down or not?"

His tone of voice sent a spark to her brain, and she glared down at him, holding out an imperious hand for his assistance. Stephen couldn't help but smile.

Seeing her in the jeweler's shop, quite obviously selling some of Laura's jewels, including, unless he was much mistaken, the beautiful necklace she had worn the night before, his temper had snapped. He wished he could explain away her actions, but her silence seemed to confirm her guilt. Still, she was quite a trooper, enduring his fit of temper and the solicitor's veiled insults and never saying a word.

He offered her his arm, which she chose to ignore. Chuckling, he followed her up the steps, walking slowly and staring up at the familiar facade.

Eleanor had softened by the time she reached the front door. She watched his ascent with sympathy, thinking how difficult it must be, facing the ghosts of his past. She wished she could be as brave when facing her own ghosts.

Stephen turned the key in the lock and pushed open the door. It creaked from disuse. Peering into the murky hall, he looked down at her and grimaced.

"Shall we?" she asked, taking his hand in hers.

"Might as well. That's what we came for," he responded, leading her inside and closing the front door.

They stepped into the drawing room. The furniture was in Holland covers, and the rugs had been removed. Their footsteps echoed in the gloomy silence.

"Is that him?" whispered Eleanor, looking at the portrait

over the mantel. It was of a young man with dark hair and bright blue eyes.

"Yes, when he was perhaps twenty years of age."

Stephen stepped closer, shivering as he stared up at the image of the grandfather he had so despised and feared.

"He's the reason I ran away to the army. As it turned out, it was the best thing I ever did. After much pleading by Charles, he even purchased my commission for me."

They continued their tour of the lower floor, ending with the study that was also a library, although all the books had been removed.

"There is something so sad about empty bookshelves," said Eleanor, walking forward and running a gloved finger along one shelf, sneezing at the dust her touch stirred up.

"I fear you'll be in a sad state by the time we leave. You're getting dust all over the hem of your gown, and you have probably ruined your gloves. Why don't . . ." Stephen paused, struck by the reflection of Eleanor's face in the mirror on the wall beside the bookcases. The color had drained out of her face, and her mouth sagged open.

Stepping closer, he asked, "What is it? Here, sit down before you faint!"

"No, no, you don't understand," she breathed, pointing to the only object that remained on the bookshelf. "You don't understand," she said again.

Stephen took the miniature and led Eleanor back to the sofa, keeping one arm around her while he threw off the Holland cover.

"Shall I fetch a physician?" he said.

"What?" she said. Then she pointed to the miniature he held and asked weakly, "Who is that?"

"This? It's my mother. Why has that upset you so? Eleanor!"

She began to giggle, the giggles replaced by a laugh; then she roared with laughter.

Alarmed, Stephen grabbed her shoulders and shook her. "What the devil is going on, Eleanor?"

Catching her breath, Eleanor felt the relief washing over

her as she explained, "Your mother had red hair, just like Simon's! I never knew that."

"Yes, I noticed that first thing when I saw the boy, but I still don't see . . ."

"No, I know you don't, but finding out has made all the difference in the world. You have no idea," she said.

"No, I don't, but we're going to stay right here until you explain."

Suddenly, Eleanor recalled her audience, and her smile faded. She bit her lip and said cautiously, "It's just that I am so surprised. Laura and I wondered where Simon got all that red hair, and now I know."

"I still don't see what that has to do with anything," said Stephen.

"It's just that everyone was taken aback by little Simon's red hair and blue eyes; he was so different from his sisters. Laura never met your mother, of course, so she had no idea Simon received his coloring from her."

"He's the image of my mother," said Stephen, looking at the picture again, his face softening. "Of course, he also gets that white lock of hair from her, just like I did. Eleanor! Are you all right? You're losing your color again!" he said, patting her hand.

She touched his cheek and turned his head to study the scar that ran across his right temple and into the hairline.

"I never noticed that you have more silver hair on that side," she said, turning his head to compare the right side with the left.

"I lost some of the lock of white hair from the scarring, and now that I'm getting older, you don't really notice what's left of it. But you see, the hair is more white there than silver," he pointed out, his hand closing over hers as she peered at his hair.

Their eyes met, and he kissed the tip of her nose before recalling their compromising situation—alone in a house without so much as a servant present to preserve the proprieties.

"I still don't understand why this discovery was so earth-shattering," he said, holding his mother's portrait up and studying it again—anything to distract him from the desire to take her in his arms. "It's not as if anyone has questioned little Simon's birthright. I'm the only one who would benefit from that, and I certainly wouldn't dream . . ."

Again their eyes met as understanding dawned. "My God! Laura believes Simon is not Charles's son."

Eleanor grasped his hand and said, "Please, Stephen, don't think badly of Laura. She loved your brother, and it hurt her so when he would go back to London to his . . ."

"His mistresses," said Stephen bluntly.

"It only happened once, after that last time when she and Charles quarrelled so and he slammed out of the house. Laura was so desperate and lonely. She had to be to take up with the likes of . . ."

"Taylor!" Stephen spat out the word, jumping up and pacing around the room before returning to her side. His eyes blazing, he looked down at Eleanor and said, "Devil take him, the red-headed snake! He's been blackmailing Laura, and that's why she sold him the land."

"Yes, only she didn't sell it to him, she gave it away. There were other things as well. We had no choice, Stephen. We would have done anything to protect Simon," exclaimed Eleanor, her eyes begging for his compassion for both her and her friend.

With a heavy sigh, Stephen collapsed onto the sofa again. "So this morning, you were selling some of Laura's pieces to pay Taylor off."

She nodded and looked away.

Turning to face her, Stephen gathered her hands in his and vowed, "We will get the land back for Laura, and all the money. As for the necklace you sold today, we'll take care of that immediately. And when we return to Ransom Hall, I'll take care of Taylor."

Eleanor shivered at his tone, but she shook her head proudly, saying, "I prefer to deal with him myself, if you don't mind, Stephen. I will enjoy telling him the news."

"As you wish," he said, smiling down at her. Then, picking

up the miniature, he said, "I think little Simon should have this picture, don't you? When he gets older, he will appreciate knowing he resembles someone in the family. He need never know what an unhappy person she was."

Their first stop took them back to the jeweler's shop, where Stephen's stern presence smoothed the way for their transaction. From there, they purchased gifts for the children and Laura, ribbons for the maids, and tobacco for the men. For Cook, Stephen chose a pretty apron frivolously trimmed in lace. Passing a leather goods store, he slipped inside and purchased a new saddle for Susan's mare and a porcelain horse for Mary.

Watching him stow these things in the boot, Eleanor shook her head, saying, "You are going to spoil them."

"And why not? I figure I've missed nine years of birthdays for Susan and six for Mary. I'm just making up for lost time," he added with a grin.

Finally, they had had their fill of shopping and began to think of the long drive home.

"I believe we need something for ourselves," said Stephen, turning the curricle around and heading toward Berkeley Square.

"Gunter's?" asked Eleanor. "I love their biscuits."

"Then we'll buy you a dozen!" declared Stephen, maneuvering around a large cart with ease.

When they were seated and served, Eleanor noticed two gentlemen entering with a pretty young woman between them. She was dressed in a flashy manner, and Eleanor averted her eyes. This was not the sort of person a lady should acknowledge.

"What is it? Some friends of yours?" asked Stephen.

"No, I've never seen her before," replied Eleanor.

Stephen twisted in his seat to look; then he whirled back around, his face, under his dark tan, turning red. He had recognized the voluptuous curves and dimpled cheeks of Miss Goodbottom. His cravat suddenly seemed too tight, and he ran his finger along his collar.

"I take it you have seen her before," murmured Eleanor,

fighting the envy she felt as she stared at the pretty young woman.

"An, uh, old friend," he said, taking her hand and scandalizing the proper dame sitting next to them.

Eleanor found it impossible to look up without staring. After several minutes of this agony, Stephen rose, paid the shot, and led her out of the famed confectioner's without tasting a single bite. Stephen climbed up beside her and turned the team toward home.

When they were finally out of town, Eleanor asked bluntly, "How well did you know that lady?"

"Not that well. Only since I returned from Belgium," he replied dully. "I told you, I'm not a saint, Eleanor."

"I see."

Stephen pulled back on the ribbons, set the brake, and turned to face her while his horses stamped their feet in protest.

"I have not seen the lady since I returned to Ransom Hall. As a matter of fact, I have no desire to see her again at all, and I'm very happy she has found someone else who enjoys her company."

Eleanor's confidence was bolstered by this news, but she couldn't help commenting, "She is very pretty, Stephen, and quite young."

Taking her face in his hands, his thumb rubbed her cheek lovingly as he said, "She was nothing compared to you, fair maiden, nothing at all."

Eleanor smiled and leaned forward, closing her eyes as he pressed his lips to hers.

"We should go home," he said, releasing the brake and lifting the reins again. Eleanor snuggled against his side, content with the world.

"I'll have to hurry if I'm going to get there on time; it will be dark soon," whispered Eleanor. "You'll go in and tell Laura? I want her to know as soon as possible."

"I'll tell her," he replied, pulling into the stable yard and stopping the team.

"Wish me luck!" said Eleanor as he swung her to the ground.

"The very best, darling," said Stephen, watching her hurry out of the stable yard and across the garden to the far end, where the secluded rose arbor stood.

Eleanor stumbled several times as she passed flower beds and pathways, fighting off the panic that threatened her. As many times as she told herself Taylor no longer had any power over Laura, Simon, or herself, she couldn't quite believe it.

"You're late. I almost left. Where's my money?" asked Taylor, stepping out from behind the arbor.

"It might have been to your advantage if you had," she said, thrusting her chin up defiantly.

"What's that about then?" he demanded.

Eleanor held out the miniature of Stephen's mother, the late Lady Ransom, saying, "This is Simon's grandmother."

"Well, what's that to me? We both know you'll do anything to keep folks from whispering. Maybe I'm not the father of the little viscount; maybe I am. People would love to have the opportunity to speculate. And then there's the question of Laura's reputation," he added with a nasty sneer.

"Oh, I think we can stand a small scandal. It will be well worth it to see you in gaol," said Eleanor, matching his bravado.

"In gaol," he muttered, grabbing her wrists and giving them a savage twist.

Eleanor screamed, trying to jerk free, but his grip was like iron.

"Not so fast, Miss High-and-mighty Webster! If I can't get my pound of flesh one way, I'll get it the . . ."

Eleanor fell back as he released her wrists, hitting her head on the flagstones. Dazed, she sat up and watched as Stephen drove home his fist time and again until the red-haired man was flat on his back and almost senseless.

Stephen sat back, spitting out blood from Taylor's one

lucky punch. Eleanor scrambled over to him, dabbing away the red trickling from the corner of his mouth.

Taylor staggered to his feet, his vile gaze singling out Eleanor as he lunged for her. Stephen pushed her to one side and tripped the big man, who fell facedown on the stones with a sickening thud.

Stephen stood up and helped Eleanor rise, smoothing her hair and apologizing for pushing her down.

"I'm fine, fine. Is he dead?" whispered Eleanor, burying her face against Stephen's chest.

"He ought to be," he said, pulling the pistol out of his coat pocket. Eleanor's eyes grew wide, but Stephen just nudged Taylor with the toe of his boot.

Taylor groaned and sat up, holding his head. He had a bloody nose and a swollen lip, but other than that, he appeared unharmed.

"Taylor, I'm going to make you an offer. Leave England or be hanged for blackmail and attempted murder."

"And if I don't want to do either one of them?"

Still holding Eleanor tight, Stephen calmly lifted the pistol and pointed it at the man's heart.

"I never kept count of the number of men I killed when I was fighting Bonaparte. I don't really think one more villain will hurt my conscience overly." Stephen paused to allow Taylor to digest these cold facts, then he added, "Leave the deed to the land, and if you are gone by tomorrow, Christmas Day, I won't even look into your accounts. Come along, man. Make up your mind. Miss Webster is getting chilled."

"I'll go," he grumbled, but he didn't so much as look at Eleanor.

"Good. I'll check tomorrow afternoon to be certain you haven't forgotten. Good-bye, Mr. Taylor."

Stephen and Eleanor turned toward the house, walking slowly through the dark garden toward the kitchen door.

"It's been a long day," said Eleanor.

"Indeed it has," agreed Stephen, pausing when they heard shouting coming from the kitchen.

The threat of the past few minutes fresh in his mind,

Stephen set Eleanor behind him and burst into the kitchen, his pistol in hand. Eleanor rushed in behind him.

"What the devil?" he shouted, his voice drowning out the servants gathered there.

When they fell silent, the very proper butler stepped forward and said, "I beg your pardon, sir. They were carried away with our news."

He held out his hand to Jane and pulled her forward.

"Jane? What's going on?" exclaimed Eleanor.

"Mr. Punt has asked me to marry him, and we were just sharing the news with everyone," replied the maid, blushing a rosy shade of pink.

Stephen pocketed the pistol and held out his hand. Punt shook it gravely, and smiled slightly as Stephen kissed Jane's cheek.

Eleanor hugged Jane, whispering, "I told you that being proper would win him over."

"Oh, no, miss, it was the captain's kisses that did the trick," said the maid, smiling happily.

As Stephen led Eleanor into the back hall, he chuckled, and she demanded, "I want to know what Jane meant about *your* kisses doing the trick."

"*My* kisses did the trick?" he said, laughing out loud, much to Eleanor's exasperation.

"Now, now, it's not quite what you think. She means the advice I gave her to kiss Punt senseless. After you told her some nonsense about maintaining her distance and being proper . . ."

"Nonsense! What you advised, Captain, was suitable only for a lightskirt, something you know a great deal too much about!" retorted Eleanor.

"Really?" he said, deliberately removing her bonnet and then taking her into his arms, giving her a thorough kiss that left her weak-kneed and breathless. "And how do you feel?" he asked, his own voice husky with pent-up passion.

"I . . . oh, Stephen, please do that again."

He shook his head and put his arm around her waist as he escorted her toward the front of the house.

"Not until we have seen the vicar at church tonight," he said. "We can have the banns read tonight and be wed in three weeks' time."

This time Eleanor stopped him, saying pertly, "I don't recall being asked if I wanted to wed you."

As always, his grin transformed his dark and devilish good looks, and he dropped to one knee and took her hand. His eyes shining with love, he said, "My sweet and beautiful fair maiden, will you make me the happiest of knights and become my wife, my love, my life?"

"I would love to, Sir Knight," she replied, her heart in her eyes. He rose to take her into his arms, but she pushed away from him, her hands splayed against his chest. "As I said, Stephen, I would love to accept your offer . . ." He kissed her cheek, and she lost her train of thought.

"Go ahead, my love," he said, smiling at her.

She took a deep breath and, in her best governess voice, said, "I love you, Stephen, but I must have your promise that there will be no other women, no excessive gambling, and no death-defying wagers."

Stephen crossed his heart. "My dear Miss Webster, I promise you, I will be as dull as . . . a governess!"

"Devil!" she whispered, sliding her arm around his neck and kissing him in such a manner that he never wanted to stray farther away from her than an embrace.

Rounding the corner and spying his sister wrapped in his friend's arms, Sir Michael demanded with mock severity, "Here, now, what's all this?"

Eleanor would have jumped back, but Stephen's strong arms held her close. His soft query was edged by steel. "Have you any objections, Michael?"

Michael gave a hearty laugh and clapped him on the back, saying to his sister, "Stephen always was too easy to provoke."

Eleanor looked into her brother's face, the face that had invaded her nightmares so many times, and she smiled.

He leaned closer and kissed her cheek, whispering hoarsely, "I wish you every happiness, my dear sister." Then he pumped Stephen's hand, saying, "And you, sirrah, you will make my sister happy or else answer to me . . . and we both know who the winner of that contest would be."

"So say you," replied Stephen with a jaunty grin.

"Come, come, we mustn't keep this wonderful news a secret," said Michael. "Let's go tell the others."

They sailed into the drawing room, where everyone was gathered playing at spillikins, a silly children's game that Mr. Ardmore had instituted.

"May I?" asked Michael.

Stephen glanced at Eleanor, who gave her nod of approval.

Michael clapped his hands for silence, and all eyes turned toward the trio.

"Ladies and gentlemen, may I have your attention!" he announced regally, pausing dramatically. "I am happy to announce the coming marriage of my sister Eleanor to my good friend, Stephen Ransom."

Mr. Ardmore jumped to his feet and shouted, "Huzzah!"

Smiling broadly, Laura started toward Eleanor only to be thrust to one side as Miss Jones screamed and made a beeline for her rival, her hands reaching up for Eleanor's neck.

Michael grabbed the young woman's arms, pinning them to her sides. In a flash, he removed her from the room, while Stephen held Eleanor against his broad chest.

His face crimson with embarrassment, Sailor Jones said, "I am so sorry, Stephen. Miss Webster, I don't know what to say."

Laura touched his arm and said, "Malcolm, we all know it's not your fault. Go to Hilda; perhaps you can help calm her nerves."

After an awkward moment, the company of friends circled the betrothed couple, exclaiming in surprise and wishing them well.

Mrs. Prentiss stole a kiss from the groom and winked at Eleanor, saying, "I knew all along, my dear, that Stephen was head over heels about you."

"When's it going to be?" asked Laura, smiling at them.

"As soon as possible," said Stephen, which caused the gentlemen to titter.

Eleanor blushed a fiery red, but she didn't want to run and hide anymore. Glancing over her shoulder, she watched Michael slip back into the room.

When the others had drifted away, Eleanor sought him out and kissed his cheek, saying simply, "Thank you, Michael."

His smile fading, he said, "Perhaps now when you see this face, you'll think of me, not Father, and you'll remember that once I did stand up for you and protect you."

Her eyes filled with tears, and she threw her arms around his neck.

"Here, now, don't waste that on your brother," teased Stephen, joining them and shaking Michael's hand. "Thank you, Michael. How was she when you left her?"

He grinned at the couple. "Well, she probably won't attend tonight's festivities, but by the time I finished talking her 'round she was relieved to have lost you to another. Of course, I'm afraid I had to paint you as a rather dull stick, but fortunately, I didn't have to lie."

"Michael!" called the major. "Come over here and set this young pup straight on what really happened at Toulouse."

"Excuse me," he said, giving Eleanor's arm a final squeeze and hurrying away.

Stephen put his arm around her and pulled her into the empty entrance hall.

"I guess the servants are still celebrating Jane and Punt's good news," said Eleanor.

"Hmm, lucky for us," murmured Stephen, pulling her close. He looked up and said, "My, my, who put mistletoe up there?"

"Probably Jane," called Mary, tripping lightly down the stairs with Susan.

Peter ran down the steps and into the drawing room. Finally, the nursemaid appeared, carrying Simon, who was dressed in his finery for the midnight services.

Stephen took Simon in his arms. Resting his forehead against the boy's, he said, "Are you ready for church, my Lord Ransom?"

"Church, Unc Stephem," said Simon, hugging his uncle's neck. Then the little viscount's eyes lit up as he spied his mother and said, "Mama! Mama!"

Stephen set him down and reached into his pocket, pulling out the miniature. "Laura, I have something for you, something I think Simon will appreciate one day, but you should keep it until he is old enough." She gazed at the picture in wonder.

"That's my mother," he explained. "Eleanor, I think she's going to faint!"

"No, I'm fine . . . I . . . Ellie?" said Laura, turning as always to her friend for guidance. "What does this mean?"

"It means it's over, Laura. The nightmare is over," said Eleanor, smiling at the tears of happiness flowing from Laura's dark eyes.

Stephen turned his attention to the girls. "Susan, I decided to take your advice." She gave him a puzzled frown, and he explained, "I have decided to marry Miss Webster."

"Did she say yes?" asked Mary, looking from one to the other, her eyes wide open.

"Indeed I did," said Eleanor, resting her hand on Stephen's shoulder.

The girls began to dance around them, squealing and laughing while Simon joined in. Stephen, with a glance at the mistletoe overhead, took Eleanor's hands and kissed her lips.

"I love you, Miss Webster."

"And I love you, you devil." For that she received another Christmas kiss.

Feeling someone tugging on the tail of his coat, Stephen reluctantly broke away and glanced down at Simon, who shook a chubby finger at them and said, "You be nice."